Birds Do It!

*lizzie starr

Dokopot Books

Dokopot Books
Lincoln, Nebraska
www.dokopotbooks.com

Book Layout © 2015 BookDesignTemplates.com

Birds Do It!/*lizzie starr -- 1st ed.
ISBN 978-0-9977542-2-3

Critique partners share much more than just the writing of our books. My thanks to Sue, Sandy, Cindy and Sheila for sharing characters' names, the drinking of tea, and love of suspense with me. Guess I learned a little by association, huh? I truly could not have created this tale without you.

 An ambulance screamed through the cross street in front of the community hospital. Birdie Simons waited patiently for the ruckus to die down as bright yellow fire trucks squealed around the corner to follow the flashing lights of the wailing rescue vehicle. Impatiently tapping her fingers against the steering wheel, she watched a young couple leaving the hospital— balloons, flowers, and new baby in tow.

Birdie sighed. Nine years before, she had left the hospital empty armed, her child dead. A second sigh tightened the shoulder strap over her chest. Even if the tiny girl had lived, Birdie would have been empty armed. A joyous adoptive family's cuddling would have taken her place. Nine years ago today.

A horn blaring behind her jerked her attention to the now silent roadway and a bright green traffic light. She waved an apology over her shoulder and left behind the hospital, but not her memories.

How stupid she'd been. At thirty-one she should have known better than to believe the attentions of a city councilman would lead to anything more than date rape. A cold chill skittered down Birdie's spine. Too ashamed to report the incident, she'd tried valiantly to go on with her life. Until the positive home pregnancy test. Birdie shuddered at the rush of memory.

Unsettled and overly emotional at that time in her life, she would never have been able to provide a decent life for a child. So she had chosen to give the child up for adoption, happy a loving couple would give her daughter a life she could only imagine.

Now the owner of a successful bird ranch providing quality avians to reputable pet stores... Birdie chuckled. It sounded so pretentious when she thought of her life in those terms. But life was good, complete, fulfilling. At least that's what she told herself in the lonely hours of the night.

After parking in front of an old farmhouse, she climbed from her sleek, dark blue SUV and leaned back against the warm metal. Arms crossed under her breasts, she succumbed to the luxury of another sigh. This was her baby now. Birdie shook her head; her baby needed a new coat of paint along the soffits, and a new lock on the front door. Even the small sign by the door proclaiming *Birdies* needed a touch up. Maybe she could get to the maintenance next weekend; today's chore was a pile of long overdue paperwork.

She pushed open the sticky door and the raucous screeching and chattering of a multitude of feathered bodies greeted her. A blonde head peeked from behind a counter and her assistant, Dot, smiled brightly.

"Everybody's fed, watered, and cleaned. No problems, boss."

"Thanks, girlfriend. What kind of plans do you have for the rest of the weekend?"

"Not much." Dot rose and eyed her curiously. "Do you need some extra help?"

The overly loud ring of the telephone interrupted the shake of Birdie's head. Immediate echoes of the sound traveled the length of room and into the next, as one mimicking bird passed the trill to the next. "I should invest in a phone that flashes," Birdie muttered as she rushed toward the small office. Behind her, Dot laughed and wandered down a row of cages, easily calming the anxious birds.

"*Birdies*. May I help you?"

The growl of a deep, resonate voice thrilled her to the tips of her toes. "I hope so."

Shaken by her uncommon reaction to a man's voice, Birdie paused before asking, "How can I..."

A touch of panic hovered behind the man's rushed words. "There's a huge blue monster in my house. I can't control the thing. She left it here for who knows how long while she went off to Bermuda or some other godforsaken place. I don't know what to do. Nine little girls are coming out here this afternoon, what if one of them is bitten?"

"Wait, sir. What monster? What are you talking about?" Just what she needed—a crazed idiot disturbing her peaceful Saturday.

The disembodied voice continued. Even with the totally masculine timbre, Birdie pictured a skinny little man dancing around the phone in panic. She had to bite back a chuckle. The daydream shattered with his terse demand. "You will come out here now and take care of this damn bird."

"Bird? What bird?"

Exasperation flowed through the telephone line. "I just told you. My mother's macaw. It's wild, a demented bird. I can't control it." The words were spaced evenly, firmly. "I need help."

Birdie covered the mouthpiece and sighed. Always an easy touch where avian creatures were concerned, she returned her attention to the stressed breathing of the ranting man. "A blue and gold...?"

"No, damn it, one of those big ones. What's it called? It's all blue with yellow around the eyes."

"A hyacinth macaw?" Birdie took a deep breath. There weren't many of the huge birds in the area, maybe this one would...

"Will you come?"

"Of course, sir. I've had fairly good luck dealing with avian behavioral problems. If we can't get the bird under control, I might be able to board it here at *Birdies* until your mother returns."

"Fine, great, whatever. Only do it quick. My daughter's birthday party starts in…" In the silent pause Birdie imagined him checking his watch. "Three hours. It'll take you about a half an hour to get here, unless you get lost."

Birdie let a defensive tone color her voice. "I have a great sense of direction, thank you." After reaching for a slip of paper and a pen, she waved the colorful page to catch Dot's attention and motioned her into the office. "Just give me the directions."

She listened with half an ear while the man listed streets and mileage. Dot stood over one shoulder, gasping at the strange street names as Birdie wrote. A wrinkle creased Birdie's forehead. These were directions to an exclusive country club on the far side of town, where each small acreage was treated as though it were a southern plantation. This would be an interesting adventure.

Dot repeatedly poked the paper with a finger until Birdie gave her a dirty look. Dot's mouth formed an open circle before she breathed, "Wow," sat in the desk chair, and propped her feet on the wastebasket.

Muffled screeching echoed through the receiver. "I'll expect you at Logan's Hollow shortly. Hurry. This bird is driving me nuts."

"And you are?"

"Garr Logan."

It took a deep breath and greater force of will before Garr could replace the handset without slamming it against the wall in frustration. The bird screamed and the flapping of wide spread, clipped wings made Garr wince as he reached for the business card he'd found stuck in the yellow pages. He glanced at the colorful rectangle before replacing it and tucking the phonebook back into the junk drawer. If the woman boarded birds, why hadn't his mother left the monster there? Why had Mom dumped that blue demon on his doorstep? She knew the bird hated him.

The sound of running feet pattered across the slate floor of his large kitchen. "Daddy." Rachelle threw herself into his open arms and planted a kiss on his cheek. "Daddy, you need a shave. You can't let my friends see you like that." She rubbed her palm against the morning stubble and giggled. "Is it time to get ready yet?"

Garr twirled his daughter in a tight circle and set her on her feet. "You know no one will be here until one o'clock. Now scoot, and let me get things ready."

"I can help you." Rachelle tried to peek around his waist but he held her steady. A dramatic child's sigh filled her chest. "You don't have to keep the cake a secret, you know. I'm not a little kid anymore."

Garr ruffled her hair, chuckling when she ducked to escape his attentions. "I know you're not, honey. Humor your old dad, okay?"

"You're not old, Daddy, not like Tammi's dad. He's ancient."

Bending nearly double, Garr peered into Rachelle's smiling face and made his words waver with an old man's voice. "I'm old as the hills, honey." He clicked his tongue against his teeth, winked, and straightened, laughing with his daughter.

A screech from the sun porch turned them both toward the French doors. Rachelle started forward but Garr stopped her with a hand laid lightly on her shoulder. "Don't go near that thing. Not until we get a muzzle for it."

Rachelle gave him a look of profound patience. "You don't muzzle a bird, Daddy. He likes me. Watch." Shrugging out of his grip, she skipped to the doorway and stopped to shake her finger into the room. "You be quiet, Brutus. Be a good bird or I won't let you have any of my birthday cake."

Immediate silence filled the air. Garr held his breath. It couldn't be that simple. Rachelle turned, gave him a bright smile, and marched up the stairs to her room. Garr's lungs burned in his chest, but he didn't dare breathe. He took a step back, paused, and turned to lean against the kitchen's expansive center island.

The second a breath passed his lips with a whoosh the screeching began. Slapping his hands over his ears, he checked the wall clock. Only five minutes had passed. That woman better hurry or he wouldn't be held accountable for his actions. Birdicide was the only possible solution.

Slamming the double French doors only slightly muted the raucous noise. The cake could wait. He'd start the outside decorations and hope one of the neighbors didn't call the cops on him. Then his mother would have to come home, take care of that damn bird, and bail him out of jail for disturbing the peace charges. Long strides took him toward the front of the house. He'd relish the silence of a jail cell about now.

"This can't be the place." Birdie held the scrap of paper at eye level and glanced past it to a wide, gently rising lawn. A crisp, white picket fence, fronted by an explosion of flowers, surrounded the lush, green area. An arch of vine-covered white-painted metal towered over the loose stone driveway. Numbers stood out in stark relief against the fence: six seven one zero one five. Birdie stared at the paper in her shaking fingers. This was the place.

She turned the SUV carefully onto the clean, white drive. The expanse of lawn stretched before her, ending at the house. Birdie slammed on the brakes and gaped at the vision before her. Most of the homes she'd passed on the way to Logan's Hollow were Greek revival, plantation style buildings with thick columned porches. This house was different.

This house was... spectacular. A true wedding cake of a house topped the slight rise. A blast of color, unexpected after the multitude of traditional white houses in the development, pleased her senses. Her favorite color, a rich purple, covered the body of the huge Queen Anne Victorian. Rose, pink, and white accented the porch rail and posts, the shutter flanked windows and high arched pediments. Birdie held her breath; the view before her was everything she'd ever dreamed of for a house, at least from the outside. A deep, longing breath filled her chest. And she was going to get to see the interior. Barely taking her eyes from the multicolored house, Birdie drove the rest of the way and parked at the top of the circular drive.

Once out of the vehicle, she paused and took a deep breath. Even this close to the city, the air smelled different, fresher. She wished she could linger forever to soak up the scenery and welcomed country peacefulness.

Until the loud, piercing shriek of a large bird rent the quiet. A man's frustrated growl answered from the side of the house. Birdie chuckled and moved in that direction. Rounding the corner, she hurried to where a flagstone patio dominated the side yard. A man's back was to her—a man's wide, muscular back. The breadth of his shoulders tapered to a lean waist and narrow hips. Encased in tight jeans, the enticing view of his backside made her mouth go dry.

Bent slightly forward, the man worked at something on a round, wrought iron patio table. Birdie took a hesitant step forward when she heard a loud hiss of air. "Excuse me?"

The man straightened with a jerk. The raspberry sputtering of an escaping balloon faded as a bright purple orb shrank into the distance. His head angled slightly to watch the escaping flight. "Hell's bells."

"Uh, sorry. I'm here about your bird."

The man turned toward her and Birdie's world turned upside down.

Sunlight glinted off the lighter strands in his dark brown hair to surround him with a halo of light. Faint laugh-lines creased the corners of his eyes. With the sun in her face, Birdie couldn't tell the color of his eyes, but felt the curiosity of his gaze.

From the front, he was as spectacular as his house. The top three buttons of his bright blue chambray shirt were undone, revealing a mat of crinkly brown hair. Birdie's fingers curled in response to his unconscious sensuality.

He canted his head to one side and hooked his thumbs over his hips. Birdie's gaze followed the downward slope of his fingers toward the fly of his snug, faded jeans, then snapped back to his face. She bit at her lower lip. What was she doing? What kind of thoughts swirled through her head? What thoughts... her face heated.

"And you are?"

Caught unaware by the casual question, Birdie took a deep breath, wiped her clammy palm on the side of her slacks, and stepped forward, hand outstretched. "I'm Birdie Simons. You called me about a bird?"

Garr took her hand and received a firm handshake. His fingers lingered a moment too long while he studied the woman before him. Golden-red waves were pulled back into a loose ponytail; a few stray hairs had fallen to a curlicue in the center of her forehead. Blue-gray eyes surrounded by dark lashes lowered, and she wiggled her hand to signal her desire for release. The rush of reluctance when the warmth of her hand left his astounded him.

Screeching rose from a low, almost conversational pitch to siren loudness. The sound faded slowly, echoing in Garr's ears. He nodded. "Yes, I called. My mother left the monster here while she went on vacation. It hates me." His hands clenched into tight fists at his sides.

"Mr., uh, Logan?"

"Garr."

"May I see the bird?"

Garr tried to shrug away the tension clawing at his shoulders. "Of course, that would make sense. I'm a bit rattled. Today is my daughter's birthday and she has nine friends coming over this afternoon. Not only do I have to deal with a maniacal bird, I have to get ready for a party, then entertain a bunch of kids. I'm concerned the bird will bite one of the girls."

"Can't you keep them away from the cage?"

"The bird loves Rachelle. And she dotes on that monster almost as much as her grandmother does. She wants to show it off to her friends." He paused and slapped the heel of his hand against his forehead. "I wanted you to take the thing away, but Rache would never forgive me for spoiling her party."

Garr sank onto a wrought iron bench and leaned forward to rub at his temples. "Are you busy this afternoon?"

No matter how desperate his problem with the bird, he had no right to ask a stranger to rescue him. A grin spread across his face—but what a lovely rescuer. Instant attraction had slammed into him when he first saw her standing in the sun and hadn't lessened, but instead curled its way to his groin. It had been a long time since a woman affected him so strongly.

"I was planning to deal with some long overdue paperwork..." A long, undulating screech interrupted her. Garr's shoulders tensed painfully. "But I can see it's more important I be here."

Hesitant, Garr lifted his gaze. Birdie rolled up her sleeves and glanced around the yard. "I'll go see the 'monster.' If I can get him to quiet down, maybe I can give you a hand out here, too."

"You don't need to do that."

"I know." An elegant shrug lifted her shoulders before she cast him a brilliant smile. "But I'm here, and I love parties. How old is your daughter?"

"Nine today." The delightful glint in her eyes faded until her eyes were a dull gray and she turned her face from him. He'd made her sad. Garr rose from the bench and struggled against the urge to pull her into his arms and kiss away the pain. When she turned back, a smile was in place, but sadness lingered in her eyes.

"What a wonderful age. You and your wife must be very proud."

Fighting his own demons, Garr looked into the distance over Birdie's shoulder. "Rachelle's mother died the day she was born."

Birdie's soft hand warmed his arm. "I'm so sorry, I didn't mean to bring up a painful subject."

Needing to keep the warmth near him, Garr covered her hand with his. A current of electricity sang up his arm. Birdie's eyes went wide and she chewed nervously on the corner of her lip. In another moment he would...

The bird's siren-like call pierced the air and broke the enchantment she'd placed on him. He gave her hand a light pat and pulled away. "I dealt with the pain long ago. I have Rache, there's not much more I could ask for." *Except someone like you.*

Startled by his thought, Garr turned toward the house. "Let me introduce you to Brutus." He glanced sideways. "Is Birdie your real name?"

Birdie giggled, more out of nervousness than at Garr's question. "Just a nickname. Guess my destiny was foretold when my parents named me." Birdie winced, both at her inane statement and at the lifelong teasing suffered because of her unusual name. She should be honored to be named after her grandparents, but she still thought her naming was just some big, cosmic joke.

The deep, rumbling vibrations of Garr's chuckle sent responsive tremors through her. Damn, this man tempted her. More than any had in the past. Even the excitement she'd felt at the councilman's attentions paled beside Garr's simple laughter.

"I suppose you were cute as a little bird when you were young."

"Nope. Gangly and awkward, hardly what I'd call cute." Luckily, they reached a set of double French doors leading to an enclosed porch before she had to confess to her full name.

Garr stood to the side with one hand resting on the latch. "The monster's in here." He opened the door slowly, backing up as he did to stay out of sight. A quick motion of his hand indicated she was to enter. When she glanced back at him, he mouthed 'good luck.'

Another chuckle threatened to explode. Imagine, a man like Garr Logan cowed by a bird. Taking a deep breath, Birdie stepped carefully into

the sunlit room. Big birds could be very
intimidating when you didn't know them.

She moved slowly into the room, placing one
foot smoothly in front of the other, glancing around.
Furnished casually in wicker and glass, the room
exuded a quiet elegance, echoing a gracious past.
Hopefully, the bird would never escape his cage.
The woven furniture would make excellent chew
toys for a large inquisitive bird.

A squawk drew her attention to a huge, steel
cage set against the wall. Birdie took a step toward
the cage, and paused, mouth open. A hyacinth
macaw posed on a thick perch, wings spread
slightly, feathers ruffled to increase the size of his
appearance as he stomped his feet. The show of
dominance—an act to gain her attention—made a
smile tug at her lips. Just like a male. Was the
beautiful avian male? If so, he could be the answer
to her hopes and dreams.

Birdie angled her body toward Garr. "Are you
sure he's a male?"

Garr made a sound of disgust low in his throat.
"My mother had him sexed not long after she got
him. The beast is male, all right. I can even show
you his papers if it's important."

"Oh, no, that's okay. Not now." Birdie tore her
attention from the definitely male body next to her
and watched the macaw. A smile touched her lips.

A magnificent bird, Brutus stretched to his full
length, chattered once, and backed into the corner of
his cage to eye Birdie warily. Advancing slowly,
despite the sudden silence, Birdie spoke soft
nonsense, telling Brutus what a beautiful fellow he
was. By the time she stood next to the cage, the bird
peered at her with one of his bright eyes and sidled
closer.

Careful to show no fear or hesitation to set the skittish bird off again, she dug into her pocket for one of the Brazil nuts she'd grabbed before leaving *Birdies*. The way to a bird's heart was often through his stomach. Wary of the powerful beak, Birdie offered Brutus the treat, softly encouraging until he climbed the side bars of the cage, moved closer, and hung upside down to accept the morsel and a scratch on his head.

Before long, she had the cage door open to stroke the large, upright bird and accept the investigative, gentle preening of the large beak. The tiny prickles of new feathers poked her fingertips; there had been a recent molt. Brutus rubbed his bottom over her hand, then along the perch, chattering happily. Birdie grinned, now she had a fair idea what the problem was. And the solution might solve one of her concerns as well.

"I don't believe it. You're magical." Garr's voice, lowered to an awed whisper, sounded from the doorway.

Turning her head to look at him, Birdie let her grin grow wider at his dazed expression. "It's nothing, when you know what you're doing. Move slowly, and come over here."

Garr shook his head and remained hovering against the doorframe.

Birdie's eyebrows lowered and she fought to make a fierce scowl. Giving up, she flashed him another smile. "Come on, you'll be okay. Just move slowly." The unreasonable urge to flirt with the handsome man tinted her playful words. "I won't let the big, bad bird hurt you." She fluttered her eyelashes at him.

Garr took a deep breath and a single step into the room, drawn more by the need to be closer to the woman who calmly stroked the blue monster than by her assurances. The bird eyed him curiously. He returned the skeptical glance and moved forward. Brutus climbed the side of the cage to hang from the top, puffed out his feathers and hissed at Garr.

"See. It hates me."

Her brows drawn together, Birdie eased the cage door closed. "I know." Her expression brightened. "Take off your shirt."

Garr took a startled step back. Unfortunately, this was not the time for his fantasies to come true. "I beg your pardon."

"It's your shirt. Do you wear a lot of blue?"

"Yes?" His response was slow, the word drawled from his lips.

"Brutus is threatened by you. Birds have excellent color vision and strong color sensitivity. Since he's blue, when you wear a blue shirt and tower over him, he gets scared. He's not angry, he's frightened. Either take off your shirt, or get out of here."

Garr liked hearing her order him to strip, it brought wicked thoughts that had no place in a day filled with a child's birthday party. He tamped down his response and tried to ease the pressure of his tight jeans as he pulled his shirt free. At her signal, he tossed the shirt behind a chair.

Birdie stared at the expanse of male chest. Oh, God, that had been a mistake. The thick sprinkling of hair tapered to a thin line down his flat abdomen, disappearing into the waistband of his jeans. Heat flooded her chest and crawled up her neck to cover her face. Those jeans were fuller than before, the tightness more pronounced over his...

Whipping her gaze back to the macaw, Birdie swallowed hard. "Okay? Now move closer—slowly. And talk softly to Brutus. Let's see if this helps."

He stepped closer and Birdie couldn't deny the pure male sensuality that blasted through her like heat from a wildfire. Unable to stop herself, she inhaled deeply, memorizing the mixture of spice and earth, tasting the overtones of desire.

Down, girl, get those hormones under control. You're here to help him with a bird, not jump his bones. The crassness of her thought calmed her enough for Garr's voice to register.

Calm, pitched low and soothing, the tone had nothing to do with his words. "Okay, monster. Let's get this straight. You're a bird. I...I am the master here. You will behave yourself, won't you, you vicious beast?"

Birdie laughed, startling both the man and the bird focusing all its attention on the soothing voice. Giving a startled squawk, Brutus hopped to the far end of his perch and glared at Birdie. She dug another treat from her pocket and offered it in apology. "You'll definitely win his confidence if you feed him. I can tell he's a greedy thing."

Garr moved closer, the simple touch of his hand on her shoulder turned her to face him. Time stopped and the brightly lit sunroom faded as she stared into his eyes. Birdie swallowed the dryness infecting her throat, and an appealing spark rose from the depths of Garr's dark eyes. The pupils dilated, his lips softened. Birdie accepted the silent invitation and leaned toward him.

CHAPTER TWO

"Daddy?"

Garr jerked back and speared one hand through his hair. Birdie turned away in time to see a young girl skid to a stop just inside the door. The girl planted small fists against her hips. "Daddy, where's your shirt?"

"I—umm. The bird doesn't like the color. Rachelle, I'd like you to meet Birdie Simons. She knows all about birds and came over to help me with the monster."

"Not a monster, Daddy. Brutus." She skipped toward the cage, reached in, and petted the bird. Garr expelled a long, harsh breath. Birdie grinned; the father could learn from the daughter.

"Rache, I told you to be careful."

"Aw, Brutus wouldn't hurt me, would ya, Brutie?" The child's bright blue gaze gave Birdie the once over before Rachelle smiled up at her. "Hi. I'm Rache. Today's my birthday. Wanna stay for the party?"

Birdie crouched to be eye level with the girl. There was something familiar about her eyes; a tremor touched deep inside the hidden places of Birdie's heart. This was not going to be an easy day. "Your dad already invited me. I'm going to watch over Brutus. If you'd like, I can tell you and your friends some neat stuff about big birds like him. And if we're careful, maybe everyone will be able to pet him." She glanced back at Garr.

"All right! Hey, Daddy, is it time to get ready yet?"

Garr glanced at his watch and groaned. "You go ahead, squirt, just make sure you don't wear blue."

"Huh? Oh, Daddy, whatever. Wasn't gonna anyway." She turned to rush away with a child's energetic exuberance, but stopped at the door. "You better put a shirt on before my friends get here." And she was gone.

Birdie chuckled, then laughed. The tension of her attraction to Rachelle's father was put into a safe place and stored away. A whisper of thought, a pain-filled memory tugged her laughter away. Her daughter could have been like Rachelle. She bit her lip to force back a tear and stood.

"How much time do we have?"

"Time? Oh, until the girls get here? Only about an hour and a half. I'll never get everything done." Panic filled his rugged features and he scrubbed at his face with his hands. "I've got decorations and favors to set out, games to get ready, and a cake to frost. The cake!"

"I'm a pretty fair cake decorator, Garr. Would you like me to do that?" She touched his arm and let her fingers slide softly over the fine hairs. His skin quivered under her palm. Suddenly uncomfortable, she jerked away. "Uh, just point me toward the kitchen."

"You don't have to do that, Birdie. I'll manage."

She pointed to Brutus. "My charge is quiet now. If he starts to get out of hand, I'll hear him. Leaving a cake half frosted might be easier than losing all your balloons."

Garr glanced again at his watch and sighed. "You've got a deal. Since I need a new shirt, I'll take you there and give you a quick tour. Warm and possessive, his hand landed on the small of her back and turned her toward the set of inner doors.

Before she had a chance to really look around the spacious great room, Garr led her to the open kitchen area. A huge sheet cake sat centered on the granite-topped island, cans of icing staggered across the counter. She turned an inquisitive glance to him and he shrugged, gave her a wry smile and turned to take a nearby set of stairs two at a time.

"Well," Birdie spoke to the still air, "so much for my paperwork."

While she smoothed a base layer of white frosting over the large cake and contemplated design choices, Birdie glanced around the great room opening beyond the wide island counter. Spacious and uncluttered, the room exuded solid, male comfort. An overstuffed couch and chairs faced a huge television. An undecipherable array of electronic equipment flanked the screen.

Even the fireplace spoke of masculine presence. A simple stone mantle held a grouping of three pictures to one side, and a plant she thought must be silk trailed from the other. Uncertain if she should feel free to explore the unknown, she ached to take a closer look at the pictures.

Only a couple of stuffed animals placed carefully in one chair shattered the aura of man. Birdie frowned to herself. Her unreasonable desire to know more, to discover everything she could about one Garr Logan, disturbed her. Garr. Even his name tasted of masculine virility when she whispered it to herself.

Summoned by her thoughts, Garr descended the stairs buttoning a crisply pressed, tan shirt. He paused on the bottom step, glanced toward the sun porch. then headed in the opposite direction. With a cheery wave, he was gone.

Birdie sighed, tried to force her curiosity and the fluttering in her chest away, and peered at the smooth, blank surface of the cake. What had she gotten herself into? A soft chattering, a strangely calm sound from a large parrot, sounded from the sunroom.

Bright inspiration flowed into Birdie and she picked up a small bowl, filled it with white icing and reached for the package of tiny bottles of food coloring.

Sometime later, she finished a final swirl around the word 'birthday' and held the decorating bag suspended above the cake. Only one thing was needed to complete her edible work of art—the birthday girl's name.

A movement, caught from the corner of her eye, startled her into squeezing a blob of bright yellow onto the center of the cake. "Oh, no."

Garr shoved his hand under the bag and caught another glop of icing in his palm. He moved to the sink, washed the color away, and dried his hands with a paper towel. "Sorry I startled you. I've been here a while. Watching."

Birdie slammed the bag onto the counter, and splattered yellow across the granite surface. "Oh, d—darn it anyway." She turned an apologetic smile to Garr. "I get so involved sometimes, I don't notice what's going on around me. No harm done. As long as you wipe up the counter."

Garr's eyes widened imperceptibly. Had she really said that? Commanded him to clean up after her? Crinkles appeared at the corners of his eyes and he smiled. Hazel. His eyes were hazel. Unable to look away, Birdie wondered if the color changed depending on his mood, or what he was thinking.

Garr turned his smile to the cake and pointed at the yellow mound. "That's not harm?"

Using a flat spatula, Birdie scooped up the offending icing and dropped it back into a small bowl. After wiping the spatula on a damp dishrag, she scraped the last of the white icing from its container and repaired the damage. Smoothing the surface with a deft flick of her wrist, she spoke. "I need to know how your daughter spells her name."

"The French way."

"And that is?" Birdie held up a hand. "Wait a sec." She reached for a second decorating bag filled with bright blue icing. After testing the flow from the tip over a bowl, she paused with the tip close to the cake. "Okay, shoot."

"R." Garr swallowed heavily. This woman, a stranger, came into his house, magically quieted a maniacal bird, and created the most beautiful cake for his daughter. Her hand moved smoothly, putting a final, flowery flourish to the large letter.

"A." She arched her shoulders forward as if easing tight muscles. Garr's fingers twitched, and he longed to soothe, to comfort, to relax her tension. That longing curled into heated tension low in his belly.

"C." Pausing, Birdie held the top of the decorating bag in one hand, wrapped the fingers of her other hand around it, and gently forced the icing toward the tip. Then, she wrapped her fingers more tightly around the bag and adjusted her grip slightly. Garr bit back a low groan.

"H." How the letter got past the lump in his throat was a miracle. Unbidden, unwanted, the vision of her fingers wrapped around him... stroking... caressing... squeezing...

His body responded painfully.

"E." A deep intake of breath filled him with her scent; spice and warm vanilla. As casually as he could, he moved to the other side of the island to hide his physical reaction. Perhaps the distance would help.

"Two L's." How long had it really been since he'd been attracted to a woman, drawn to someone so intimately? The tip of her pink tongue peeked between her lips as she concentrated, moving slowly along her full lower lip as if it traced the letters as well.

"E." By God, if she didn't stop caressing that damn bag...

"There, finished." Birdie looked up at him. A triumphant smile made her face bright and beautiful. She sucked an icing covered finger into her mouth. "What do you think?"

I think I want to know you better. Much better. Realizing she waited for an answer, Garr cleared his throat and tore his gaze from her face to look at the cake. A large blue bird covered nearly a third of the surface; the yellow-circled eye watched him much as the monster did. "It's remarkably like Brutus."

Her grin widened. "That's what I was trying for. Oh, wait." Scrounging through the mess on the counter, Birdie came up with a candle shaped like a nine. After placing it carefully, it looked like the bird held the candle in an outstretched claw. The bright yellow 'Happy Birthday' above the deep blue name made the cake an artistic masterpiece.

"Amazing. Rache will love it. How can I ever thank you?" He inched back around the counter to stand beside Birdie. "I'm in your debt. First for helping with the bird, and now this."

Birdie spread her hands. The movement tugged her blouse tight across her breasts. Garr moved closer. The blue in her eyes deepened until the gray disappeared. He sank deep into her gaze. He was going to kiss her—again and again if she would let him. Her eyes told him she would. The space between them narrowed.

Garr put his hand on the counter, right into a bowl of icing. Muttering under his breath, he turned away. This was not the time for... for what? What happened here? Keeping his back to Birdie, he washed his hands. "I think we're nearly ready for the party now." With a quick glance at his watch, he nodded. "Yep, the girls should be arriving soon."

Deep inside his head an inner voice echoed with frustration. But not leaving soon enough. Alone. How could he get this woman alone?

"Garr? Is something wrong?"

He failed at keeping a sarcastic laugh contained. "No, just dreading the onslaught of little girls."

"Why don't you start with the outside games, then when they get a little worn out, bring them in and I'll tell them about Brutus. Then cake and..." Birdie came to stand beside him at the sink. "You have ice cream?"

"Of course we do." Rachelle's happy voice sounded from the stairway. "Daddy wouldn't forget my ice cream. Would you, Daddy?"

When Garr didn't answer right away, Rachelle ran across the room to hug his waist and peer up into his serious expression. "You didn't forget, did you?"

Garr ruffled the top of her long, golden-brown hair. "Of course not, sweetheart. I got chocolate and butter rum just like you ordered." He winked at Birdie and received a warm smile in return. A family moment. This felt like a family moment, one missing in his and Rachelle's lives. Emptiness slammed into his chest. Kneeling, he engulfed Rachelle in a hug, holding her until she squirmed out of his arms.

The doorbell rang and Rachelle sprinted for the front door. "They're here, they're here."

It had been a long time since Birdie had been even slightly involved with a child's birthday party. Now here she was, deeply immersed in party games. The shrill cries of the active girls pushed at her thoughts, shoving away possibilities.

In the kitchen, Garr had seemed so... so interested in her. Closing her eyes, Birdie shook her head. How many times would she read a man's intentions, or even just his attention, incorrectly? When would she learn that no man could really find her interesting? Or that he was only interested in his own agenda? Garr was only taking advantage of the help she could give him with the party. A loud squawk from the house reminded her of the real reason she was there. The bird.

Brutus was a beautiful bird, well-formed and sure of himself. Much like Garr. No, keep thoughts away from Garr, concentrate on the bird. On anything else. But even as she tried to force her mind from thoughts of Garr, her eyes sought him out. He'd hung a piñata from the swing set, and now he tugged on the short rope to pull the papier-mâché creation out of the reach of a broomstick-wielding child.

The movements bunched the muscles of his shoulders and upper arms and stretched the material of his shirt tight across his chest. Birdie licked her lips and tried to draw moisture to her dry mouth. Her eyelids drifted closed; she had to get away.

Birdie returned to the sunroom and watched Brutus happily destroy a large block of wood. Hopefully, she would convince Garr to listen to her plan, and fulfill the hopes that had been growing since she'd first seen the bright blue bird. It would soon be time for her to show Brutus off to the crowd of girls. First, she needed to make sure the bird was calm, and willing to be handled. There was no way she would jeopardize her chances with an ill-behaved bird. But which chances? The chance of her plan for the bird, or a chance with the man who intrigued her so greatly?

Garr took a deep breath of relief. After a barrage of games, the girls were finally tired. He was exhausted and glad of the respite. It would be brief, he knew—kids had such boundless energy. He'd better let them visit the monster bird before the excitement started again.

A quick glance around filled him with a strange sense of loss; Birdie was nowhere in sight. That woman had gotten under his skin much too quickly. He'd have to play it carefully or… or what? He shook his head to clear it and headed for the sun porch, hoping to find Birdie there.

Cautiously, he opened the door. Dimmer than the bright summer sunlight outside, it took a few moments for his eyes to adjust. When they did, a painful longing settled in his chest.

Birdie sat easily on a hard, straight-backed chair, cuddling the monster bird in her lap. She stroked the bright feathers and paused to scratch lightly over the bird's large head. In return, Brutus took one of her fingers in his thick beak and nibbled softly.

The need to be closer to Birdie pulled him into the room, and the longing sank lower in Garr's body. The rough sound of him clearing his throat rang loud in the comfortable silence.

Birdie glanced up and met his gaze. The smile froze on her lips and something unreadable passed through her eyes. Wanting to chase the elusive emotion and discover the cause, Garr took a step closer.

Brutus ruffled his feathers noisily and climbed from Birdie's lap to perch firmly on her shoulder. He hid his head in her hair and after an emphatic hiss, began to preen the shoulder length strands. Garr's fingers twitched.

"I'm sorry. I hope I didn't cause any problems by interrupting." He took another step.

Birdie's blue-gray gaze skittered away from his. "No, no problem. Brutus is pretty calm right now. It might be a good time for the girls to meet him."

Reluctant to leave her presence, Garr nodded. He was even more reluctant to share the moment with a troop of giggling nine year olds. Then, he blinked. What moment? "Uh, sure. I'll go get them."

"Tell them to come in quietly. No loud talking or sudden movements."

His concern at letting his daughter's guests near the huge bird must have shown, for Birdie smiled gently and encouraged Brutus to leave her shoulder for the security of her lap. "Everything's under control, Garr. We just don't want to startle Brutus. Go on now." Her smile turned mischievous. "Don't give Brutus a chance to have second thoughts about his good behavior."

After returning her smile, Garr backed from the room. That was another thing he hadn't realized he'd been missing. The lighthearted banter, the teasing that made his heart lurch. The women he'd dated since Melissa's death had been too concerned with impressing him to have fun.

The lovely, unassuming Birdie Simons truly impressed him. Something about her was different, delightful, and he had to know what that something was.

"Okay, girls, I know Rache told you about the bird we have staying with us."

A chorus of affirmations interrupted him. Palms forward, Garr lifted his hands for silence. Prolonged shushing kept him quiet as well, and he waited until he again had the full attention of the ten little girls.

"Right, then. Now, this is a huge bird, but even so, he scares easily. You don't want to frighten Brutus, do you?"

Ten heads solemnly shook from side to side. "So when we go in, you'll be quiet, right?"

The heads nodded up and down in unison. Garr grinned when Rachelle rolled her eyes at him. "The woman taking care of Brutus right now is named Birdie." He paused until the scattered giggles subsided. "She'll introduce you to the bird and tell you all about him. When we're done there, maybe Rachelle can tackle that pile of presents before we have the cake."

The girls rose silently and walked toward the house. Garr lifted his eyebrows in amazement at his daughter, and Rachelle smiled before taking his hand and tugging until he bent to her level.

"I told 'em how to behave, Daddy. It'll be okay."

Sometimes Rache's insight and maturity astounded him. He hadn't been so... adult... when he was nine, had he? The way the world was now had to be the reason. A sigh for lost innocence lifted his chest before he joined the girls waiting at the sunroom door.

Clustered around Birdie, the girls leaned forward to hear her soft-spoken words. Timid hands reached out to stroke the bright feathers, gradually becoming more assured, but always awed and gentle. Garr leaned against the doorframe, folded his arms over his chest and crossed one foot over the other. His concern faded and his lips twitched into a smile.

Even while she was speaking to the girls, Birdie remained uncomfortably aware of the pure male essence of the man planted so casually in the doorway—and of her reaction to him. Forcing the tremor from her voice, Birdie gave the girls a brief explanation of pet birds in general, and the specifics of the larger parrots. Although she knew the kids only wanted to touch Brutus, she continued with her education.

Brutus, much to his credit, was calm and quiet, only uttering a few softer calls and chatters. He clearly enjoyed the attention and petting and happily preened the hair of any girl who moved close enough.

Birdie breathed a soft sigh of relief and glanced at Garr. A mistake. The gentle curve of his mouth, the relaxed softness of his full lips, halted the breath in her lungs. He looked— kissable. Then, his gaze lifted from his daughter and the glint in the dark, hazel depths made her heart flutter. Butterflies danced around her belly, every muscle felt quivery, and she was glad to be sitting down.

Sensing her unease, Brutus became restless and climbed onto Birdie's shoulder. His strong claws clenched painfully through her shirt and into her skin, and she fought to keep her gasp of pain from escaping. Garr moved forward, lifting one hand, but Birdie shook her head.

"Brutus is tired now, I think it's time for him to go back into the cage. He'll feel safe there, just like you do at home." Birdie held one hand against the large bird, and her fingers soothed through the blue feathers.

"Okay, girls. Let's leave quietly." Garr motioned for the girls to move away from the bird. "There's a pile of presents on the table, and after Rache opens hers, there's one for each of you, too. And then, what you've been waiting for—the cake."

Rachelle turned to her friends and began pushing them gently from the room. "Yeah, and Birdie decorated it, too. Wait 'til you see it. It's so cool."

"Can we see Brutus later?" a petite blonde asked shyly.

Birdie rose from the chair and smiled at the girls. "Maybe just before you go home you can come in and say goodbye."

Garr's deep voice was a counterpoint to the high, excited whispers of the girls. "Will you join us? When the monster is comfortable, of course."

Turning toward the cage, Birdie nodded. "I'll be right out. Wouldn't want to miss the fun stuff." She heard the group leave. The cold, emptiness at her back told her Garr had gone as well. How could he affect her so completely, so quickly? Taking a firm stand with herself, Birdie reminded her heart that her snap attractions of the past had not been healthy, nor had any led to a satisfying relationship.

Her head agreed with her assessment, but her heart argued.

Somehow, this time was different.

Once the macaw was settled with a fresh block of wood and a thick, green pepper ring, Birdie crossed the patio and immaculate lawn to stand to one side of the gift table. Scraps of torn paper floated on the light breeze. The girls' happy chatter brought contentment to her jangled nerves.

Rachelle tore into the gifts while her fine, golden hair blew across her face. The girl shoved a strand ruthlessly behind one ear, then ran one finger down her cheek in a gesture that made Birdie pause. She knew that movement—that flick of square-tipped fingers—but from where?

Rachelle's bright blue eyes crinkled with happiness and she hugged a stuffed animal. She smiled up at Birdie. Deep sadness centered in Birdie's chest, the pressure strong around her heart. This could have been a party she'd given to her own daughter. The sense of familiar hovered over her again at the dimple gracing Rachelle's cheek, and the sting of tears burned behind her eyes.

Turning away, Birdie paused to catch her breath, then rushed toward the house. One hand held back the sobs burning her nose and throat. Why this year? Why didn't the ghost of her child stay buried? Watching the party through tear-blurred eyes, she leaned heavily against the kitchen counter. She had to get herself together. But the tears fell anyway, tracing down her cheeks to plop into the stainless steel sink.

"Birdie? What's wrong?"

Birdie jerked at the concerned voice and turned toward the island as she rubbed her eyes fiercely with her sleeve. "Just thought I'd get the cake ready." She reached for the large cake, but pulled her shaking hand back to cradle it against her stomach.

Garr's hand became a gentle pressure on her shoulder and he encouraged her to turn toward him. "What's wrong? Did we do something?"

"Oh, no," Birdie hurried to reassure him, but even more tears spilled down her cheeks. "I'm usually able..." She took a large sniff. "To keep this under control."

His hand moved from her shoulder and Garr's fingers curled into her hair. Inching her closer, he wrapped his arm around her and pressed her cheek against his shoulder. "Can you tell me?" He swayed from side to side, rocking her gently.

"I can't. It might ruin the day."

Garr held her away from him for a moment and stared into her face. One thumb dried the tracks of tears. "Looks like yours is already ruined." He cuddled her against him again before she had a chance to speak.

The words spilled out before she could stop them. Muffled against his shirt, somehow speaking would be a cleansing. "Nine years ago... today, I gave birth to a baby girl. She was fine. They told me she was fine, but suddenly... suddenly. Oh, Garr, there was no reason."

"What happened?"

"She died."

The absence of emotion in the simple statement ripped through Garr's heart. He lowered his head and pressed his lips against Birdie's hair. "Oh, baby, I'm so sorry."

Her shoulders shook and she cried silently. The tears made a warm, damp spot on his chest. Garr held her tightly, and his lips moved in nonsense words of comfort against the top of her head, her cheek.

Inviting him to brush his mouth across hers, Birdie's face tilted upward. Intending only to offer comfort, Garr was surprised when Birdie's arms snaked around his neck and her lips sought his for an urgent kiss. She pressed against him and he responded, dragging her to her toes and tasting her lips. The softness parted and they groaned together when he stroked his tongue carefully into her mouth.

Birdie jerked away. There was no rejection in her eyes, only the deep sadness from losing a child. A welling of tenderness brought a deep breath to fill Garr's chest and he reached to dry the last of her tears with his fingers. "I'm sorry, baby. I know what it's like to lose someone."

"I'm sorry, too. This must be a bittersweet day for you as well. I shouldn't..."

He moved his fingers to cover her lips. "I think this may be..." Garr paused and closed his eyes for a moment before continuing. "...what we both need today."

Taking Birdie back into the circle of his arms, Garr held her tightly. This was right. He was right. He needed her. Wanted her. Using one finger to angle her chin, he claimed her lips, teased with the gentlest of pressure, until the need and the want settled deeper within him.

A rhythmic chant from the yard and the pounding of small fists against the patio furniture broke into his growing sensual haze. Garr lifted his head and peered around in confusion.

Birdie stepped back, but leaned forward to place a quick kiss on his cheek. "The natives are restless."

"Cake. Cake. Cake. Cake. Cake."

A rumble of deep laughter burst from Garr. "Will you be able to help me?"

"Of course." Birdie turned to the sink and ran cold water. Bending, she cupped the water over her eyes. One hand patted the counter to the side and Garr reached into a drawer and handed her a clean towel. "Thanks." She turned to him. "My nose isn't too red, is it?"

Garr took the towel from her and looked closely into her face. Dropping a quick kiss on the tip of her nose, he shook his head. "Nope. Now, I'll take the cake, if you can grab the ice creams. I think I've got all the plates and other things we need outside already."

"You got it, boss."

"Birdie?"

She stopped with one hand on the freezer door and turned back to him.

"I really am sorry. I don't want you to think I took advan—"

"I was the one who kissed you first, Garr. I took advantage of your concern."

Wanting to lighten the sudden seriousness, Garr lifted the cake and winked before he turned toward the back yard. "You can take advantage of me anytime, baby."

And the funny thing was—he really meant it.

CHAPTER THREE

Party over. Guests gone. Yard and kitchen cleaned. But Birdie still hadn't had a chance to talk to Garr about her suggestion for Brutus. She folded a dishtowel and laid it on the counter, patting the material gently as if to gain courage from the cotton weave. Garr carried Rachelle into the great room and dumped her on the couch before turning to Birdie.

"I have one more favor to ask of you, Birdie."

"Shoot." This might give her a little more time.

"I have one more present for Rachelle, but I need a little time yet. I was wondering—"

"Daddy!" Rachelle leapt to her knees on the couch and hung over the back. "What is it?"

"If you would keep her company for a bit while I finish up." Garr turned to his daughter. "It's a surprise, of course. Now, you two stay here." One of his hands lifted to stop Rachelle's questions. "Promise me?"

"Cross my heart." Rachelle did, and looked expectantly at Birdie.

"Uh, me, too." Birdie followed suit before crossing the room.

"Sit here by me." Rachelle patted the warm, tan leather couch and reached for a remote. "Can we watch TV?"

Garr nodded. "If Birdie doesn't mind. I'll try not to take too long." He disappeared up the stairs.

Rachelle flicked through the channels and paused at a drama. "I saw this one before. It's about a couple of babies that get switched at the hospital. It's really sad because one of the girls gets cancer. That's when they discover the switch."

Unease tingled the back of Birdie's neck. "You don't want to watch a sad show on your birthday, do you?"

"Naw." Rachelle scooted closer and snuggled against Birdie's side. "Can we watch cartoons?"

"Not some of those crazy new ones, okay?"

"I like the classics, just like Daddy. That and Japanese anime."

"I've never watched anime. What's it like?"

Rachelle punched buttons on the remote and tossed it to the side when a Looney Tunes™ cartoon filled the huge screen. "There's all kinds, kid stuff like those gaming cards, martial arts stuff. Some of it Daddy won't let me watch cuz it's too bloody." She giggled into her hand. "Or too sexy."

Taken aback, Birdie leaned away from Rachelle and looked at her profile. "What do you know about sexy?"

"Oh, not much really. Just that it's adult stuff. Daddy keeps those videos and DVDs locked up. Ooh, this is one of my favorites."

Letting her mind relax into the action between hunter, duck, and rabbit, Birdie eased back in the leather cushions and wrapped her arm around Rachelle's shoulders. The lonely, emotional pain hovered, but she kept it at bay and enjoyed the special moment.

Garr heard shouting, so he rushed to the landing and leaned over the railing. Birdie and Rachelle stood practically nose-to- nose in the center of the great room.

"Duck season."

"Wabbit season."

"Duck season."

"Duck season. Shoot him now."

Birdie made a popping sound and, laughing, Rachelle fell to the floor. Birdie sank cross-legged next to her and they rocked back and forth with their laughter.

Garr's chuckle eased into a deep sigh. Another of those picture moments; a family moment. He shook his head to clear the wistful thoughts before leaning further over the railing. "Hey, birthday girl. Whenever you're ready."

Rachelle let out a whoop, leapt to her feet and ran toward the stairs. She skidded to a stop before she mounted the bottom step. "Can Birdie come, too?"

"Sure, squirt." A play of emotions crossed Birdie's expressive face. Unable to categorize the fleeting moments, he gave her a nod and motioned for her to join them. A deep breath pulled the material of her shirt tight across her breasts. The tantalizing sight, along with the smile finally touching her lips, made the blood course hot and heavy through his body. He turned to gather Rachelle in his arms and they waited until Birdie joined them.

"In your room."

Confusion turned to hope in her young face as Rachelle glanced at Garr and rushed through a door. Garr took Birdie's hand and ran his thumb across the smooth skin of her knuckles before tugging slightly to pull her closer to his side. They followed Rachelle into her room.

The fashion doll pink room startled Birdie and she blinked twice before glancing at the man who held possession of her hand, and her raging emotions.

Garr grinned, shrugged, and leaned closer to whisper, "It's what she wanted."

"Daddy, is it real?" Rachelle stood motionless before a large desk. A bright purple computer monitor flashed Happy Birthday in tall letters. She reached toward the computer. "This is for me?"

Garr gave Birdie's hand a squeeze before he released her to kneel beside Rachelle. "Didn't you want your own computer?"

Eyes fixed on the screen, Rachelle nodded.

"And I thought you'd be responsible enough to have one." Garr gave her a hug. "Now, I can use mine when I want."

Rachelle's small arms wrapped tightly around his neck. "Oh, thank you, Daddy. I love it."

Garr's response was muffled against her hair. A tiny tickle, a strange tightness grew low in Birdie's belly. The dreams she'd held as a young woman, the plans for children and family slinked past the walls she had built to keep them out. A shudder shook her shoulders and she fought to keep back a fresh flow of tears. She would not embarrass herself again. She would not.

Chewing on her lower lip helped to focus her emotions so she could turn her attention back to the duo before her. With a touch of the mouse, Garr showed Rachelle the varied programs loaded onto her new computer. With each new program, she planted a wet, noisy kiss on his cheek.

"Internet, too? Daddy, this is too much!"

"You don't want access to the world?"

She slapped his shoulder playfully. "You know I do. And I promise to be careful. Really. Thank you so much, Daddy. You're the best ever."

Garr sat back on his heels and watched the ease with which Rachelle maneuvered through the programs. Birdie wished he would turn back to her and ease the loneliness of her life. The emptiness threatened to overwhelm her.

The brief tilt of his head toward her brought their gazes crashing together with a force that made Birdie take a step back. "Will you be okay, squirt?" Garr rested one hand on Rachelle's shoulder as he spoke, but his eyes never left Birdie.

Rachelle shrugged. "Course. You go away."

Garr nodded and stood. The intensity of his gaze, the deepening of the clear depths both frightened and excited Birdie. She feared her reaction to the welling of emotion, but welcomed the responding warmth spreading through her to pool low in her belly. When he took her hand and led her from the room, the warmth turned to heat such as she had never felt. She tugged him to a stop at the top of the stairs. She had to stop this, now. But did she want to?

"I'd like to talk to you about Brutus." Did her voice really crack and expose the emotion she was trying to hide?

"Brutus?" A shake of his head tossed his dark hair back from his high forehead. Brilliant emotion faded from his eyes and Birdie had to bite her lip to keep from saying the words she thought would bring back the light. She couldn't, she wasn't willing to take the chance.

"I think I may have a possible solution."

"Let's go downstairs. How about some coffee while we talk?"

"You've said a magic word, sir. It's been too many long hours since my breakfast half a pot."

His strong, white teeth glistened when Garr smiled in response. "At last, a woman who shares my love of plain, old coffee. Or do you prefer cappuccino, like so many women of quality?"

"Only if I have to. You're right. Black, hot, and strong's my preference."

"Have a seat then. It'll only take me a few minutes."

Birdie sank again onto the warm, soft leather couch, leaned her head back, and closed her eyes. Her plan would keep her in contact with Garr—a thing she both desired and dreaded. If only she could trust what she believed she saw in his eyes. But the last time desire had flared in a man's eyes, nearly ten years ago, events had set in motion that still filled her with pain.

Unbidden, the attractive, crooked smile of the councilman, the father of her child, filled her inner vision. She'd discovered his desire was real, but he'd lied about his feelings to the point of laughing at her when she became pregnant. The shudder of memory shook through her, and dampness filled the line of her closed lashes.

"Are you okay?"

Birdie's eyes burst open at the soft concern in Garr's voice. "Memories."

Setting a large mug on the coffee table, Garr eased his long body next to her on the couch. "I wish I could take back the pain of this day, baby."

"Why do you call me that?"

A slight bronzed flush tinted the angles of his cheeks. "I... don't know. It seems right. Does it bother you?"

Considering her answer, Birdie paused. "No, it doesn't." She reached for the cup and, after testing the heat, took a leisurely sip. "Oh, that's good, food for my soul."

Angling so he could rest one arm along the back of the couch, Garr tasted his own coffee. "Always much better with a friend. Now, what about the monster?"

Birdie held the cup against her lips. This was a delicate subject, one she had no idea how Garr would take. Best to just blurt it out. She lowered the cup and rested it on one of her thighs. "I think I know the reason for some of his behavior. He's gotten old enough and he wants to mate."

Oh, great. Just what I need—a horny bird. I'm gonna strangle Mom. Garr blinked twice. "Mate? As in...?"

Birdie's face was a study in concentration as she obviously tried not to laugh. "As in, he needs a girlfriend."

"Umm, how can you tell?" Looking over the rim of his mug at Birdie, Garr took a long sip of coffee. The heat from the dark beverage felt like it was wrinkling the inside of his nose, so he lowered the mug.

"Well..." Increasing his discomfort, Birdie drew out the word. He didn't like not being in control of a situation, and this bird tested him to his limits. "You saw how he was trying to feed me when I was holding him?"

Garr nodded, the memory of Brutus rubbing his face against Birdie's cheek brought a strange rise of jealousy. Of a bird? "And have you seen him rubbing himself on his perch?"

"And that means—what?"

A faint pink covered Birdie's neck and face. Garr grinned at the endearing blush. A true blush was a rarity among women these days. "He, er…" She took a deep breath. "…is, um, relieving sexual tension."

"What?" Garr's loud exclamation surprised him. Carefully, he lowered his mug to the coffee table and lifted his arm to point toward the sunroom. "I've got a bird mast—uh, doing that? In my house? I've got a young girl here." His face grew hot and behind his outrage, feared he blushed as well.

Birdie's grin told him he did, but she continued without further acknowledgement of his discomfort. "Like I said, I might have a solution. I've thought about this from a number of different angles, considering the circumstances."

"I won't have that bird doing—that—in my house."

"Garr, it's just a part of life. Rachelle has some ideas about such things. She told me about your videos." Birdie's mouth dropped open, her eyes grew wide as if surprised at her words. She held her breath in with her fingers pressed to her lips.

Disbelief rose in Garr's chest. "She knows about my videos?" Then, he lowered his voice, the tone questioning and concerned. "Just what did she say about them?"

Birdie's breath blew out and she swallowed. The motion of her throat drew Garr's attention. Although he fought the uncomfortable sensation, it fascinated him. "Only that you have some anime you won't let her see because there's too much violence. Or they're too sexy."

"Sexy?" Garr's voice rose an octave before settling back to fierce determination. How much did his little girl understand? He'd take her out of the public school, put her in the safer environment of private classes. Maybe he'd just hire a tutor...

The soft touch of Birdie's hand on his arm brought him back. "Garr, all she knows is that they're adult stuff. Her words exactly. I wouldn't worry about it. I've had lots of school groups come in to Birdie's on tours. If a bird exhibits that kind of behavior, I just tell them the bird is playing. Having some fun."

She giggled and Garr found himself responding with a soft chuckle. "I suppose they are."

A deeper blush tinged her cheeks. Garr brushed the back of his fingers across the smooth, warm skin and leaned forward.

Birdie shook her head and the intriguing touch fell away. She couldn't afford to let him get too close. Her feelings were too fragile, too confused. "N—now, about Brutus."

Dark lashes lay against the angle of Garr's cheeks, and when he opened his eyes only polite curiosity remained. A flare of disappointment brought a faint sting of tears to her eyes. This was what she wanted, wasn't it?

"What do you propose?" The businesslike tone calmed her, enabling her to respond in kind.

"I have a female hyacinth who has also been exhibiting the desire to mate. I had begun to think I would never find a suitable male since I have no desire to ship her out of state."

"And you think Brutus would be suitable?"

"Oh, yes. He's beautiful. His configuration is perfect. He's young and healthy. And hopefully available." Birdie let the question hover in her eyes.

"As far as I'm concerned. But he is my mother's bird. And I don't know when she'll be back from her 'vacation'. As much as I need some peace and quiet, I don't feel comfortable letting the monster leave the house without Mom's okay."

"Oh, I understand. And I wouldn't want to cause any problems. I have a possible solution, although it may cause some additional problems."

Obviously waiting for her to continue, Garr lifted his eyebrows.

"I propose to bring Molly here. I have a reasonably portable cage that I could set up close to Brutus. We can't let them in the same cage until we're sure they'll get along. Unfortunately, it can take some time for birds to become accustomed to each other. And even longer to bond enough to mate."

"There'd be two monsters here?"

Birdie sighed; this wasn't going to be easy. A flutter deep in her soul told her Molly would find this candidate acceptable. Now, how was she going to convince Garr the noise and trouble was worth it?

"Any chance having a second bird here would calm the monster down so he'd be quieter? Or would two birds equal twice the noise?"

"Macaws are one of the noisiest birds."

"Of course they are." Garr picked up his mug and stared into the contents. "Would you like more coffee?"

"Uh, sure. A warm up would be great." The lithe movement of Garr crossing to the coffeepot dried her mouth. A man should not look so good in his clothes. He pressed the refilled mug in her hands. She hoped it wouldn't be too hot when she took a sip. She needed the moisture to be able to talk.

"So, I'd get to be the guardian of what you hope will turn into two lovebirds."

Birdie took another deep breath. This was the tricky part. "I know this is an unusual request, but it is a strange situation. If I could have frequent access to your house..." She paused as wrinkles appeared over his lowered brows and amended her statement. "At least to the sunroom, and maybe the kitchen, I'd take care of both birds. With any luck, you'll hardly know they're around. Or me, either."

Garr nearly said he could care less about the birds, but the thought of seeing Birdie on a regular basis had his heart pounding, beating a rapid rhythm against the walls of his chest. "What about your business? Won't coming over here so often cause problems?"

"Oh, no. I have an assistant who cares for the birds every day anyway. And I have an arrangement with the college. Ornithology, biology, and veterinary students take shifts overnight and on weekends as needed. And by writing research papers, they earn credits by working for me. Actually, that's how Dot, my assistant, started out."

Garr nodded. "Sounds like a good deal for everyone."

"Sure is. I'd never be able to have a life if I didn't have the help."

What was Birdie's life like? Was there a way to become more a part of it—other than as a bird donor? A fledgling thought tickled the back of his mind, but he immediately rejected the notion. She'd never accept—or would she? How could he even imagine offering—oh, he imagined a lot where Birdie was concerned.

Before he let doubts cloud his idea, he cleared his throat and spoke. "Would it be easier if you stayed here? Then you could have access to the birds anytime." He held up his hands to silence the protests forming on her lips. "We've got a guest suite on this floor, so you wouldn't be too far from the sunroom. Rachelle will be gone during the day for school, I'm in and out with my business..."

"Business?"

A small smile twitched one side of his lips. "I've been working mostly out of my home, during the construction of a small office complex. I'm an architect."

"That's why your house is so unique."

"I suppose. I've never thought of it in those terms. Now, back to our business."

"I couldn't stay here. I'd be in the way."

"Do you cook?"

"Well, of course. But what does that have to do with anything?"

"Although I'm sure taking care of two monsters is a large enough duty, if you'd cook a meal or two while you're here, it would be repayment enough. I've never been able to get beyond the barest of basics, and Rachelle gets tired of the same things over and over."

"And you think I could do better? Parrots need a more varied diet than just seeds, so I often fix chicken and potatoes for Molly. I'm sure Brutus would enjoy a bit of cooked rice now and then." She relaxed, and the tense set of her shoulders loosened. After taking a sip of coffee, she continued. "How long will your mother be gone? This could take a while. But when she returns, perhaps I could get permission to take Brutus back to *Birdies*."

Garr shrugged. "I never know. It could be days, it could be weeks. If you need a break, I suppose we could arrange for one of your students to cover here as well."

Birdie shook her head. "You've got it all figured out, don't you?"

"Uh, no. We can work things out as they come up, can't we?"

Crazy as it was, she was close to accepting Garr's proposal. How could she think of staying in a strange house, living with strangers? But such an attractive, appealing stranger. And Rachelle—for a short while she could believe her daughter had lived and was part of her life. Birdie sighed. This was headed toward another failure to be added to her short list of relationships.

No, not a relationship failure. There was no relationship. Despite the way Garr kissed her earlier—the wonderful way Garr kissed her earlier—she could keep this on a business level. Couldn't she?

And what about Molly? Didn't her favorite bird deserve a chance at the happiness she'd never found herself? Her eyes rolled to the ceiling. There she went again, giving the bird human characteristics.

"You must be thinking pretty hard."

Birdie's gaze angled to Garr. "Huh?"

"Your face is very expressive, you know. There's been a wide range of emotions passing over your face. It's interesting trying to figure out what each one means." Garr leaned back against the arm of the couch and crossed one leg over the other. "I hope this means you'll take me up on my offer."

"I hardly know you, and I'm not the kind to suddenly take up with strange men." Not anymore, anyway.

Resting his forearms against his crossed leg, Garr stared at her. Uncomfortable with the intense scrutiny, Birdie squirmed. Suddenly, Garr uncrossed his legs and leaned forward to take her hands. "This is a business proposition. One that should prove profitable for each of us."

It sure didn't feel like business, it felt like...

The word slipped past her lips before she could think of more negative reasons. "Okay."

"Okay what, Birdie?"

"I'll bring Molly here, and stay for a while to make sure the birds get along safely. Then, when your mother gets back from wherever she is, I'll see if I can talk her into letting Brutus come back to *Birdies* with me."

Garr's smile warmed her insides dangerously. What had she just done? He squeezed her fingers, rose, and pulled her to her feet. And into his arms.

The feel of Birdie's body, warm and alive next to his, caused Garr to stumble back a step. He took Birdie with him, and let no space come between them to cool the heat building low in his belly, and lower still. Her lips parted in surprise; her hands lifted to his chest to balance herself. It was easy to angle his head lower.

He covered her lips, soft, tentative, barely caressing. She stood stiff in his arms, but her mouth responded and he touched the tip of his tongue to her tender inner lip, but entered no further. For some reason, she didn't respond as she had that afternoon. It was difficult, no, it was torture, but he would honor her reluctance. Garr ended the kiss and held her away from him, immediately missing the feel of her in his arms.

"Then, we have a deal?"

Birdie nodded mutely. He took her hand. "Let me show you the room."

Digging her feet into the carpet, Birdie shook her head. "No. That can wait until tomorrow. I think I'd better go. How early do you want me to show up? I warn you, I'll make a lot of noise with that cage." Finally, the tense, hesitant lines of her face relaxed into a smile. "It'll be midmorning at the earliest, since I've got a few arrangements to make."

Garr stuffed his hands into his jean pockets to keep from touching her again.

"Whenever you get here will be fine. I've got nothing planned and I doubt we'll see Rachelle much. I may have to use a pry bar to get her away from her computer."

"No way, Daddy." Rachelle paused on the stairs. "I'm not a geek, you know."

"I know. Birdie's got to leave now, so you'd best say goodbye."

Rachelle skipped down the stairs and flew into Birdie's arms. "I don't want you to go."

If only he could be as free with his emotions as his daughter. He wanted Birdie to stay as well, but for much different reasons. Still, she would return tomorrow, unless she changed her mind. Unless, Rache knew she was coming back. He doubted she could disappoint the child.

"Don't worry, honey, Birdie will be back tomorrow. She'll even be staying with us for a while. And bring another bird to be Brutus's friend."

"That's so cool." Rachelle wrapped her arms around Birdie's neck and planted a noisy kiss on her cheek. "I'm glad. Will you teach me more about birds?"

Tears shimmered in Birdie's eyes and she hugged his daughter closer. "Of course I will." Her gaze lifted to Garr and his heart lurched. If this caused her so much pain, maybe it wasn't a good idea. As if reading his thoughts, Birdie shook her head and mouthed, "I'm okay."

Birdie patted Rachelle's narrow back and leaned back to look into the young, hopeful eyes. "I'll be back tomorrow, kiddo, and I'll give you a special introduction to my macaw, Molly."

Rachelle gave her a timid smile, and reached up to take Garr's hand. "Now, you walk her to her car, Daddy. Be a gentleman."

Garr sketched a brief salute and offered the crook of his elbow to Birdie. "Yes, ma'am."

The happy giggles erupting from Rachelle spilled over into Birdie's heart and filled her soul. The time here would be both wonderfully pleasant, and a painful reminder of what might have been. And that was without even considering the virile man offering his arm and his home.

She rose and let Garr lead her to the front entry. Full dark had fallen, but the path to the drive was illuminated by glowing lights hung from tall posts. As they passed under one of the lights, Birdie paused and stared in wonder at the sinuous dragon suspended from the pole as if in flight. Tiny claws supported the ball of light. She turned her astonished gaze to Garr.

He smiled proudly. "One of my better designs. I've always loved dragons, think of them as guardians. So these guard the way to my home. Keeps me and Rache safe."

"Your house is like a fairy tale anyway. Now I find fanciful creatures at every turn." She glanced back at the last light post before stepping onto the crushed, white stone drive. Even this close to the city, it was as if she was in another place, a completely different world. And, compared to her dingy apartment, this was a new, wonderful world.

The stones crunched under their feet; the sound comforting in the evening's quiet. The hum of insects rose from nearby bushes and a single firefly illuminated the underside of a leaf. She turned to Garr. "This has been an interesting day." Her voice sounded too loud and she winced.

Garr leaned close and trapped her against the side of her vehicle. "Mm, very interesting."

The heat from his body was too much, and much too inviting. An undeniable pull arched her forward and she found herself cradled against him, her ear pressed to the heavy beat of his heart. Her heart beat irregularly, then eased to match the intoxicating rhythm of Garr's.

His body moved against hers. Long forgotten desires swirled to the tips of her breasts and hardened her nipples. She actually tingled; a feeling she thought was reserved for novels. Her lungs filled with a deep breath and pressed her sensitized breasts firmly into Garr's chest. His breath caught.

Clutching the material of Garr's shirt, Birdie lifted to her toes. She wanted to kiss him, to see if she could recapture the feelings he'd created in her that afternoon. Her lips brushed the sharp angle of his jaw. His arms circled her and pulled her tight against him. Trapped by the feelings churning through her, more than by the strong press of his hand splayed on her back, Birdie sighed, lifted her lips a fraction and kissed his full, sensuous mouth.

Garr took control of the kiss. No longer tentative and tender, his mouth crushed hers and she welcomed the slow, persuasive thrust of his tongue. He devoured her, stroking his tongue against hers, exploring her mouth completely. Birdie clung to him, only the strength of his shoulders and the press of cold metal at her back held her upright. Never, never had she been kissed like this. She wanted more and lifted her hands to inch her fingers into his hair.

Garr pulled back, covered her hands with his, and tugged them down to hold them firmly against his chest. His chest rose and fell with his rapid breaths. There was a soft, disappointed moan. Heat flared over Birdie's face when she realized it came from her.

"We have an audience." Garr's voice was rough, almost harsh.

"Huh?" Birdie could barely put one thought together, let alone comprehend the meaning of Garr's words.

Nodding toward the house, Garr said, "Rache is watching from the guest room window. And if we don't stop now, she'll learn more about adult stuff than she needs to know right now."

"I... I'm sorry." Her gaze sought the ground, but only found the wall of Garr's chest.

His strong fingers lifted her chin. "There's nothing to be sorry about. I'm not. We'll see you tomorrow morning?"

Unable to trust her voice, Birdie nodded. Warm lips brushed against her cheek before Garr reached around her to open the SUV's door. She dug the

keys from her pocket, slid into the seat, and
fumbled with the ignition. After checking to make
sure she was in, Garr shut the door and moved
around the front of the vehicle.

He tapped twice on the windshield to catch her
attention and waved. When she reached the end of
the drive, she glanced into the rearview mirror. Garr
stood at the top of the drive, one hand still lifted in a
gesture of farewell.

CHAPTER FOUR

Another wooden chew toy landed haphazardly in the cardboard box. Grinning, Dot shook her head at Birdie, removed the toy and returned it neatly to the box.

"So, you're really gonna do this?"

"I can't believe it, but yes." Birdie leaned her hip against a counter. "I just can't believe it."

"This is just all for Molly, isn't it?" Dot cast her an appraising glance.

"Of... of course it is." Birdie turned to an open cupboard and shuffled through the contents.

"Uh-huh. So, is this guy a hunk?"

Birdie swallowed heavily. "I wouldn't know."

"Uh-huh. Tell me another one, Birdie. The back of your neck is bright red."

Curving one hand over the offending skin, Birdie reached back with the other to loosen the clip holding her shoulder length hair in a high ponytail.

Dot laughed. "And you colored your hair last night, too. Didn't you?"

Birdie turned to face her assistant and crossed her arms. "It was time."

"Uh-huh. New color, too, isn't it?"

A shrug lifted Birdie's shoulders, and a sudden sense of relaxation washed over her. All this over-thinking about the situation with Garr, and Brutus, had made her defensive. A chuckle tickled her lips. "You know I never remember what color I picked out the last time. As long as it's red and appeals to me at the time, that's the box I choose. What do you think of this one?"

"Better than that time you went almost orange." Dot joined her in laughter.

Birdie groaned at the memory. "Yeah, but it was kinda fun. Now, can you think of anything else I need before I take off for the fine life?"

"Wish I could have some vacation time in one of those estates."

A cobweb decorating a corner caught Birdie's eye when she rolled her gaze to the ceiling. "This is no vacation. You know how hard it can be to introduce birds to each other." She glanced at the carrier where Molly, eyeing her warily, clung to the thick wires of the door. "I know, Molly darlin', you don't like the carrier. We'll be leaving soon and you'll meet a nice young man. I'm sure you'll get along just fine."

"You really better get going, before Molly decides to destroy the carrier. Remember what happened the last time you tried to take her somewhere?"

Birdie did, and stifled another groan. Molly had escaped from the carrier and had taken her frustrations out on the upholstery of Birdie's old van. "Ah, I'd sure like to keep this vehicle looking good for a while longer. I'll grab Molly if you'll bring the box of supplies."

When the carrier was settled in the van and the bungee cords holding the broken-down cage were secure, Birdie turned to face Dot's smile. "You sure you won't have any trouble?"

"Of course not. I'll call the college tomorrow and arrange for additional student help. Otherwise, it should be pretty quiet. It's not like you're off to Borneo or somewhere like that, you know."

"I know." Birdie sighed. Was this really the best solution for everyone concerned? Maybe she should just wait until Brutus's owner returned. Her heart lurched at the mere thought of not seeing Rachelle again. The child had wrapped herself around Birdie's soul in just those few hours. There was something— special about the friendship Birdie thought might develop between them. Some unidentified connection she wanted the chance to understand.

"I've got my cell phone and I'll call as soon as I have the number there. I can't believe I didn't get it yesterday."

"Uh-huh. Bet your mind was elsewhere."

Telltale heat filled her face. Her thoughts had strayed to places better left unexplored. The frown she bestowed on Dot did little to stop her assistant's knowing chuckle. So instead, Birdie patted Dot's shoulder. "I'm off, then. I'll keep you posted."

"Sure. And let me know how the birds are doing, too." Laughing, Dot returned to *Birdies* dim interior.

Birdie wanted to stomp her foot in frustration. If it were up to her romantic assistant, she'd be married off by the end of the week. A soft smile touched her lips as she slid into the SUV and revved the engine. What would it be like to be married to Garr? The strange tingling began in the center of her chest and spread to her breasts and nipples. She looked down at herself. Maybe she shouldn't have worn a T-shirt. Marriage would be interesting, but the honeymoon...

Enough. She slammed her palm against the steering wheel. "Don't be foolish, Birdie. He's not interested in you. Ain't no way."

She pulled out of the parking space. A low, shiny, classic sports car pulled away from the side of the road and into *Birdies* drive. It sat there a few moments, facing her. The positions of the vehicles reminded her vaguely of a standoff, or some old 'B' movie where the teenagers played chicken on deserted roads. Irritation reared its head. She was ready to advance on the solid, immobile vehicle blocking her path when the driver put the car into reverse, whipped back onto the road and zoomed away with a squeal of tires. Relieved, Birdie drove forward. "Well, Mol. Ready for an adventure?"

A loud, extremely irritated squawk, followed by agitated chattering, came from the back seat. "I know, Mol, but we'll be there soon." Too soon.

"When's she gonna get here? Da-a-a-d?"

Garr held a finger to the slick cookbook page to mark his place and let out an exasperated breath. Being a parent tried his patience as much as the monster bird did at times. At least the animal was quiet. "For the millionth time, I don't know. Why don't you give up looking out the window every two minutes and give me a hand? That'll make the time go faster."

"Oh, sure, Daddy." Rachelle tugged a tall stool out from under the counter and climbed up, slammed her elbows onto the granite, and propped her chin in her hands.

Unfortunately, Garr knew exactly how she felt. His ears were tuned to the sound of tires on the drive, and his heart had lodged thick in his throat every time the phone rang. Every telemarketer in the country must have called. Everyone and their brother. Everyone except Birdie.

He'd lain awake most of the night, his thoughts alternating between disbelief at his offer, fear she'd change her mind, and heated memories of the feel of her in his arms.

"So, Dad, trying a new recipe?" Rachelle swung the cookbook around so she could glance at the brightly colored picture. "Mexican?"

Garr shrugged. "Would you help chop some veggies? I thought we might have a salad to go with the enchiladas."

Rachelle slid from the stool and started taking crisp vegetables from the refrigerator. "Pretty fancy for just us." She cast a glance back over her shoulder. "Are you trying to impress someone? Are you gonna burn this, like you did the last time you tried something new?" Rachelle giggled as she pulled a cutting board from a lower cupboard. "That would be really impressive."

Returning the cookbook to its original position, Garr peered at the directions. "Seems simple enough. I know you don't trust your old dad to cook much beyond boxed mac and cheese, but maybe there's a chef hidden inside me just waiting to get out."

"Oh sure. And I know the number for pizza delivery by heart." A large wooden bowl joined the pile of vegetables before Rachelle climbed back onto the stool. "Will you hand me a knife, please."

Garr took a small ceramic knife from the wooden knife block and turned the handle toward his daughter. "Be careful."

"I always am."

They worked in comfortable silence and soon the bowl of lettuce and mixed vegetables waited on a refrigerator shelf. A flat casserole dish of enchiladas sat on the counter while they waited for the oven to heat. Rachelle shook her head and rolled her eyes dramatically at the awkwardly rolled enchiladas.

Garr moved the dish to the top of the stove and crossed his arms defensively. "Once I put the cheese on, you won't be able to tell how they look."

Rushing around the counter, Rachelle launched herself into his embrace. Her small arms wrapped tightly around his neck and she kissed him soundly on the cheek. "They'll taste great, even if they don't look like the picture."

With his eyebrows lifted, Garr asked, "Think so, squirt?" Rachelle was saved from answering by the soft chimes of the doorbell. She squirmed to be released. "It's her. I'll get the door." Her bright athletic shoes tapped over the slate floor as she rushed toward the front of the house.

Garr forced himself to take a deep breath, put the enchiladas into the oven and wipe his hands on a damp towel. His muscles ached with the strain of the slow, controlled movement. He really wanted to rush out the door with Rachelle and welcome their guest properly.

He wanted to know Birdie better. Hell, simply put, he wanted Birdie. She excited him like no woman had since Melissa. But, for some reason, she was frightened. Not of him he didn't think, but of her own feelings. Some bastard must have hurt her badly. During the night he made the decision and had vowed to give her the time she needed to feel comfortable with him.

By the time he reached the wide-open front door, Birdie and Rachelle had the back of her SUV opened and their heads were together while Birdie explained something to the child. Sunlight glinted off golden strands in Birdie's red hair and the smile she gave Rachelle sparkled. Garr fervently hoped it wouldn't take too much time.

The smile froze on her face when Birdie noticed him, and her gaze collided with his. Her eyes were more blue than gray today, and the intensity invited him closer. But, when he took the steps onto the drive, her eyes became wide and wary. Garr took a deep breath and silently reaffirmed his personal vow. Time. She needed time.

"Welcome. What can I help you with?"

Rachelle's arms stretched around a large, brown box. "I've got this stuff. I'll take it to the sunroom, 'kay?"

"Great, Rache." Birdie's eyes remained firmly locked with his. "I... uh... could use your help to get the cage inside. It's heavy."

Garr nodded and moved toward the back of the SUV. A loud screech stopped him cold and he eyed a beige carrier on the middle seat warily. Great, this bird didn't like him either. And he made sure to wear neutral colors.

"I'm sorry, Garr. Molly doesn't travel well. She's a tad irritated with me."

Loud calls echoed from the vehicle and were answered from the back of the house. "We'd better get her inside before the neighbors call the cops on us for disturbing their Sunday peace and quiet." Garr reached for the carrier and jerked his hand back when the thick, black beak snapped at him.

"Let me take Molly. If you could bring in the pieces of the cage, I'll start setting it up. The sooner she's in a place she feels is home, the better."

Like owner, like bird. Garr stepped back so Birdie could reach the carrier, and watched her take the awkward case into the house before he reached for the black metal cage. He concentrated on wrestling the heavy pieces from the back without scraping the vehicle's finish. When all the parts lay on the grass, he hefted the largest piece and carried it to the back of the house.

He lined the pieces up on the patio before he entered the sunroom. Birdie and Rachelle were cooing over the huge blue bird cradled in Birdie's lap. Silently watching them with obvious curiosity, Brutus hung from the top of his cage. Birdie produced a treat from a pocket and offered it to her bird. When the large beak daintily accepted the large nugget, Birdie handed one to Rachelle. Brutus snatched his treat from Rachelle and turned his back on the females.

Birdie chuckled. "It will take a while for them to grow accustomed to each other. We'll start by putting Molly's cage across the room then gradually move them closer. We don't want either bird to get stressed out by being too close, too soon."

Garr wondered if she was really talking about the birds, or if it was their situation that colored her words. When she looked up to discover him standing in the doorway, her startled eyes told him she wasn't sure either. He'd keep it businesslike—for right now.

"I've got all the pieces outside. Let me know what you want first, and I'll bring the parts in as you need them."

Birdie nuzzled the bird in her lap. "I'm sorry, honey. You've got to go back in the carrier for a little bit. I'll hurry, I promise." She looked at Rachelle. "Would you sit by the carrier and keep Molly company?"

Rachelle's face lit. "Of course. Take as long as you want."

With the bird safely tucked away, Birdie turned to Garr. "Ready?"

It took longer than Birdie anticipated to get the cage back together. Frustrated, she longed to kick the stupid pile of metal and scream. Yet, somehow, Garr's calm presence kept her in check as he methodically fit one angle of the cage to the next. *Well, he is an architect.*

Finally, with the cage situated just right, Molly was freed from the carrier and left to examine the new surroundings. The noise of two birds trying to assert dominance bounced from one wall to the next. Rachelle covered her ears.

"We have to leave them alone. If we stay here, they'll never shut up."

The trio entered the kitchen to find smoke billowing from the oven. A smoke alarm squealed, adding to the din. Garr rushed to the stove and flipped on the vent. Rachelle pulled a stool under the smoke alarm, climbed up and easily removed the batteries, bringing relative quiet to the kitchen. Garr flapped a towel to direct the smoke up to the vent.

Birdie laughed at their well-choreographed movement. "Looks like you've done this before."

Garr shook his head wearily. "More times than I care to count. You'd think after all these years..."

"Pizza?" Rachelle lifted the phone.

"Do you need to stay here while the birds scream?" Garr's hopeful, puppy dog eyes melted Birdie's already dangerously soft heart.

"No, they should be okay. Loud, but okay. Obnoxious, but okay."

Garr lifted both hands. "I get the picture. How about we do lunch far from the high decibel level?"

Lunch out? Sunday dinner was a time for families; how could she...?

Rachelle took her hand, looked up with bright blue eyes and smiled a smile so familiar it took Birdie's breath away. "Please?"

Garr took the smoking pan from the oven and set it in the sink. His shoulders sagged. Birdie blinked at her twinge of guilt. He'd said he was a terrible cook; he must have been trying to impress her. Endearing, but totally unnecessary. She couldn't let him suffer, could she?

"Okay."

Garr turned and smiled. "Then, the OK is where we'll go."

From the only booth available at the rear of the small restaurant, Birdie was able to take in the full impact of the décor. Train related signs covered the walls, glass lanterns and antiques filled shelves over the service area. But most amazing was the model train that periodically circled the room on tracks placed near the ceiling. Feeling almost sorry for the engine pulling a long string of cars, each advertising a different area business, Birdie chuckled.

"This place is wonderful. I can't believe I didn't even know it was here."

Garr barely glanced up from his menu. "Food's good, too." He tossed the plastic covered pages to the table. "Don't know why I bother to look, I know what I'm having."

Birdie glanced at the Sunday dinner specials. "Um, I guess I do, too, unless I change my mind before the waitress gets here." Nervous about being there with Garr and Rachelle, Birdie didn't think she could eat very much—even though she had skipped breakfast. A salad and the stuffed baked potato would be about right. And it shouldn't be too messy; she was good at dropping food all over herself.

Full of banter for Garr and Rachelle, the waitress arrived to take their orders. A knot formed in Birdie's stomach but she ignored it. She refused to dignify the uncomfortable emotion by naming it.

She fiddled with a napkin from the black, metal dispenser while she waited for the waitress to leave. "So, you come here often?"

Startled eyes met hers. Garr chuckled. "Great line."

Oh, God, that sounded like a pickup line from a bad movie. She glanced away quickly and stared out the clear windows lining the front of the restaurant.

Letting his fingers linger just a moment too long, Garr reached over the table and touched her hand. She was so cute when she got flustered—faint pink drew a soft line across her cheeks. He took a deep breath and leaned back in the booth, letting his arm rest around Rachelle's shoulders. That should keep him grounded.

"This is one of our favorite places, isn't it, squirt?"

Rachelle nodded, reached for her glass of soda and blew bubbles with the straw until Garr tapped her shoulder and she stopped. An innocent smile graced her young face.

Garr turned his attention back to Birdie. A strange look filled her eyes as she watched Rachelle. It was a look of recognition; as if she met someone she hadn't seen in years. Confused, he studied her, and waited until her gray-blue eyes returned to him. He smiled to offer comfort for something he didn't understand. Yet.

"Originally this restaurant operated right next to the railroad tracks, actually not too far from here. This location is much larger than the first OK Café."

Smoothing the wrinkles in her forehead, Birdie's eyebrows rose. "Larger?"

"Yep. There they catered to the railroad workers and the locals who dared to try the shabby place. My grandparents used to take me there. Now, well, you can see the results of a good reputation, excellent food..."

The waitress appeared with their meals. Birdie's eyes widened at the size of the overstuffed potato set before her.

"And adequate portions." Garr chuckled.

"Adequate?" Her voice squeaked. "Good thing nothing comes with this besides the salad. I can't eat all this."

"It's good, you may be surprised." Garr turned to his meal, cut a bite of roast from the pile on his plate, and placed it next to Birdie's potato. "Try this. They have some of the best beef in town."

Trying to swallow the dry lump in her throat, Birdie watched Garr and his daughter a few moments while they happily attacked their meals. She looked at the roast resting so innocently on her plate and glanced at Garr from under her lashes. He watched her.

Birdie picked up her mug. She needed to get a life. She'd been around birds too long. She glanced again at the offered bite. Feeding the female was a typical male mating behavior. Humans didn't do the same thing... did they? She didn't know, couldn't seem to think clearly.

After a few swallows of good, rich coffee, she was ready to tackle her meal. First, since Garr was waiting for her reaction, she tried the roast. It was good. Tender and moist, so she smiled at him and nodded. He smiled around a mouthful of food and pointed at her potato with his fork.

The blend of toppings whipped through the potato was as good as the beef, and Birdie found she was hungrier than she thought. Soon, she'd eaten the entire potato and the others were done as well. Rachelle stared out the window.

"Daddy? Is there a car show in town?"

"Don't think so, squirt. Why? Have you taken a sudden interest in cars?"

Rachelle's hair flew across her face when she shook her head. "Eww. Of course not. There's just been this old car driving down the street. See it? This is the fifth time it's gone past here."

A faint niggle of concern tickled the back of Birdie's neck. The dark, classic sports car had been at *Birdies* that morning. She rolled her eyes. It was a beautiful, sun shining Sunday. Of course the local car lovers would be out showing off their vehicles. Certainly more than one dark sports car cruised the city streets.

"Daddy, can I go out and watch the pigeons?"

"Don't you want your ice cream first?"

"Naw, I'm full. Can I?"

Garr slid from the booth and let her escape. She gave Birdie a knowing grin and skipped from the café.

"Pigeons?"

"You saw that windmill when we came in? They've built a cage around the base and keep a variety of fancy pigeons. Rache loves to watch them, she even coos at them."

"So, you've raised a bird lover."

"Given the right circumstances, I could become one, too."

No, he couldn't mean what she thought he said, could he? Birdie closed her eyes and lifted her coffee for protection. This was a fantasy, only wishful thinking. He meant something totally different.

But, the changeable colors of his eyes had darkened, the pupils becoming larger. They drew her closer, pulling her deeper into the fantasy. She blinked, shook her head, and turned to peer out the window. This was a trap she couldn't fall into again. She would not let herself be set up for the pain. Business. This was all business.

The touch of Garr's hand brought her back to the café and the reality of the man seated across from her. He was warm and real, and... it was business. She jerked her hand away.

Garr pulled his hand back across the table and glanced at his fingertips. A long breath lifted his chest. What had he done? Why did she reject him so easily? Most of the women he'd dated had nearly drooled and draped themselves all over him. He tossed away the uncomfortable, confusing thought. Birdie's reaction startled him. Desire had darkened her eyes last night. Wasn't that evidence she returned the heat he felt for her? Was she playing him for a fool, just to get a mate for her damn bird?

He crumpled his paper napkin into a tight wad and tossed it on the table. Fine. It would be business only. And once his mother returned home, it would be over. His heart lurched painfully, but he shook the feeling away. How could anything be over when nothing had started?

"Are you ready to go then?"

"Y-yes. I'd better check on the birds."

"Fine." Garr stood, held his hand out to Birdie, but jerked it back to his side. Instead, he pulled his wallet from a hip pocket and tossed a few bills on the table. "I'll pay the bill and meet you at the car."

Birdie stared at his wide back as he wound his way through the clustered tables toward the register. This was what she wanted—a reasonably cordial, business relationship. But why did it feel so empty, so cold and impersonal now? She rose from the booth and didn't even look at Garr when she passed behind him.

Birdie leaned against the car and crossed her arms. This was going to be tougher than she anticipated. How could she remain cool and aloof when her nerve endings sang each time Garr was near her? She took a deep, determined breath. She'd just have to stay out of his way as much as possible. Maybe his mother would return soon.

"Rache, let's go." Garr called from the other side of the car. "Now."

All smiles and excitement, Rachelle rushed to the car. "Daddy, can we..."

She glanced from Garr to Birdie then back at her father. The smile disappeared from the young face. "Never mind." Rachelle's words fell dull and lifeless. She slid onto the backseat and Garr slammed the door behind her.

What about Rachelle? Birdie climbed into the car and leaned her head against the headrest. She couldn't let those thoughts, or that fantasy affect her relationship with the child. What was she going to do?

The view from the side window blurred from the tears she didn't want and didn't understand filling her eyes. She had to think of Molly, and Brutus. They deserved the chance to find avian happiness. So she'd straighten her shoulders, hold her head high and...

Heavy, oppressive silence filled the car the entire trip back to Logan's Hollow.

Four days passed more quickly than Birdie thought possible. Always polite, but seldom warm, each morning Garr asked if she needed anything. Then, he took Rachelle to school and she was alone until late in the afternoon. The birds behaved well and she was amazed at how quickly they became adjusted to each other. However, macaws were social creatures, and she had suspected Molly might have been lonely for one of her own kind.

Each day, watching both birds for signs of stress, she moved the cages closer together. The large birds chattered happily and the screaming became less frequent, but twice as loud with two voices. Both birds continued to exhibit pre-mating behaviors, and her supply of wooden chew toys rapidly disappeared.

She had prepared a meal each evening and suffered through the silent, nearly conversation-free time. Even Rachelle remained subdued, only showing interest in the daily lessons Birdie gave her in caring for birds. Then after supper, saying she needed to do her homework, the girl would disappear upstairs.

Garr shut himself away in his home office in the evenings, but Birdie didn't think he got much work done. If the sounds of pacing and restless rustling of papers were any indication, he rarely even sat at the wide desk or drafting table.

And each day, Birdie fought the depths of a depression threatening to overwhelm her.

Four days cooped up in his small, temporary downtown office had nearly driven Garr over the edge. His partner and the office manager each gave him increasingly strange looks the longer he spent at his desk. He'd scheduled as many appointments as he could and struggled to maintain a professional attitude, but the woman at his house drove him to distraction.

She spoke barely three words to him in any given day, and spent all her time either with Rachelle or the birds. Of course, he hadn't been very friendly, either. But he couldn't be friendly without being *friendly*. So, he spent the long evening hours alone, pretending to be ultimately busy.

The scattered papers covering his desk gave him no satisfaction, and his footsteps had mashed the carpeting, creating a path from the desk to the door. Too many times he'd stopped with his hand on the doorknob, ready to confess his feelings. And exhaustion did little to fight the agony of his imagination when she retired for the night in the room just below his?

Once again, he stood at the door, his ears tuned to the soft sounds of her movement in the great room. The television played softly but the sounds of movement against the leather furniture told him she was restless, too. Garr took a deep breath, held it, and let it whoosh slowly past his lips. This pretending was foolish, he was foolish. He should be pursuing the woman. He'd never backed down from obtaining a desired objective. Before he could rethink his action, he opened the door.

Unable to stand being alone in the guestroom any longer, Birdie sat in the family room, her eyes on the large television, her thoughts elsewhere. She chewed on her lower lip until the pain made her stop. She should never have agreed to stay here. Garr was dangerous to her senses—dangerous to the world she had built for herself. And Rachelle—as much as she now loved the little girl, with the resemblance--

The door to Garr's study flew open and he filled the doorway. "I... um." He cleared his throat. "I was thinking of making a pot of coffee. Would you care to join me?"

That was more words in a row than he'd said all week, and relief eased into Birdie's strained thoughts. Perhaps they could form a truce. "No need. There's a fresh pot waiting. I just haven't gotten up for any yet."

"Stay put." Garr's easy stride carried him quickly across the room. He moved as if he were afraid she would disappear when his back was turned.

And she should. But, not this time. She'd waited for this moment since Sunday, hoped for a chance to make some amends for her reactions. He held her favorite, thick mug in front of her, and sat carefully on the far end of the couch. "Okay?"

Birdie wasn't sure if he meant where he sat, or the coffee, so she just nodded. Both were fine. "Garr, I..."

"Shh. I know. I've been an ass these past few days. Do you think we could start over?" He leaned forward, his mug of coffee held between his hands like an offering.

"I haven't been exactly cordial."

Garr's eyebrows lifted and a tentative smile finally tugged at his full lips. "Can we start again? Please?"

"A truce?" The mug in her hands shook and the surface of the dark beverage erupted into tiny coffee waves.

"I was hoping for something more like—friendship?"

Birdie fought the tingle of desire his hopeful expression created. Friendship was good. A good start, anyway. "I think that would be a good idea."

The tension holding his shoulders high eased away. The tight knot at the base of his neck dissolved. Garr hadn't realized how much Birdie's answer meant to him. "Me, too." He glanced toward the stairs. "I'm sure Rachelle will be happy, as well. She's not normally such a quiet child. In fact, she's usually about as loud as the monster. How are our lovebirds, anyway?"

Garr watched Birdie over the rim of his mug. The tiny lines around her eyes and the double crease that had hovered between her brows for the past few days had disappeared. Even the firm set of her voluptuous mouth softened to remind him how kissable she was. He tried to cover the change in his breathing by leaning back and setting the mug to one side.

Luckily, she warmed to her subject, and her eyes sparkled with excitement. "They're getting along great. I keep moving the cages closer together so by the time your mother gets home, they may be sharing living quarters. But, if I want them to mate, I may have to have to create an aviary for them. They need lots of room. Just for the nest box, not to mention those long tails."

Garr chuckled. He liked her like this, flushed with excitement. A shame she wasted the excitement on birds. The glow dusting her skin should be directed toward him. Caused by him. And no one else. Garr squirmed against the buttery soft leather couch. He had to curb such thoughts or his body would betray him.

"Tomorrow I need to go back to *Birdies*."

"What?" He'd let his thoughts wander and had no idea what she was talking about. Did she mean forever?

"The birds have chewed their way through my supply of toys. They need more." She leaned forward to whisper, "Chewing can be a sexual behavior, you know."

"Uh, no, I didn't." The pull of fabric across her breasts, the brief view of cleavage at the neckline of her blouse dried his mouth. He would love to nibble at her neck, or softly chew a response from her breasts and nipples.

Something must have shown in his face, because Birdie leaned back suddenly. Her posture and her expressive face closed to him. God, he'd gone too far. Again.

Birdie took a deep breath. They needed to talk about something other than sex, even if it was bird sex. His hazel eyes had become almost brown, filled with dangerous promise. Her traitorous body responded, hot and heavy, to those unspoken promises.

"Anyway, I need to pick up some more toys and check in with Dot."

"Rache has only a half day of school tomorrow. Then I need to drop her off at a friend's house. They're having a sleepover." He sighed. "Better her friend's mom than me. So how about if we pick you up, have a quick lunch, then stop at Birdie's before dropping off Rachelle?"

Hesitant, she watched him. Only honest interest filled his face.

"Besides," he continued, "I know Rache would love to see where you work. Actually, so would I."

"How could I refuse?" Birdie would never hear the end of it from Dot if she didn't introduce her to the famous Garr Logan when she had the chance. "I'll be ready when you get home."

"Do you think we should tell Rache?" He glanced meaningfully at the stairs. "She'll be relieved we're getting along."

Birdie nibbled on her lip, and winced when she hit a sore spot. "I'm sorry I've caused her distress."

Garr leaned forward. "No, it wasn't just you. In fact, I think she's been the only one acting like an adult here."

Birdie couldn't help it. She chuckled. Garr's face brightened. He stood, paused a moment, and held one hand out to her. "Shall we go tell her?"

Pausing as long as he had, Birdie contemplated his outstretched hand. She lifted her own and let him wrap his fingers around hers and tug her to her feet. He stepped back before their bodies touched, but kept a firm hold on her hand. The tingles burned a path from her hand to cover her body. His simple touch burned her. But she dared not pull away, for she refused to lose the feelings she had just discovered. After her nod, they crossed the room and mounted the stairs to the second floor.

After dropping an exuberant Rachelle at school, Garr made a side trip to the city library before checking in at the office. The librarian had been happy to help him and cast frequent looks in his direction, even after they had located the books he requested. Scanning the volumes quickly, he selected a few, checked out, and hurried to the office.

Despite the thrill of designing and constructing his own building, it had been a long time since a project interested him, excited him as much as this did, and he couldn't wait to get started.

 Even with the drab, chipping paint, the front of *Birdies* was a sight filling her with immense joy and proprietary pride. She glanced at Garr as he put the car in park and wondered what he thought of her converted building. He was sure to see something different with his architect's eye.

"Come on in. I'll introduce you to Dot first." Rachelle grabbed Birdie's hand and pulled her toward the door. "Hey, slow down, sweetie. Don't go rushing in, you might scare the birds."

Rachelle slowed immediately and turned her head to look back over her shoulder. "Hurry up, Daddy."

Garr's presence behind her and the warmth of his body seeped pleasantly into Birdie. It was all she could do to keep from leaning back against his strong body, the world be damned. But a loud squawk from inside made her take a step forward and the moment evaporated. A variety of bird noises filled the air when she opened the door and escorted her guests inside the building. "May I help you?" Dot moved from behind a tall, leaning pile of boxes. "Oh, Birdie. What're you doing here?"

"Showing off my place. And I need to talk to you. And, I really need more wooden chews."

Dot patted the pile of boxes. "Just got in a new shipment. They're here somewhere. We may have to dig." She fisted her hands and jammed them against her hips. "And who are these fine folks?"

With her hands gentle on the girl's shoulders, Birdie pushed Rachelle in front of her. "This is

Rachelle Logan, my hostess while I'm taking care of her grandmother's bird."

Dot bowed slightly. "Nice to meet you. Are you a fan of birds?"

"I sure am. Birdie's been teaching me lots. Can I see the birds here?"

"I'll show you around in a sec. First, Birdie has to introduce me to your dad."

Rachelle giggled, and the sound was mimicked from the far end of the room. Her eyes grew wide and she turned to Birdie. "Hurry up."

Allowing Garr to move forward in the narrow space, Birdie stepped to one side. "And this is Garr Logan." She winced inwardly at how much her voice softened when she said his name. A quick glance at Dot confirmed her suspicions, her assistant's wide smile flashed at Birdie before she held out her hand to Garr.

"Nice to meet you. I'd say I've heard a lot about you, but I haven't. Yet." Dot winked at Garr and turned a wicked grin to Birdie. "I'll let you two take care of gathering what you need while I show Rachelle around. Have fun. Hey Rache, can I call you Rache? Let's start down at the end where the giggler is." Dot led the way and Rachelle gawked at everything as she followed.

Birdie turned to Garr. "Probably shouldn't have done that. Once Dot gets warmed up, it may be hours before you see your daughter again."

"This should be quite the experience for her. Where do we start?"

Birdie bit her lip to keep from giving the answer her heart screamed for her to give. Instead, she pointed to the small area set aside for her office. "I've got some paperwork I need to take with me. If you could start looking through these boxes..." Her hand moved to the angling stack of boxes. "The chews shouldn't be too hard to find."

Twenty minutes later Garr had packed a small box with bird toys, and Birdie had a folder of papers stuck under her arm. Garr wandered past the multitude of cages looking for his daughter. The girl's crestfallen expression when they returned to the entry brightened only slightly when she was reminded how much she had been looking forward to her sleepover.

Dot patted the young shoulder. "Maybe your dad will let you come by again sometime. If we arrange it right, you can help me feed the birds."

Garr answered before Rachelle could even ask. "I don't see any problem with that. As long as you promise to do what Dot says and you don't get in the way."

"I promise, oh, I promise, Daddy." She wrapped her arms around his waist. "Thank you."

Garr hefted the box. "Ready?"

Birdie hesitated. "Can I meet you in the car in a couple of minutes? I have something I need to discuss with Dot."

She waited until Garr and Rachelle were far from the door before she turned to Dot's curious gaze. But the young woman spoke before she could.

"I needed to tell you something, too. But I didn't want to say anything in front of our guests."

"Is something wrong with one of the birds?" Birdie's heart lurched. Had she neglected the rest of her charges by spending all her time with Molly and Brutus?

Dot lifted one hand and waved dismissively toward the rows of cages. "Don't worry about them.

We've been having a fine time. Actually, it's probably not a problem."

"Something's worrying you, girlfriend. Spill it."

"Well, there's been a number of calls asking for you."

"I do have a business here, you know." Hopefully her flippant response would ease the worry from Dot's normally calm face.

"I know, but he refused to leave any sort of message. I guess that's really not so strange, but then, I got this barrage of hang-up calls. Something about the whole thing just doesn't feel right."

No, it didn't. But Birdie didn't know why. Hang-ups—rude as they were—happened all the time. She forced a chuckle. "Ah, a suspicious mind. Guess it comes with the territory when you're dating a cop, huh?" Birdie paused a moment. "Speaking of said cop, are you going to see Roger tonight?"

Dot grinned. "I don't doubt. We had a huge fight last night, so I'm sure as soon as he gets off duty, he'll be over with flowers. Maybe even a bottle of wine. We'll have a great evening making up."

Birdie's face heated. The sensual implications reminded her she would be alone with Garr that evening.

"Why Birdie, you're blushing. We're going to have to talk soon. You really like this guy."

Ignoring Dot's curiosity, Birdie glanced out the door. Garr and Rachelle were looking around the area and talking as they waited by the car. "I need you to ask Roger something, a legal question."

"Okay." Dot shrugged. "Just remember he's not an attorney."

"I know. And if he doesn't have any idea, that's okay. I need to know if I can look at my chart, my records from the hospital. There's something I want to check out."

Dot hesitated, then spoke slowly. "I'll ask him, but don't be getting yourself in trouble. Is this about when... about nine years ago?"

Not trusting her voice, Birdie nodded.

"You'll talk to me if you need to? I don't want you reopening an old wound better left scabbed over."

Too late. It was much too late for that. "I know. You're a great friend, Dot. Just ask Roger. I'll give you a call tomorrow and see if he knows anything." The escape the door offered was a welcome relief.

Dot held the door open and called after her. "Not too early, 'kay?" Dot's delighted laughter cut off with the closing door.

Birdie shrugged at Garr and moved to the passenger side of the car. She wasn't sure what she'd just set in motion, nor if she really wanted to discover the possible truth. Or revisit truth's pain. And what did it really matter anyway? Those nine years were long gone, never to be recaptured.

Garr grilled steaks and opened a bottle of wine, two things he said he could do without messing up ninety nine percent of the time. After the meal they sat on the couch and gradually the space between them narrowed until Birdie curled comfortably against his side. The stereo played an assortment of soft classical music, and he'd even found a thick candle to light the otherwise dim room, creating a moment to savor.

Birdie remained quiet, and he could almost hear the wheels in her head grinding together with deep thoughts. But he didn't want to think — he wanted only to experience, to feel. Still, he needed to honor her thoughts.

"May I use an old cliché?"

Startled, Birdie's wide eyes turned to him. "What?"

"Penny for your thoughts."

"Oh." Birdie straightened and sat cross-legged, facing him. "Does Rachelle look like your wife?"

That was hardly the type of question he expected, and he wasn't about to let the specter of his past love color this night. "No. Melissa was dark like I am. Somehow, we still ended up with a golden, blue-eyed darling."

"Was she born in the hospital here in town?"

"Yes."

"That means your wife and I were there at the same time. We might have even seen each other."

Unsure where Birdie was headed, Garr hesitated. Nor did he like morbid direction of her thoughts. "It's possible. Although Melissa was taken to surgery almost immediately after we got there."

Birdie nodded. "And I was in the labor room for a long time. Did you see Rachelle right after she was born?"

"Birdie, why are you asking me these things?"

She shrugged as if she didn't know, but kept her eyes lowered and wouldn't look at him.

"Baby..." At the endearment, her eyes lifted slowly. "That wasn't a happy time for either of us. Why bring it up now? Can't we talk about something else?"

"I—I'm sorry. You're right." She attempted a wavering smile. "You ask me a question now."

Garr lifted his eyebrows and rubbed his chin in thought. He held one arm out to the side; she sighed and snuggled against him again. Angling his long body, he lifted her onto his lap. His lips touched her earlobe. "What's your real name?"

Birdie jerked, stared at him and chuckled nervously. She seldom admitted her full name, but immediately trusted Garr with her awful secret. With her eyes lowered to the rise and fall of his chest, she spoke softly. "Burdetta Opalina Simons." She peeked at him but he wasn't laughing, so she lifted her gaze to his. "I was named after my dad's parents. See why I never tell anybody?"

Garr took her face between his hands. She identified the small, callused area caused by holding a pencil in the smooth texture of his fingertips. The warmth of his palms calmed her, made her feel cherished. Her eyelids drifted closed.

Those wonderful fingers traced the line of her closed lids, the curve of her cheeks, before barely brushing over her lips. He was close, and the warmth of his wine scented breath sent shivers coursing along her spine.

"Burdetta Opalina Simons." Garr's voice was raw, harsh and vibrated delightfully through her. "I'm going to kiss you." One of his hands continued to cup her cheek, the other moved between her shoulder blades to press her closer.

Birdie's lips parted at the first touch of his firm mouth against hers. A sound made deep in her throat invited him to explore. His kiss tasted of wine and the indescribable flavor she would always remember, always associate with Garr. One kiss melded into another. She clutched at his head, and the silky press of his hair against her palms increased her delight.

The warmth of his lips traveled over her face to linger gently over her closed eyes. He traced the shell of her ear with the tip of his tongue before he sucked softly on the lobe. When the kisses trailed the length of her stretched neck, she fought to keep from crying with pure delight.

Garr supported her with one hand and arched her back while he ran the other hand up and down her side. The position pressed her bottom into the firm presence, the burning heat of his desire. Birdie captured his roving hand, lifted it to kiss the palm, and lay it over her breast. She bit back a cry of delight.

"Baby?" The harshness of Garr's voice made her open heavy lids. His hand was motionless upon her body and she wiggled her shoulders to create a wonderful friction. "Baby, are you sure?"

Leaning forward, she captured his hand between them. "Sure? Very sure." Garr groaned deep in his chest. She traced his lips with her tongue and sank into his soul-rending kiss.

A flash of lightning brightened the dark windows. A few seconds later a crash of thunder rattled those windows. Lost in the sensuous movements of Garr's lips and hands, Birdie accepted the wild change of weather as part of the experience of loving Garr.

Until a frightened scream sounded from the sunroom. Lightning flashed and the scream repeated. After a third crash of thunder and answering scream, Birdie jerked from Garr's embrace and slid to the floor on her rump. One of her hands lifted to cover the 'o' of her mouth.

"Molly." She crawled toward the sunroom. "Molly's terrified of lightning," she called back over her shoulder.

Enjoying the view of her lush bottom moving away from him, it took a few moments before her words, and the screaming bird, registered. Jumping to his feet, Garr blessed the fact he wore sweats rather than his tight jeans and followed Birdie.

Molly hung from the side bars of her cage, her mouth open as she panted in distress. Birdie advanced slowly, her voice soft and cajoling. By the time she stood next to the cage, the bird was silent, but eyeing her warily. "I'm going to take her out of the cage and bring her into the great room. The lightning might not be so bright in there. Can you bring a couple of towels?"

Garr turned, but before he could move away Birdie clutched his arm. "I'm sorry, Garr."

He kissed her cheek. "It's okay, baby. Take care of Molly." Strangely, he felt no jealousy toward the bird, and understood the need to calm the frantic macaw. Quickly grabbing a couple of towels from the bathroom, he hurried back to the sunroom, but slowed his pace as he entered.

Birdie had Molly cradled in her arms like a baby. She looked up and smiled. "I think she'll be okay now." But another bright flash of lightning and crash of thunder sent the bird cowering against Birdie's chest, the loud cries of her distress making Brutus join in the fracas.

"I think we need to bring Brutus into the house, too. Can you get him?"

"Me? I don't do birds."

"Garr, please. I can only handle one at a time." Her pleading blue-gray eyes were his downfall.

"What do I do?"

"Move slowly and open the cage. He'll probably come to you without any trouble, then hold him like I've got Molly."

Sure he was going to lose at least one finger the second the monster bird was free of the cage, Garr took a deep breath. But, to his surprise, Brutus climbed right into his arms. They followed Birdie and Molly into the great room.

The storm raged outside; the wild pounding of rain against the side of the house made human talk nearly impossible. So, he followed Birdie's silent example and wrapped a towel around the shivering bird, held him close, and talked nonsense to him. Garr let a grin stretch his lips. This wasn't much different from comforting Rachelle.

Rachelle. The grin froze for a fraction of a second before fading quickly away. She and her friend had planned to sleep outside in a tent. He hoped they had been called back inside before the storm started. Of course they had. He sighed; his daughter was safe.

The storm passed and Brutus became restless, fought his way out of the towel, and climbed to Garr's shoulder. The strong beak nuzzled through his hair and tugged softly at individual strands. Garr held himself still under the strange ministrations.

Birdie smiled. "Looks like I've got two converts. Brutus likes you."

Garr's eyebrows lifted. "Oh, really?"

"Yes. He's decorated you with bird blessings."

"He what?"

"He pooped on your shoulder."

"Eww." Garr lifted a corner of the towel toward his shoulder.

"No, don't rub at it. That'll just push it into the shirt and possibly stain. Let the area dry and you can just pick it off." Hiding her smile from him, Birdie fussed with Molly.

Garr watched her until her gaze lifted to his. "Whatever you say. You're the bird boss."

"And this boss says these birds are tired. Since it sounds like the worst of the storm is over, I think it's time they went to bed." Her face flushed and his groin tightened. "It might be better if they went one at a time. Would you mind taking Brutus and I'll give Molly a little extra support until you come back?"

Trying to ease himself from the couch with a heavy bird perched on his shoulder was difficult, until he was able to persuade Brutus into the crook of his arm. The bird made a few happy noises and yawned. Garr moved carefully to the sunroom and eased Brutus into the cage. He offered a fresh chew from the box and fastened the wide door securely.

Birdie's eyes were closed, her head propped against the back of the couch. Molly paced along the couch, and stopped to pick at the towel covering Birdie's lap. Garr leaned over the couch and held his hand out to Molly. He lowered his voice to a mere whisper. "Shall we let her sleep, pretty bird? Come on, I'll take you home."

His eyes widened when the bird sidled next to his hand. Caution warred with elation as he lifted the calm bundle of blue feathers and carried her to the sunroom. Garr glanced from her to Brutus and back. The yellow-rimmed eye blinked once and, if it were possible, she seemed to smile.

"Guess you don't want to be alone tonight, either." So he opened Brutus's cage and let Molly take her time entering. She found a place on a perch and cocked her head at Brutus. Garr chuckled. "You are a little flirt, aren't you?" He watched the birds for a few minutes until their actions convinced him they would be fine together.

"Goodnight. Don't do anything I wouldn't do." The heavy cover slipped easily over the cage to block the light and after a few curious squawks and feather rustlings, the sunroom was bathed in silence.

Birdie slept peacefully, one hand tucked under her cheek. He was tempted to simply cover her with an afghan and let her sleep, but couldn't bear the thought of her cramped and uncomfortable in the morning. Garr knelt beside her and ran the back of his fingers along her cheek. "Time for bed, baby."

Birdie's eyes opened to sleepy slits. "Bed?"

"Yes, bed. Stand up now and I'll help you get there."

Her movements were slow, as if she were still asleep. Garr took her hand and guided her to her room, folded back the bedcovers, and pressed on her shoulders so she would sit. He knelt again and fumbled with the laces of her shoes.

"Molly?"

His face was close to hers when he looked up into her sleepy concern. "Molly's safely tucked into bed, too. Lift your legs." She was pliant under his hands, and Garr got Birdie situated comfortably before he turned out the bedside lamp. The faint, reflected light from the great room highlighted the feminine curves of her face, the slight pout of her mouth in sleep. Garr bent to place a kiss against her forehead and turned away with a sigh.

"Stay with me." Birdie's voice was muffled against her pillow. "Please. Don't go."

Garr's eyes narrowed. "Are you sure?"

There was no answer, just the soft passing of her breath. A wry smile touched Garr's lips. He kicked off his shoes and carefully removed his bird stained shirt. Laying on top of the covers, he eased his body next to Birdie and wrapped his arm over her waist.

"Thank you." Birdie's words were softly slurred with sleep. Garr closed his eyes and let the feel of the woman beside him lull him into a strange contentment.

Birdie woke with a start. A heavy pressure on her hip made her breath catch. Cautiously, she glanced down. Garr's arm rested over her hip, his uniform breaths stirred the hair against her cheek. A moment of panic gripped her until she realized, with the exception of his shirt, they were both fully clothed, and he was on top of the covers.

She chewed on her lip, slid carefully to the edge of the bed, and held his arm steady while she slipped from underneath it. She didn't want him to wake. The red-orange numbers of the bedside clock read just after four. Stretching the kinks from her shoulders caused her to stumble as she made her way to the bathroom.

A nightlight gave enough illumination for her to see and she peered closely at her reflection. No, she didn't look any different, but something deep inside had changed. And even though she knew what it was, she didn't want to face the fact— refused to think the words that would make it real.

Birdie slipped out of her wrinkled clothing and tugged an oversized T-shirt over her head. There was a thick afghan on the couch; she could sleep there. Birdie shook her head. No, she'd check on the birds, then slip back into bed. Perhaps being next to Garr would warm the cold chills from her skin. She reached the bedroom door, paused and listened. It was quiet in the sunroom; the birds were fine.

So, she reached around the doorjamb and fumbled for the switch that would turn off the remaining lights in the great room. The soft, comforting patter of rain accompanied her back to the bed. The lights from the city reflected off the low clouds gave her enough light to see Garr. His dark hair was tousled and curled delectably around his ear. Relaxed in sleep, he was a marvel. That such a man seemed to desire her had to be a gift from the heavens.

Birdie sank slowly onto the edge of the bed and curled her legs onto the mattress. Inching her hand under Garr's, she lifted and slid back against the curve of his body. With a soft exhale of breath; she closed her eyes.

"I didn't know if you'd be back." Garr's arm tightened, drawing her closer.

Birdie turned to her back so she could look into his face. His soft smile greeted her. "I almost didn't."

Garr's smile didn't waver. "You're here now." His lips barely touched her cheek.

Birdie swallowed heavily. Her body throbbed. It was time to free herself to do the things she had imagined over the past week. "Garr?"

His lips tickled her ear. "Yes, baby?"

"I... I want... to have sex with you."

CHAPTER SIX

The bed shifted. Garr angled his upper body over hers and his large hands cradled her face. "Look at me, Birdie."

Birdie shook her head. If she opened the eyes she'd closed against his rejection, the tears hovering there would fall. And he would know what a fool she'd been.

"Baby, look at me." The gentle pressure from Garr's thumbs traced the line of her lashes. "Don't cry, baby. Just look at me." Birdie's indecision made her chew on the inside of her cheek. Before long the area would be raw, but she couldn't seem to stop. Or look at Garr. The gentle strokes of his thumbs encouraged her, and finally she looked blurrily at him. His eyes were dark shadows in the dim light—serious, thoughtful shadows.

"I don't believe in casual sex."

Birdie closed her eyes and tried to turn her face away. She must have misread his earlier interest and the response of his body against hers. The soft pressure of his hands held her in place.

"Open your eyes." The earnest demand was impossible to ignore. "I'll admit I've engaged in sex for sex's sake, for the physical release. But not for a long time. I couldn't stand the emptiness afterward."

Cognizant thought fled, and all Birdie knew was the hard body against her, the heat of the hands holding her face, the desire that swelled the tips of her breasts and curled into a delicate ball between her thighs. But he didn't want to...

"Baby, I ache for you. I want you so badly, the taste of your kisses is imprinted forever in my brain." He arched his hips against her. "My body betrays me. I want you, Birdie. But, I will not have sex with you."

"Garr. I—"

His thumbs moved to cover her lips. "Shh. You deserve more than the hollow emptiness of no commitment, of sex only." His lingering kiss replaced his thumbs. "And I want more. I won't have sex, but if you wish it, I will make love to you. No, we'll make love together."

Birdie drew her brows together in confusion. Her hazy mind didn't understand the distinction he was making. But her heart must have, for her lips moved. "Make love?"

"Yes, baby. If you want it." His voice was tight, strained.

The movement of her head created a caress of his fingers. "Yes."

The warmth of Garr's hand traced down her side to cup the curve of her hip and rested there while his head lowered, lips searching for hers. The firm pressure of his kiss, the soft, yet insistent touch of his tongue brought burning desire—and understanding. Now, now she understood his words, the distinction he made, and her love for him grew.

Her eyes popped open to find his open as well, watching her as the movement of his mouth upon hers seduced her already willing senses. Garr drew his mouth from hers and smiled softly at her surprise. Propping his head on one hand, he leaned back and just looked at her. His eyes were dark and unreadable.

The caress of his gaze pulled her already tight nipples to firm peaks and filled her breasts with a sweet, aching heaviness. The hand at her hip moved, slid across her body, and bunched the soft T-shirt beneath his palm. The unexpected touch of skin upon skin made her gasp with delight.

"So soft." Garr's eyes closed. His face became a mask of concentration as if he memorized each inch of skin he touched. "I could touch you forever, never asking for more."

Birdie arched her back, pressing up against his hand. "Garr, please."

Low and sensuous, his chuckle created quivers along her skin. "But I won't." With a mock growl, he pushed the material from one breast and dipped his head to take the hardened nipple between his lips.

"Oh, my God." Birdie's hands flew to capture Garr's head, to hold him in place while he suckled. Gently at first, then with increasing pressure, until she whimpered with need. She guided his head to her other breast and he pulled the T-shirt away with his teeth before fastening his lips on her in a powerful kiss.

"Garr, I..."

His head lifted. "Yes, baby?" The soft, breathless words stopped her remaining concerns and she tugged gently on his ears. "What do you want, sweetheart? Tell me."

There was nothing else she could say, but "love me."

The groan vibrating from Garr's chest as he gathered her in his arms and held her tightly raised tiny chill bumps of excitement to cover her body. His kiss was long, searching, demanding, and she never wanted it to end.

Her hands splayed against his back, moved in ever more frantic circles, and smoothed lower until her fingers slipped under the waistband of his sweats and stopped over the taut muscles of his buttocks.

The mingled sounds of their pleasure wove together sighs and moans; pleasure's cacophony increased the tension between them. Their hands touched, stroked, caressed, until Garr captured Birdie's restless fingers and held them above her head.

He nuzzled her neck and sucked the lobe of one ear into his mouth. Gasping and squirming, Birdie tried to escape the sensual onslaught, yet, knowing if she did, she would surely die. Garr's lips moved against her hair. "You still have clothes on."

"Oh," Birdie panted. "So do you. Take 'em off."

His hot lips trailed along her jaw to hover by her other ear. "Yours? Or mine?" He loosed her hands, traced the shell of her ear with his tongue and teased the sensitive skin of her neck with soft puffs of breath.

Birdie moved her hands to his chest and lingered on the crisp curls. She pushed firmly, to make him roll to one side. "Both, you idiot." After swinging her legs over the side of the bed, she rose. Her legs wobbled weakly and she let her loosened panties fall to the floor. The T-shirt followed but she turned away from Garr's avid, burning gaze.

Garr's sweatpants flew over her shoulder and slumped to the floor. On his knees behind her, Garr wrapped both arms around her waist and tugged her back onto the bed until she sprawled on top of him. Rolling quickly, he trapped her beneath him, one knee wedged high between her thighs.

"Baby..." Birdie parted her legs willingly and he settled between them. He nuzzled the hollow at the base of her throat. "Birdie, I don't know if I can wait much longer."

"I can't. Garr, please, I've waited long enough." Lifting her shoulders, Birdie reached between their damp bodies and, intending to guide him to fill the empty ache deep inside her, wrapped her fingers around his firm length.

Garr's lower lip was caught tightly between his teeth, and his neck arched back as his hips followed Birdie's insistent direction. Suddenly, he looked down on her and covered her hand with his. "Oh, God, baby. No. Stop."

Frozen by his impassioned words, Birdie's fingers loosened and he let her hand drop away. "What?"

Hiding his expression from her, Garr's head dropped forward. His chest rose and fell with agonized, panting breaths.

"Garr? What have I done?"

When his eyes lifted, the deep pools of desire were tinged with sorrow. "You've done nothing but right, Birdie. It's what I've done. No, what I haven't done." The satiny hard length of him twitched against her leg and the depths of her inner core responded, muscles clenching rhythmically as if to draw him deep within her.

"Birdie, baby—I don't have any protection."

A hysterical giggle bubbled from Birdie's throat. "Is that all?"

"All?" Garr's voice rose an octave. "All?"

"Garr, I don't care. I want you, need you. Now, not after you run to the drugstore."

"But—" He gasped when her hand touched him with a slow, stroking motion and his body leapt into her grasp. "But, what if..." She caressed him and thought followed the trail of his lost words. She slipped her other hand up to cup the back of his neck. He gave little resistance when she guided his lips to hers, lifted her hips and positioned him.

"No what ifs."

Garr gave a soft cry and entered her with one long, slow stroke. Birdie arched her hips and allowed her body to adjust to the wondrous presence within her. She wrapped one leg over his hips, and tensed the muscles to push him deeper.

The rocking movement of his hips and the slick friction within her body tightened the curl of desire until her cries and moans grew insistent. Garr kissed her face, took her cries into his mouth, and returned the dance with his tongue against hers. Braced on one forearm, he tormented her breasts, the rough pad of his thumb brushing over and around her nipples.

The rhythmic meeting of their bodies continued; at times a slow sensual agony at others a rapid, undeniable force carrying her far beyond her celibate daydreams. The harshness of Garr's breath became music to her ears and she knew his release was near. She met his thrusts, planted her feet on the mattress, and lifted her hips to increase the contact between them.

"Baby, I can't... longer..."

"Yes, Garr. Now, please."

"You... haven't..."

"'S okay. I don't. Please? For you?"

Garr trembled and shook his head in denial. Birdie captured his face between her hands and kissed him deeply. She matched the thrust of her tongue with the movement of his hips.

He arched his back so his lower body pressed her deep into the mattress. Smiling, Birdie welcomed the pulsing heat pouring into her, then cherished the sweat soaked man who collapsed on her steaming body.

Garr felt complete. Wonderfully complete and utterly guilty. What good was he as a lover if his partner didn't find the fulfillment he did? After all his pretty words about the difference between casual sex and making love, he didn't take her with him. His eyes closed as he sought forgiveness.

"Birdie, I'm sorry."

Her smile was content, but her body still thrummed around him. "I'm fine, Garr, really. That was wonderful."

He drew breath to speak, but she stopped him with a kiss. "I accepted long ago that I'm one of those women who never have orgasms." The shrug of her shoulders scraped the still firm tips of her breasts over his chest. "It's really not a big deal."

Garr eased to her side and wrapped one arm under her shoulders to hold her close. "You've never had one?"

Confusion filled her eyes for a moment. "I don't think so. Nobody's ever asked me before."

Unable to withhold his chuckle, Garr touched the tip of her nose with a finger. "You'd know it, baby."

Sadness replaced the confusion. "Perhaps. It's all academic anyway." She looked away, her lower lip hidden between her teeth.

She was one of the most naturally sensual women he'd ever met. Birdie needed no artifice or games to make a man go crazy for her. And she had no idea of her appeal. Garr vowed silently he would show her, teach her the joy her body could feel—with him. It would be a surprise to her, a very pleasant surprise.

Repositioning himself so his back rested against the headboard, Garr angled Birdie to his side. Nipping gently at her swollen lips, he kissed her. "May I try, baby? To bring you pleasure?"

"I had pleasure, Garr. You don't need to do more." She shivered delicately.

The response of her body delighted him as it accepted what it needed, even though her mind denied. "But I do, baby. I do."

"Try, then. But Garr, I can't promise anything." He grinned at the note of hope in her voice.

"All I ask is that you relax and let me pleasure you. And tell me what you like."

Wide blue-gray eyes watched his face and slowly, ever so slowly, she nodded. Garr gave her a wide smile, tucked her head against his chest and kissed her hair. He would love her simply, learn her responses and lead her to her peak. Even if it took the rest of the night—the rest of his life.

His brain acknowledged the dream of his heart, but he stored the feelings away, knowing somehow, it was too soon. Birdie was still frightened. "Will you trust me, Birdie?"

She turned her face up to his. Her honest acceptance of him smoothed the confusion from her brow. "Yes."

Garr kissed her. A simple, gentle kiss that made her sigh and her soft breath flowed past his ear. As he teased her lips, he stroked her side, curved his hand under her breasts, and skimmed the fullness. He smiled to himself when she arched into his touch. His fingers traveled lower, paused to circle the dip of her navel, and lay flat and still over the soft roundness of her belly.

He tangled one hand in her hair and tipped her head back slightly to allow full access to the length of her neck. She trembled. How had no man cared to take her beyond this point?

While he traced the pulse throbbing at the base of her throat with the tip of his tongue, he inched his hand inched lower to rest over the thatch of curls at the juncture of her thighs. Birdie tensed, and lifted her hands to push him away.

"Trust me, baby." He waited until her hands rested on his shoulders. "Thank you."

Slowly, he slipped one finger into the cleft hidden by the triangle of hair, touched the moisture there, and drew it upward. Birdie cried out and clutched his shoulders. Again he dipped lower and covered the small, throbbing nub with smooth friction. Circling his finger over her, he pressed lightly on the nub. The motion changed, and he rubbed back and forth before circling again.

Birdie held her lip between her teeth, and even after Garr kissed her and tongued the irritated redness she held her lips tightly together. Though she would not speak, her body directed him and, becoming attuned to the subtle signs, he angled his fingers one way, then another—over her, around her—until her hips lifted from the bed.

Entering her with one finger, Garr swirled his finger into her hot, moist core. He angled his hand so his thumb now slowly caressed the firm nub. He withdrew, entered again, and circled, all the while his thumb remained relentless in the sensual assault.

Birdie moved with him. Her skin flushed and became covered with a fine sheen of sweat.

Her breath came in gasps she no longer tried to control. Her cries of delight and desire grew in intensity. Garr captured her mouth once again and timed the entrance of his tongue so it alternated with the movements of his fingers.

Unable to stand the double onslaught, Birdie twisted her head away.

"That's it, baby. Just let it happen."

"I can't. I can't stand it. Stop."

"No. Close, so close."

A spring, deep inside her, winding tighter and tighter, connected to his fingers. He was winding her, over winding, and she was going to break into millions of pieces. She'd never find herself again.

A wave of tremors washed over her, followed by a second, and a third. Each wave brought a moaning gasp to her lips until, at last, she cried his name.

"Yes, baby, that's it."

He pressed his palm against her, ignited the tight coil, and sent her into a burning flight. A wordless cry burst from her lips. She raced like a comet though worlds of feeling she'd never imagined. A never-ending delight shook her solid life.

When she thought she could breathe again, she opened her eyes. Garr held her tightly with one of his palms pressed to her cheek. His smile caused another tremor to jerk through her.

Tears filled her eyes and spilled onto his hand.

Garr wiped at the dampness on her cheeks with his fingers. "That's okay, baby. Now, it's okay to cry."

"I... I can't believe... oh Garr, it was as wonderful as people say."

He chuckled. "And will be again."

"Again?"

"You're an innocent aren't you?" His eyes twinkled—he teased her.

Birdie slapped at his shoulder. "I know it's not a once in a lifetime thing. I just never imagined being able to experience anything like that. I can't imagine feeling that way again. Ever."

Garr's eyes grew dark and serious. There was a long moment of silence before he asked, "You will let me?"

A hot flush covered the deep blush of her satisfaction. She glanced away, but then returned her gaze to hold his. "Yes."

CHAPTER SEVEN

A high-pitched, irritating trill woke Birdie. She reached toward the nightstand and her cell phone, but couldn't reach the edge of the bed. Tangled in a mess of arms and legs, she could barely move. "Garr," she said as she shoved at the immobile, sleeping weight, "Garr, get off me."

Unintelligible mumbling answered, and his bulk eased only slightly away from her. Birdie grabbed the phone and flipped the mouthpiece open as Garr pulled her back against him and wrapped his leg over hers. "This is Birdie."

"Hey, boss. Did I wake you?"

"Umm." Birdie slapped over her shoulder, trying to keep Garr from nibbling on her back. "Uh, what time is it?"

"If you don't know, then I did wake you. Sorry. But, I was up early. Rog had to take first shift today. Really cut into my plans, you know."

"Is there something wrong, Dot?" Bringing giggles too close to the surface, Garr caressed her side with his fingers. "Stop that."

"Sounds like your night was even better than mine. Dare I hope..."

"Hope away." Birdie's mood was light, unbelievably contented, and she really didn't care who knew.

"'Bout time, girlfriend. Anyway, I won't keep you long. Just wanted to pass on the info I got from Rog."

"Info? Oh!" Birdie shrugged out of Garr's embrace and struggled to sit on the edge of the bed. "Tell me."

"You're lucky. This is one of the few states that allows patients access to their past medical files. The only problem you might face is the fact the hospital is transferring all their files to computer. So, if you wanted the original files, only the data transfer company knows where they are if the files have been computerized. And I doubt they would let you see the originals."

Birdie sighed. "I don't know if an original is important or not. Do you know where I need to go?"

"Got that little bit of news from the hospital this morning. The data company has all the archived files. That's where they'd be. Of course, you won't be able to talk to anyone there until tomorrow. Want the phone number?"

"Yikes," Birdie yelped into the phone. Garr traced patterns along her spine with his cool, wet tongue. "Sorry, Dot." She covered the mouthpiece. "Will you stop that?"

Garr paused as if in thought. "No, I don't think so. Just hang up the phone and come back to bed."

"Uh, Dot. I've got to go—"

Dot laughed. "I don't doubt."

"I'll stop by tomorrow and get the information from you, okay?"

"No problem. See ya." The phone went dead. Birdie stared at it a moment before she turned her gaze to the clock.

It was late, and she needed to check on the birds. Minute particles of guilt floated across her mind. She should have checked on them earlier due to the distress caused by the storm.

After reaching for a short robe that miraculously remained on the end of the bed throughout the night, Birdie unwrapped Garr's arms from her waist.

"I need to check Brutus and Molly." She stood and shrugged into the robe. Garr tugged on the hem until she turned back to him. His little-boy pout and sad, puppy-dog eyes begged her to stay. "I can't. The birds were pretty stressed last night."

Garr flopped on his back and clasped his hands behind his head. Birdie took a long moment to study his nude body. Defined muscles corded his arms and legs and were softened by the fine hairs covering them. The same soft hair was sprinkled liberally over his chest and tapered over a flat belly to the nest that surrounded...

"Like what you see?"

Birdie merely cocked an eyebrow at him and turned toward the door before she could embarrass herself. The delighted sound of Garr's laughter followed her across the great room.

Standing frozen in the sunroom doorway, Birdie's mouth moved soundlessly in disbelief. Molly's cage stood uncovered and empty. Tears sprang to her eyes. "Garr." The croaking whisper barely made it past her lips. "Garr." This time the sound was a little louder. Straining her voice, her muscles tensed with the effort as she called a third time. "Garr."

An answering shout echoed from her room, followed by a loud curse. She couldn't turn away from the empty cage; it was as if her dreams had disappeared with the large bird. Garr rushed to her side and took her hand.

"Birdie?"

Sobbing, she sank into his arms. "Molly's gone. She's not in her cage. Where is she? What did I do wrong this time? Molly..."

Garr rubbed her back. He was confused, until he recalled putting the birds to bed after the storm. "Come with me." He guided Birdie into the sunroom, stood beside her in front of Brutus's cage, and kept one arm securely around her shoulder.

"What if Brutus is gone, too?"

"Shh, look." Garr took one corner of the cage cover and tossed it back. Two irritated squawks echoed Birdie's gasp.

Brutus and Molly perched next to each other. Molly had one claw lifted to push the male bird away. Brutus eyed the humans, and advanced toward Molly, who accepted the food he offered. Unaffected by human concern, both birds turned their backs.

Birdie turned wide eyes to Garr. "How?"

"I, umm, thought they might like each other's company last night, since they had both been frightened. Did I do wrong?"

Tears drying suddenly, Birdie laughed. "It often takes years for a pair of macaws to bond, it seems you have hurried the process along."

"They've bonded? Isn't that what you wanted?"

"Yes, and I thank you. We'd best leave them alone as much as possible now, so they can get to know each other better."

"Hmm, I like that idea." When he turned to lead her back to the bedroom, the towel he'd wrapped precariously about himself at Birdie's call slipped to a pile at his feet.

Birdie looked him up and down. "I could really use a cup of coffee." Leaving him to deal with his makeshift kilt, Birdie rushed into the kitchen.

Drawn by the sway of her hips and the bounce of her messy hair, Garr stared after her. There was a depth to her he longed to explore, needed to know. A secret to be discovered.

The pot of coffee was long gone, but neither Garr nor Birdie wanted to leave the soft leather couch and the comfort of the other's company. Leaving Garr to guess at her thoughts, Birdie had often lapsed into silence. His thoughts were easy to guess. He'd had to change position often to hide his arousal; the towel across his lap offered little effective cover.

His avid gaze skimmed the length of leg showing beneath the hem of Birdie's short robe. The deep vee above the robe's belt showed an equal amount of cleavage. Despite the coffee, his mouth was dry. Leaving the towel in a pile on the floor, Garr knelt beside her, took the mug from her hands and eased her to a prone position on the resilient leather. With a sharp tug, the belt fell away. He pushed the robe from her breasts and gathered the soft globes in his hands.

"Birdie—"

"Don't talk." Birdie rested her hands on his cheeks and angled his head toward her breasts. Needing no further encouragement, he tongued the nipples to stiff peaks and drew a damp trail between them, then moved lower. And lower, until his mouth rested just above her triangle of hair. Birdie's essence called to him, begged for him to taste, to devour, to experience.

The muscles in her legs and belly tensed. Birdie held her breath. Garr lifted his head, blew a soft breath across her skin, and placed a kiss against her womanhood.

The front door slammed and the quick taps of small feet crossing the foyer clenched his belly with panic. His arousal was suddenly, painfully gone. Birdie's eyes went wide and she struggled to cover herself, pulling the robe over Garr's head in the process.

The footsteps stopped at the bottom of the stairs. "Daddy? Are you here?"

Thankful the furniture arrangement kept them hidden from his inquisitive daughter and hoping she couldn't see past his bare shoulders, Garr straightened.

"Oh, there you are. I'm really tired, I'm gonna go take a nap."

"A nap? Did the storm keep you awake last night?"

"I was at a sleepover, Daddy. Nobody sleeps then. We had so much fun." Dragging her backpack, Rachelle started up the stairs to her room. "Is Birdie here? She was gonna tell me more about macaws today. But I'm too sleepy."

Birdie's head popped up next to his, and she gave him a grimace before answering his daughter. "I'm here. We can talk anytime."

A smile twitched Rachelle's lips and her eyes moved from one adult to the other. "Great. Can we do something fun for supper? I think I'll stay in my room until then. "'Night."

Rachelle hurried up the stairs and closed her door quietly. Garr was about to turn to Birdie in relief when a happy whoop echoed down the stairs.

The bright sound preceded an emphatic, "Yes," and the pounding of dancing feet.

Birdie sat in her SUV watching the glass entryway of Tech Data Storage for nearly half an hour before she summoned the courage to even open her vehicle door and step onto the hard, gray pavement. With one hand resting on the hood, she took three deep breaths. Wasn't three a magic number? Maybe she'd be calm by the time she reached the building.

She peeked through the smoky glass door. A lone woman sat behind a high counter and sipped from a large mug. Dealing with the receptionist shouldn't be hard. If she wanted to learn anything from her old hospital records, this was the only way. Birdie grasped the handle firmly and tugged open the door.

Thick brows drawn together, the receptionist glanced up. "May I help you?

"I—I hope so. I need to see my medical records from the City Hospital. They told me that the year I need to see is already at your facility. Is there any way I can get to my files and—"

The receptionist slapped a brown clipboard on the counter. "Fill out this form. It releases TDS from any liability." One of her long-nailed fingers pointed toward a grouping of hard, fiberglass chairs.

"Uh, thanks." Birdie clasped the clipboard to her chest and fumbled in her bag for a pen while she crossed to the chairs. Squirming into the hard seat, she rolled her eyes toward the ceiling. These chairs had to be rejects from thirty years ago.

The form was simple and only took her a few moments to complete. The receptionist double-checked Birdie's two forms of identification and sighed dramatically before disappearing down a long hall into the depths of the building. Waiting was never easy for Birdie, and the bleak room had no artwork or fake potted plants to hold her interest. Even the parking lot, made grayer by the smoked glass, was boring.

Until a sports car, green enough to shine through the glass, slowed and waited at the lot entrance. Birdie leaned forward, and a sharp trill sounded from the depths of her purse. Still watching the ugly car, she dug through her bag for her cell phone.

"This is Birdie."

Silence. A snap. Static. Birdie snorted softly. She hated wrong numbers when the caller didn't even bother to acknowledge they'd misdialed. As she dumped the phone back in her purse, the car rolled into the parking lot, circled her vehicle slowly, then fishtailed in its speed to reach the street. Strange people were out and about.

Birdie glanced down the hall wondering about the receptionist. Then the actions of the driver drew her thoughts. Her vehicle was close to the building; there was more than enough room just inside the lot entrance for such a small car to turn around. So why did it drive all the way around her SUV? There wasn't anything remarkable about her transportation, nothing she could think of that would warrant the interest of another driver. Not even a magnetic sign advertising her business.

Slumping in the uncomfortable chair, Birdie closed her eyes and took a deep breath. A figure filled her inner vision; a dark haired, hazel-eyed dream come true. A dream come true with a beautiful daughter she felt she knew.

Garr and Rachelle trusted her. So what was she doing here, sneaking around, looking for information that might not even exist? Her mouth formed the shape of his name. No, she had to keep her mind off Garr, and how lonely her night had been without him sharing her bed.

He'd been just as restless through the long night. How many times had she heard the bedsprings groan and she imagined him tossing and turning? She felt more than heard the muffled thumping she convinced herself was his fist against a pillow. And for long minutes, she counted the soft footsteps of his pacing. She wanted to go to him, but didn't know if she would be welcomed in his bedroom with his daughter sleeping across the house. Had he felt the same?

"You can come back now."

"Oh." Birdie jumped, and dumped her purse on the floor. Luckily, the snap held, so she didn't have to chase her belongings across the linoleum. As collected as she could pretend to be, she rose and followed the receptionist.

The woman's bored words, obviously repeated many times, led Birdie to a small room. "We have had similar requests. It seems many people still fear the complexities of data storage and wish copies of their records. There is a copier available." She handed Birdie a small, beige box. "Just slip this into the slot in the machine and it will count the copies you make. The copier will not work if the counter is not inserted properly. Return the box to me as you leave. Copies are fifty cents per page."

Birdie laid her purse and the counter on the table centered in the tiny room. "Thank you."

Finally, the receptionist smiled. "It should only be a few minutes until your files are located. A tech will bring the documents here." She pointed to a small box that once held file folders sitting on a stand next to the copier. "Just leave the files in this box when you're done. They'll be returned to storage before anyone else uses this room. We do pride ourselves on adherence to privacy. I hope you find what you're looking for."

Birdie nodded to the woman's back and sat in a chair only slightly more comfortable than the ones in the reception area. The wait for her files seemed an eternity, although by her watch, only about four minutes passed. After knocking once, a young man stepped into the room and handed her a thin file.

"Thank you."

He shrugged a response, backed out the door, and pulled it closed as he went.

Birdie stared at the folder, placed it on the table, then arranged and rearranged it precisely. Opening the dark green cover and exposing the contents of her medical records might open the proverbial can of worms. What did she expect to find there—a written statement proving her child had lived and was switched by some well-meaning nurse? A dry laugh choked past her throat. She shouldn't let television influence her thoughts.

This investigation very well could damage her burgeoning relationship with Garr. The possibility he would think she snuck around behind his back might make him throw her from his house. From his life. She glanced at the far wall and traced the vertical lines of the dusty paneling with her unseeing gaze. That's what she was doing—sneaking around—wasn't it? If nothing else, she should have asked him more questions about the day Rachelle was born and his wife died. She should have discovered more about the condition of his daughter, a child born under trauma and stress.

Admitting to herself how much this could hurt Garr, Birdie shoved the file across the table. Who did she think she was— harboring the belief that her child might not have died? A lonely birth mother, that's who. She held her breath, pulled the file back in front of her, and opened the cover. If there was nothing in the file, she wouldn't need to admit her folly to anyone. No one would be hurt.

The first few pages were insurance and medical history information. Nothing interesting there. Scanning the slightly yellowed sheets, Birdie flipped rapidly through the pages until she came to a section of nurse's notes. Written in three differing colors of ink, the notes covered her admission, labor, and delivery. Confused by the inks, she studied the pages until she realized each nursing shift had used a different color. An organized portion of her mind applauded whoever came up with such an efficient system.

She paused, sucked her bottom lip in between her teeth, and held it there while she read entries by the nurses in the natal unit that described her daughter's condition. The tiny child's vitals and appearance immediately after birth were normal, at least there was no concern shown by the nursing staff. Birdie sniffed back a tear. Afraid the sight of the being who once shared her body would make her change her mind, she'd chosen not to see her child. Now, years later, the written words brought a sharp, vivid picture of her daughter to her mind.

Small, only six and a half pounds. Blue eyes and the finest of pale golden hair covering her head.

Birdie imagined the tiny child, wrapped in a pink blanket, lying comfortably in her arms. Her mind's eye watched the girl grow until she appeared as Birdie had seen Rachelle just that morning before leaving for school. Denial, strong and painful, centered around her heart. It couldn't be, could it?

Birdie forced herself to continue reading. She absorbed the shock as the nurses described the sudden concern for the infant's condition. But then it seemed her child began to breathe normally again, and returned to a more stable condition. At the bottom of the page, she stopped reading, ripped a tissue when she pulled it from her purse, and wiped her eyes. When she flipped the page up and over the clip at the top of the file, a thin strip of paper slid to the center of the next page.

About to brush the torn scrap away, Birdie noticed a bit of handwriting at the ragged edge. She peered closely at it then lifted it to the light. The writing looked like part of a date and a set of initials. Birdie set the paper on the table and watched it as if the rest of the page would suddenly sprout from the scrap.

With a flash of inspiration, she compared the scrap to the top of the previous page. Dated and initialed by the nurse who started the page, the shape of the few numerals and the ink color were close enough to the scrap for Birdie to examine both closely. Slowly, she turned to the next whole page of notes. Again, the papers and numerals were similar.

She checked the date and times of the last entry on the first page and the opening notes on the next. Confused, she flipped back and forth between the pages. There was something missing, some important information. The entry on the top of the second page was timed two hours after the last entry from the first page. The last page described the infant's death. What happened in those two hours to change a stable condition to death?

Birdie flipped rapidly through the remaining pages. Something wasn't right. Where was the missing page? There had to be more charting, more about the condition of her child. Her attention returned to the ripped scrap of paper.

Had someone torn the incriminating page from her chart when they replaced her living child with a dead one?

Rising to pace the small room, Birdie berated herself for such fanciful thoughts. She would have been better off never even considering such possibilities. And if she found out it was the truth, what would she do? Could she confront Garr with the information, or tell Rachelle she was her biological mother? Better to close the file, leave the room, and forget it.

Instead, Birdie slipped the small, rectangular counter into the copier, unfastened the clip at the top of the file, and copied the few pages of nurses' notes. There was nothing else of importance in the thin folder. She slipped the copies into a manila envelope she'd brought along and put the file back together. A quick toss landed it in the return box.

Throughout it all, the ripped slip of paper lay on the table, taunting her. With nothing but half a date she didn't think there would be any way to prove a page had been removed from the file. Yet, she had to try—needed to know the truth. Wondering if it would be considered stealing, she slipped the scrap into the envelope with her copies, yanked the counter from the copier, and paid the receptionist before she could rethink her actions.

Dot would ask too many questions if she returned to *Birdies*, so Birdie took her investigation to the public library. An isolated desk next to floor to ceiling windows gave her privacy and a great light source to study the copied records. Her untrained eyes noticed the two entries surrounding the page she thought might be missing were written by the same person. Of course, the matching initials proved her right.

But the first entry was neater, the language more precise and informative. The second appeared rushed, sloppy. Birdie's imagination kicked in. A harried nurse, looking guiltily over one shoulder, ripped a page from the chart and replaced it with another before moving into the small nursery and switching the occupants of two tiny cribs.

Birdie shook her head to clear it. Things like that didn't happen in real life, in mid-sized cities like this. Did they? The scrap of paper held tightly between two of her fingers seemed to pulse, repeatedly drawing her attention. With a grimace of determination, Birdie checked the phone book section of the library before she returned to her vehicle.

Using her cell phone, she called the hospital and asked for human resources. Her voice disappeared when a man answered on the second ring, but after a cough, she was able to croak out her request.

"Can you tell me anything about nurses who may have worked in maternity nine years ago?"

"I'm sorry, ma'am. We aren't allowed to give out personal information on any hospital employee."

"I understand. I should have known— confidentiality and all that."

"Yes, ma'am."

Birdie sighed. Where was her mind? Of course they couldn't tell her anything.

The voice from the hospital office continued. "However, I can tell you that a majority of those nurses have retired. To honor the years many of them worked in the nursery, the hospital displays their pictures in our lobby area. Good luck on your search, ma'am."

"Oh, thank you. You've been a great help." After flipping the phone closed, Birdie tossed it to the seat and dug through her copied documents. She wrote three sets of initials on a wrinkled half sheet of paper from the bottom of her purse and circled the letters naming the nurse who had written the controversial sections.

The hospital was located across town, but the streets flew by without her comprehension. Her mind tried out different scenarios, imagined what would happen if one of the retirees' initials matched the letters scribbled on the paper clutched in her hand. What ifs circled her mind like vultures, but she ignored them, intending only to concentrate on finding the truth about her daughter.

Rachelle dropped her backpack on the end of the couch and slouched next to it. "Are you gonna be in your office all night again?"

Garr sank next to his daughter and wrapped an arm around her shoulder. She curled her legs up on the couch and snuggled closer. Realizing that while avoiding Birdie, he'd inadvertently ignored Rachelle as well, Garr made a silent promise. He'd make it up to both of them—somehow. He'd started with Birdie, now it was Rachelle's turn.

"I know it's not much fun, but I need to change the sheets on my bed. Wanna help?"

"Oh sure, Daddy. That'll be the highlight of my day. Glad I finished all my homework at school so I have lots of time to help make beds."

Garr brightened. "No homework tonight? How about pizza? Your choice. And you can choose a movie, too."

Cautious disbelief filled her young, blue eyes and Rachelle leaned back. "Pizza, and a movie, on a Monday?" She pressed her palm against his forehead. "You feeling okay, Daddy?"

"I feel wonderful, squirt. So, how 'bout it?"

"Race ya." Rachelle leapt to her feet and rushed toward the front staircase. Garr followed, gained, but refused to overtake the sudden lightness of her mood. His own moodiness affected her more than he realized.

Together they pulled the rumpled sheets off the king-sized bed and tossed them into a pile near the bathroom door. While Garr shook the pillows out of their cases, Rachelle opened the hall linen closet and called back to him. "Can I pick?"

"Sure." Thinking she would choose his favorite deep purple, he was surprised when she returned with her arms loaded with cream colored satin. Why would she pick sheets given to him long ago by a woman who'd hoped to join him in those sheets? He hardly believed he'd even kept them. The bedding made a shimmering pile when she tossed the pile to the center of the mattress.

"Why those, Rache?"

She shrugged and sat on the edge of the bed. "You like Birdie, don't you, Daddy?"

Garr reached for a pillow and a smooth pillowcase. "Yes, I do. Very much. How about you?"

Rachelle's hair hung around her lowered face and hid her expression. "I wish..."

"What, sweetheart?" Garr suspected they each harbored the same wish, but neither wanted to voice the words.

Rachelle's face lifted and mischief filled her eyes. "Are you gonna invite her up here tonight?"

"What?"

"Oh, come on, Daddy. I'm not a kid. Jon, this boy in my class, he tells us how his mom has lots of different men spend the night with her."

Garr sat slowly. Was he facing that discussion? He didn't know if he was ready. "What else does he tell you?"

"Well..." Rachelle paused dramatically before she grinned up at Garr. "Gramma told me the facts of life, Daddy. I know you think I'm too young, but she didn't. No big deal."

Garr's mouth dropped open. His mother took it upon herself to... His mouth closed with a snap and he smiled. The wonderful woman had saved him a lot of grief. "Do you have any questions now?"

"Yes, I do."

Fiddling with the stuffed pillowcase, Garr held his breath and waited. The rapid flow of possible questions racing through his mind baffled and frightened him. How much did Rache really know? How would he answer her?

"Are you gonna invite Birdie up here tonight?"

"Rachelle."

"I know, it's none of my business. But I wish you would. I wish she'd stay here with us. For always."

His heart sang with agreement, along with purely adult wishes of his own. Pulling Rachelle into his arms for a huge hug, he whispered into her ear. "Me too, squirt. Me too."

CHAPTER EIGHT

Wearily, Birdie opened the door and stepped into the wide foyer of Garr's home. The day had been emotionally exhausting and she was almost beyond thought. All she wanted to do—.

"Help, help!" A scream echoed from the upper level—from Garr's room.

Birdie took the front stairs two at a time. Rachelle. Rachelle was in trouble. Her footsteps faded in the thick, plush carpeting of the upper hall and she slowed. A heavy candlestick sat on a console next to Garr's door. She hefted it, lifted it shoulder high, and inched into the room.

Rachelle had Garr trapped on the bed. Holding his shoulder down with one hand, she tickled with the other. With a mock growl, Garr reversed their positions and Rachelle squealed with glee. The candlestick fell to the floor with a dull thud, making enough noise to interrupt the tickle fight.

Both Garr and Rachelle froze then scrambled off the bed to face her. Rachelle didn't try to withhold her giggles, and soon Garr's deep chuckle joined her. Birdie only stared at the surprising family moment.

Finally she found her voice. "I'm sorry, I didn't mean to interrupt." She pointed out the door. "I heard screaming when I came in and was worried."

Rachelle glanced sideways at Garr, who nodded slowly. Two sets of hands raised, and with fingers moving, they advanced toward Birdie. Rachelle called out, "Tickle fight."

Birdie backed into the doorframe. "No, I don't..." But it was too late. The hands connected with her, tickling unmercifully until she slipped to the floor in convulsions of laughter.

Gasping for air, she held her hands up in surrender. If she'd ever been in a tickle fight before, even as a child, she didn't remember. "Enough. I can't take it anymore. Please."

Rachelle plopped beside her on the floor. "We're having pizza and a movie tonight. Cool, huh?"

"Yeah." Her gaze lifted to Garr. His chest rose and fell rapidly as he tried to catch his breath. Just past him, the unmade bed tempted her senses. She couldn't imagine being able to survive without being with him again. But her suspicions could damage any chance she might have for at least a short while being part of his life. He might not want her... if he knew her thoughts. He might even-- hate her. She tore her gaze from him and turned to Rachelle. "What movie?"

"Will you help me pick? Come on, we can look now." Rachelle grinned innocently at her father. "While Daddy makes the bed." Scrambling to her feet, she held out one hand to Birdie.

Placing her hand in the girl's small one made Birdie's heart thumped hard in her chest. . She let Rachelle believe she helped her to her feet and tried to smile at Garr. His brows drew together, his eyes dulled with concern. The smile failed. Rachelle tugged on her hand and pulled her into the hallway and down the back stairs.

Garr stood frozen for a moment before he bent to pick up the forgotten candlestick. Birdie would be a wonderful mother. She'd exposed herself to the unknown to save a child. The candlestick found a place on his tall dresser and he turned toward the bed. Smoothing wrinkles from the satiny sheets, Garr imagined Birdie's skin under his fingers. Before he spread the top sheet, he held it to his face and let the cool material caress his cheek. He needed her, ached for her. And yes, he silently told his daughter, he was going to invite her to his room that night.

He took extra care in making the bed and arranging the pillows. And rearranging them. Everything had to be perfect for her. Satisfied he could do no more, Garr shut the door behind him and instead of following Rache and Birdie to the back stairs, he took slow steps toward the front staircase.

A manila envelope balanced on the bottom step next to Birdie's purse. He glanced at it before placing it and the purse on a side table. Laughter from the great room drew him—Birdie's lower chuckle was an amazing counterpart to Rachelle's happy laughter. They were a good pair, a match. For a brief moment he wondered if Birdie's child would have been anything like Rachelle.

Shuddering away the rise of morbid thoughts, he started toward the great room and slipped on a folded piece of paper. He frowned then realized it must belong to Birdie as well. He didn't mean to look at the boldly printed name as he picked it up, didn't mean to pause and consider why Birdie would have the name of a registered nurse, didn't mean to pry into her private life.

A nurse? Was Birdie ill? He cast a quick glance at the large, brown envelope. Did the name on the paper have anything to do with what was in the envelope? He carried the paper with him into the great room.

"Hey, Daddy, guess what movie we picked?" Rachelle jammed one fist against her hip as she angled it sharply to one side. High and nasally, her voice rose. "People. I ain't people. I am a shimmering, shining star in the cinema firm-ma-ment. Says so. Right here." Laughing, she collapsed onto the couch.

Garr lifted his eyebrows. "Hope you like old musicale pictures, Birdie. I've raised a fanatic who could probably do the entire script for you."

The smile Birdie turned to him was relaxed and natural. "We could do it together. I love musicals."

"Shall we order the pizza and get set up? I'll start the movie after the food gets here, okay?"

"Can we have pepperoni and mushrooms?" Rachelle bounced on the couch until Birdie agreed with her choice. Garr made the quick phone call and returned to the great room, three cold cans of soda balanced in one hand, paper plates and napkins in the other.

Rachelle looked from him to Birdie and back before she spoke and broke the solid eye contact between the adults. "I'm going to go talk to Brutus and Molly until the pizza gets here. If that's okay, Birdie."

She blinked and nodded. "I think they'd like that. There's some fresh peanuts in a plastic container on the counter. Why don't you give them each a few for a treat."

Garr waited until Rachelle's voice came softly from the sunroom before he pulled the paper from his shirt pocket and held it out to Birdie. "I think this is yours. I found it on the floor in the foyer."

A deep pink crawled up Birdie's neck and infused her face. With agonizing slowness, she reached toward the proffered paper then snatched it from his fingers. The reaction surprised and confused Garr. Something was wrong.

"Birdie, are you okay? I mean, are you ill?"

"Oh, no."

"Why are you seeing a nurse?"

"I—I haven't seen her yet. Uh, she lives in a nursing home now."

"Then...?"

Her body trembled.. Her lips quivered as if she were afraid. He couldn't imagine anything he'd done to make her fear him?

"Garr."

The sheer panic on her face catapulted pure male protectiveness into every pore of his body. His muscles tensed. He clenched his fists. "Whatever it is, baby, we can handle it. Will you let me help you? Don't deal with whatever this is alone."

The doorbell rang and Rachelle paused only long enough on her headlong rush to the front door to snatch money from Garr. He leaned closer to Birdie. "Will you talk with me later?" Swallowing heavily, he took the plunge. "Upstairs?"

His eyes drifted closed as her lips came close to his. The softness of Birdie's kiss astounded him, stealing the breath from his lungs. "Yes." She kissed him again. "And yes."

Birdie glanced at the envelope waiting innocently by her purse as Garr led her to the floating staircase and up to his room. She had promised to talk to him, but how much could she tell him? Dreams and possibilities? Surely not. Garr was a man of absolutes and she could only tell him half-truths until she knew for herself the whole of what happened all those years ago.

Even distracted by her thoughts, Birdie marveled at Garr's sanctum, his private space. The bed, dressed with a bold geometric comforter, dominated the large room. A chair and loveseat formed a cozy grouping in the round turret. Earth tones covered the walls and polished wood furniture gleamed. It was perfect. It was Garr. And she wouldn't change a thing.

Well, maybe something. A few plants at the tall turret windows and some candles might be an improvement and soften the aura of man. Birdie grinned down at her feet.

Square, male fingers lifted her chin. "What are you thinking?"

"Only that you need some plants and candles."

Garr held up one of his fingers and turned to a highboy chest. After rummaging through a drawer, his proud flourish produced a fat candle. The dark wax settled easily into the candlestick she'd dropped earlier. He turned back to her with hands spread wide. "Can't do anything about plants right now."

"You must be more of a romantic than I thought."

Garr pressed one palm against his chest and bowed his head. "At your service." He reached back into the drawer and removed a small box of matches. "Actually, I keep a candle here in case the electricity goes out." He lit the candle, stretched to turn out the overhead light and turned a wry grin to Birdie.

The flame cast glowing highlights through his hair and brought a magical twinkle to his eyes. As if he weren't already hard enough to resist. Birdie forced her feet to remain motionless or she'd run into his arms and forget the sorrow of her investigation. If she could simply forget and spend the rest of forever in his arms...

Garr took her hand and drew her toward the loveseat. He placed the candle on an end table, sat next to her, and wrapped her in the safety of his arms. Birdie tried to relax into the comfort he offered, but remained stiff and unyielding fighting the tears hovering so close to the surface.

"Birdie, will you talk to me now?"

Relief at being able voice her sorrow-filled suspicions flowed through her. Words rose to her lips and bubbled out so fast, Birdie couldn't have stopped them, even if she'd wanted.

"After nine years, I haven't let go. I... I need to find closure. I have to know the truth of what happened to my child. I... I just don't know. I wanted to check my hospital records, but I had to go to this cold, awful building where everything is being saved to computer."

"Did you get to see your records, baby?" Garr rubbed small circles on her back.

Nodding against the front of his shirt, Birdie absorbed his warmth. But his comforting did nothing to lessen the deep, fear-filled chill.

Birdie pushed away from his chest and leaned back far enough to watch his face. For a moment the play of candlelight across his features distracted her.

"Birdie?"

She took a deep breath. "Yes, there was even a copier available. I copied a few pages. What I read confused me."

"Are the pages downstairs? Do you want me to get them for you?"

Birdie clutched his arm. "No. Not now. Please? Can't we just talk?"

"Why are you so afraid, baby? I see it in your eyes." Garr's arm slipped from her loosened grip; his fingers slid along her thigh. He gathered her hand between his and leaned closer. "Can you tell me? Will you?"

She didn't want to confess what she thought. She only wanted to sink into the deep, mysterious, candlelit pools of his eyes. Eyes so unlike his daughter's. The realization made her jerk and his brows drew together in concern. He remained silent, waiting. Birdie took another deep breath, praying to get through the words without falling apart.

"Garr, the nursing notes described how my daughter had difficulty breathing. Then, she seemed to be okay. But the next page... on the next page..." Her voice dropped to a strangled whisper. "She died. How could that happen? She was there, then she was gone."

"Birdie, I understand how you feel."

"Do you? I planned... it was arranged she would be adopted. I was afraid to even see her, hold her. Afraid I'd change my mind. I couldn't provide for a child then. So, I planned to never see her, never know about her. Why does it feel so different, like I made a colossal mistake when she may have died?"

"May--"

Birdie rushed on to cover her slip. "When I was reading the notes, they didn't make sense. It was like something was missing. And I think there was. In between two pages I found a strip of ripped paper. Like someone had started a page, then tore it out. Like they were hiding something." She paused and chewed on her lip. "I took the ripped paper."

A tiny, consoling smile touched Garr's firm lips. "My little thief. I doubt anyone would notice a missing scrap of paper."

"I'm not worried about that. Only about what it might mean. Anyway, I called the hospital to see if I could find out the names of the nurses who worked in the nursery back then. I knew, legally, they couldn't tell me anything, still, I had to try. Human resources told me all the nurses had retired and that they'd been honored by having their pictures placed in the hospital lobby. For their years of service."

"I've seen the wall of fame there. A nice way to recognize dedicated employees. The RN you have written down—was she one of the maternity ward nurses?"

Birdie nodded. "I had the initials from the nurses' notes and I matched them to the names under the pictures. She's the only one still alive."

"Do you think she'll remember anything? The number of babies born each year must be astounding."

"But there were two unrelated deaths that day." Birdie rushed to cup Garr's cheek with her palm before he could turn away. She winced at the sorrow in his eyes, but knew of no way to make what she had to say any easier. "I'm sorry. I don't mean to hurt you, too."

"You believe that day might have stuck in her mind?" Garr rubbed his cheek against her palm.

Birdie drew her hands away, folded them in her lap, and stared at the entwined fingers. This search for truth could cause so much pain to those she loved. Crushing the material of her shirt into a tight, agonized ball, her fingers tightened. She loved Garr Logan, and his beautiful daughter, Rachelle. No matter what happened, she would always love them. Then why this overwhelming need to open the proverbial Pandora's box?

Garr's large hand covered hers and rested lightly against her nervous fingers. She looked into his face. His earnest, concerned expression stilled her heart as well as her twisting fingers. "Birdie, baby, what can I do to help?"

"Nothing. I think I need to figure this out myself."

"Why?"

Birdie didn't know the answer to the soft-spoken question. Instead of admitting her confusion, she plowed forward. "Miss Ansley is in a nursing home now. She's very confused, but I need to try and talk with her anyway. I have to."

"I understand. We can go tomorrow."

"No. I mean, you don't have to go with me."

"Only as emotional support? Wouldn't you like someone there in case she does remember? Someone who's not quite so intimately involved?"

If he only knew. But then, he wouldn't make the offer. She wouldn't even be there—in his house. In his arms. There was so much she couldn't tell him.

"Okay." Although hesitant, the word made him smile. She would wake and leave early, before he was even alert and out of bed. He didn't know which rest home so he couldn't follow her. That way she'd protect him from... from what? What *would* she do if the nurse remembered and she had to face the truth of her fears?

Garr stroked her arms. "You're very tense. How about a bath? It might help relax you."

The play of emotions through her mind didn't allow much room for thought but she did manage a nod. Garr tugged her to her feet and wrapped his arm around her shoulders. She stumbled as they crossed the bedroom and Garr stopped. He turned to wrap his hands around her upper arms. "Are you okay?"

"Fine." She tried to reassure him with a half-smile. "It's been a rough day. Besides finding my records and Miss Ansley, I've gotten a lot of weird phone calls."

The circle of a masculine arm pulled her closer. "How so?"

"First, there've been hang up calls at *Birdies*. I guess that's not necessarily so unusual. But now I've been getting them on my cell. But there's no identification other than the phone number."

"Are the calls from the same number?"

Birdie shook her head. "Oh, I'm sure it's nothing. Either kids fooling around or someone with thick fingers keeps misdialing."

"Hmm, could be."

Garr kissed her cheek and silently led her to the bathroom. Even with the confused swirling of her thoughts, Birdie's mouth dropped open in amazement when he turned on the light. A massive, free-standing jetted soaking tub filled fully a third of the room. Natural stone filled with sparkling flecks to catch the light covered the walls. The tub was huge. Big enough for...two. "Oh, my."

Garr chuckled. "That's often the reaction when someone sees this room for the first time. I've opened the house for builder tours, and most of the comments are about this room." He moved to the tub and adjusted the taps on one wall. A wide waterfall of water burbled over a stone ledge and into the tub. "It does take a while to fill, though."

Birdie stood in the center of the room as he moved to lay a stack of thick towels next to the tub. He brought the candle from the sitting area and turned off the light. Filling the room with a soft glow, the flame reflected from the mirror, off shiny tiles and the sparkling stones and into the water. "You really are a romantic."

"No, I'm more of a sensualist. When I bother to take the time, I think it's important to appeal to all the senses."

Birdie's mouth went dry. Her senses were definitely appealed to, and the ache low in her body sent whispers to her heart and mind. *Don't ever let him go.*

Showing her his backside, Garr leaned over to check the temperature of the water. "Looks pretty good."

Birdie licked her lips. It certainly did.

"The switch for the jets is right here." Garr stretched to point to a hidden alcove at the foot of the tub.

Birdie couldn't breathe.

"I'll leave you alone, now. Enjoy."

"Garr?" He froze at the doorway, but didn't turn toward her. Birdie unbuttoned her blouse and slipped out of it. "Garr." With tortured slowness, he turned and she dropped the blouse to her feet. "Don't go."

Garr glanced at the tub. Desire swirled through him like the flowing water. When he looked back at Birdie, her slacks had joined the blouse. She moved toward him and her skin glowed softly in the candlelight. With her arms around his neck and her body pressed against him, he truly understood the meaning of sensual. The touch of her lips against his ignited him and every inch of his body responded.

The feel of her lips twitching into a smile closed his eyes in delight, but she drew away before he could join her kiss and show her his deep longing. His eyes remained closed when Birdie drew away and, with his new sensitivity, he heard her finish undressing. The soft lapping of water as she slipped into the tub lifted a silent groan from the depths of his chest.

"Don't just stand there." Gentle laughter colored her words. "Take off your clothes and get in. I'm lonely."

His eyes popped open. Clear water covered Birdie to just above her breasts; the shimmering reflections both hid and accented the charms of her body. She scooted the length of the tub and started the whirlpool, her delighted gasp audible above the swirling water.

Birdie reclined against the softly angled backrest, sighed, and closed her eyes. Thankful for the reprieve, Garr stripped quickly and entered the churning water. The whirlpool had nothing on his churning emotions. He stroked his foot along Birdie's thigh. She opened her eyes and smiled at him.

That smile shattered a small, hidden box of reserve within his heart. A wave of well-being and rightness replaced his long loneliness. Letting his eyelids drift closed for a moment, his mind reached out and captured the fleeting approval. Melissa would be happy he found love again. He loved Birdie Simons, deeply, completely, forever.

Opening his arms, he invited her into his embrace. Birdie turned, slid her back against his chest, and rested her head against his shoulder. He placed a kiss on her temple. She snuggled against him, took his arms, and wrapped them over her chest.

The pressure of her warm, slick bottom against his groin made him swell. Garr tightened his arms and angled his legs around her to pull her even closer. Inordinately thankful he'd put all the tub controls out of the way on the wall, he reclined, lifted Birdie slightly and let his erection slip between her thighs.

They lay together, silent, letting the warm water bubble over them. If there were a heaven, this was damned close. Birdie tightened her thighs around him. Garr shifted and gasped. Seeking to return the exquisite feelings, he cupped her breasts and twirled the nipples between his finger and thumb. She arched into his hand and the movement captured more of his length between her legs. Garr tasted fresh, wet skin when he kissed her neck.

"Baby... my God."

"Garr, I think I'm wrinkled enough. But I don't know if I have the strength to get out of the tub."

Garr shifted his body slightly to one side and gave her a tiny push. "Will you join me in bed?"

"Do you really need to ask?" Birdie climbed from the tub and grabbed a towel. The swish of the terrycloth over her rose tinted skin fascinated him, and he leaned his arms on the side of the tub to

watch her. Birdie glanced over her shoulder and
tossed the towel over his head. "Come on,
slowpoke."

After reaching back to turn off the whirlpool,
Garr wrapped the towel around his waist as he rose
from the water. Birdie was already halfway to the
bed by the time he'd stepped onto the plush
bathmat. Springing after her, he caught her at her
waist and spun her around. He'd ached forever to
kiss her, to taste the depths of her mouth, so he took
fierce possession of her lips.

Leaving her breathless, Garr turned down the
comforter and, after plumping two pillows, lay on
his back. "Well?"

Birdie scrambled onto the bed, stretched out
next to him and tugged on his shoulders. Garr
remained still, resisting the urge to comply with her
desire and cover her with his body. Finally, she sat
up. Confusion filled her expression.

"This is for you, baby. Your chance to take
charge." Garr took her hand and kissed the palm.
He smiled wickedly. "Take me, I'm yours."

When she only stared at him, Garr closed his
eyes and spanned her waist with his hands. Using
gentle pressure, he encouraged her to straddle his
hips. Comprehension dawned in her desire glazed
eyes and she rose, positioned him, and sank down
with a cry.

Growing harder, longer as she moved upon
him, Garr struggled to let her choose the tempo of
their mating, the force of their thrusts together. He
groaned and whispered her name. Even in his
hormone charged youth, he'd never been this hard
for a woman, been this frantic in his need. Teasing,
caressing, guiding her to new angles of delight, his
hands roamed her heated body.

Birdie's sounds of pleasure excited him and filled him with an age-old need. He slipped his hand between them, stroked into her curls and found the swollen bud. Her moans changed to muted, wild cries, her movements urgent. She clutched his shoulders pressing her nails into his skin.

Her eyes popped open wide. "Oh. Oh, Garr. I'm..."

"Yes, baby."

She ground against him and whimpered. Shudders trembled along her body. Garr pulled her down to his chest and held her. She was his. Now and forever. Always his. The tight, rhythmic convulsions of her inner muscles drew him deeper and with a cry of his own, Garr surrendered and followed her burning path to ecstasy.

CHAPTER NINE

A soft knock, followed by louder, continuous knocking woke Birdie from safe, sated slumber. Garr mumbled crossly and flopped to his back. "What?"

"You forgot to set your alarm, Daddy. I've got to leave for school in less than fifteen minutes."

"School?" Garr jerked to sitting. "Sh—, okay squirt. Give me a couple of minutes. Go have some breakfast."

Rachelle's giggles brought a responding smile to Birdie's lips. "I already did. I'm ready to go when you are."

Birdie leaned up on one arm. "The birds." Realizing she'd spoken out loud, she covered her mouth with one hand and stared an apology at Garr.

More giggles came from the hall. "I took care of them, too. Hurry. You've got ten minutes. I'll be in the car." The carpet muffled sounds of her footsteps disappeared.

"I'm sorry. Now she knows I was here."

Garr kissed the tip of her nose. Angling back slightly, he gave her a look filled with strange longing before he captured her mouth with a burning kiss. "I'm not. And, she hoped. She asked me yesterday if I planned on inviting you up here. Rachelle loves you, Birdie."

A welling of hope and sadness filled Birdie, rendering her unable to speak. Garr's fingers traced the side of her face, his soft gaze told her he understood. But he didn't. He couldn't, not really. Maybe today she'd find out the truth.

"Hurry up, baby. If you can be ready in seven minutes, we'll drop Rache off at school, then go visit your nurse." He moved toward the bathroom, reached around the door and tossed her a bathrobe. "So you can get to your—the guest room."

Birdie slipped on the too large robe and wrapped the front tightly closed. Garr stopped her at the door, gathered her tightly in his arms, and kissed her. "Maybe later," his breathy words flowed past her ear, "we can move your things up here."

The offer pleased her more than she was willing to admit, but she couldn't accept right then, not with the specter of the unknown hovering over them. She nodded to forestall actual agreement, and sighed at the joy infusing Garr's face. He swatted her lightly on the bottom.

"Hurry. Six minutes."

Five minutes later, she had thrown on jeans and a T-shirt, and was searching for a pair of socks to put on in the car when her cell phone broke the rushed silence. Tempted to leave it on the dresser, she glanced at it. It might be just another of those hang-up calls. But, much to her dismay at times, she'd never been able to just let any phone ring.

"Hello? This is Birdie."

"I got you. Thank goodness." Dot's harried, breathless voice made Birdie pause with one shoe dangling from her hand. "I don't know what I'd've done if you didn't answer."

"Dot, what's wrong?"

"You've got to come over here. Now."

"Here?" Panic rose to a knot in her throat. "*Birdies*? What happened? Are the birds okay? Are you?"

"Calm down, girlfriend. Just get over here. The birds are fine. There's someone here... someone who..."

Dot's frustration in trying to tell more than she was able to say was evident. Birdie lowered her voice to a whisper. "Are you in danger?"

Dot laughed, a brittle forced sound. "Nothing like that. For me, anyway."

Birdie looked up at a small noise. Garr stood in the doorway; questions filled his eyes. Forcing an apology to Garr into her expression, she spoke into the phone. "I'll be right there." Flipping the phone closed without hearing Dot's reply, she tossed the phone into her purse and slung the strap over her shoulder.

"I've got to get to *Birdies* right away."

"It will only take a few minutes to drop Rache at school."

Birdie shook her head, perched on the edge of the bed, and yanked socks over her bare feet. Shoes followed quickly. She stood and faced Garr squarely. "I need to do this myself. Get Rachelle to school and go to work. I'll tell you about it tonight."

"But—"

She shoved him in the center of his chest. "Get going. We're past the ten minutes, don't make her late for school." Garr turned and she continued pushing him from the room. "I was late once and hated it. Had to go to the principal's office. It was traumatic."

"Okay, I'm going. Sure you'll be all right?"

"Of course, I'm a big girl. I've been on my own a long time." She pressed a kiss to his cheek and rushed out the door, afraid to see the confusion that had to be filling his wonderful, hazel eyes.

Her SUV was halfway down the drive before he'd backed out of the garage. Impatiently holding her foot on the brake pedal, Birdie waited at the end of the drive until the car pulled up behind her. Pasting a confident smile on her face, she turned and waved over her shoulder before turning onto the street.

Giving the expensive, late model rental car only a cursory glance after she parked next to it, Birdie had no thought as to whom it might be that Dot thought she needed to see. Options had sped through her mind as she navigated the busy streets crossing town, but she'd rejected each. Had Garr's mother had returned and for some reason gone to *Birdies* instead of his house? She moved from the parking area and peeked through the entryway door. No movement indicated anyone was present in the cramped space.

Foolish to keep guessing when all she had to do was open the door. But a sudden sense of dread washed over her and turned her muscles to frozen piles of mush. Just when she thought she had her life planned and settled, all these emotional upheavals piled up at her door. She took a deep breath, opened the door, and entered a world of chattering birds—and the unknown.

The murmurs of voices filtered from the office. Dot's distinctive tone followed the low rumble of a man's voice. The dread crawled across Birdie's shoulders and caressed her tight muscles with pinpricks and tingles. The man's voice rang too familiar, too long a part of her memories to ever be forgotten. It couldn't be.

But it was. The casual stance, the way he threw his hip slightly to one side to mask the intensity of his posture, how his crossed arms pulled the soft material of his polo shirt tight across his back—too familiar. Birdie took a hesitant step into the office just as Dot noticed her and the man turned.

"What the hell are you doing here?" Shocked, both by his presence and her outburst, Birdie fought the rise of heat to her face.

"Now, is that any way to welcome a long-time friend?" He spread his hands as if in supplication— or to welcome her into his embrace.

"Friend?" Birdie snorted and gratefully allowed anger to replace her confusion. "You're no friend of mine, Stan Davis. I can't believe you'd ever show your face in this town again, let alone come to me with words of friendship."

Dot rose from her chair. "I, uh, think I'd better check on the birds." She touched Birdie's arm as she passed. "I'll be right out here if you need me."

Birdie nodded and sank into the chair Dot vacated. She focused a glare on the man standing before her. "Well?"

Bright blue eyes sparkled as Stan tried one of his patented, charming smiles on her. The shine faded when she refused to acknowledge the charm. She clenched her jaw and stared at him, determined to not show an ounce of doubt, a tiny bit of anything to encourage him. All he ever needed was the smallest opening...

"Birdie, how I've missed you."

"Yeah, right. That's why you disappeared. Raped me, left me pregnant, and that was that."

"I didn't rape you, Birdie. You just didn't know you consented."

"Great logic, Stan. Get out of my business, stay out of my life."

"I've done a lot of thinking lately. About you, about us."

Birdie rolled her eyes then returned her stare to him. She didn't dare take her eyes off the snake, not for a moment. "Sure you have. What? Were you in jail and had no guards to charm?"

Even, white teeth glistened when he smiled. "I've managed to avoid incarceration. Not that there would be any reason for me to be concerned. Birdie, I'd like to try again."

Tight, constricting bands of fear circled her heart. A calculating glint filled his eyes, and harshness not present when he served as a city councilman flared in the bright depths. He'd changed, and Birdie knew it was definitely not for the better.

"I need something, Birdie, and only you can help me obtain it." Bracing himself on his hands, Stan leaned over the desk. "There's no one else."

"No mob connections? No out of work gangsters to help you out?"

A muscle in his cheek jerked and a wild light entered his eyes. Birdie cocked her head to one side and watched him fight his emotions. She'd struck a nerve, all right. If he was in trouble, she needed to get rid of him. Now.

"Get out. I can't, no, I won't do anything to help you. Where were you when I needed help? Where were you when I struggled to make decisions affecting the rest of my life?" Birdie paused and chewed on her lower lip, willing the impending tears away. "Get. Out."

Stan sat on the edge of the desk and stroked his finger along his cheek in thought. Birdie gasped, then coughed to cover her reaction. It was the same movement Rachelle used when deep in thought. She peered carefully at Stan. The set of their lips were similar, but the amazing blue eyes were the same. Birdie collapsed against the back of the chair.

"Perhaps I can help you change your mind, babe."

The use of an endearment, so close to the one whispered by Garr such a short time ago, made her shudder.

Stan angled his upper body closer and reached for the arms of her chair. "I see I still make you tremble." His face came closer, but he paused, enabling her to jerk away. "I'll be in town a few days, at the Inn 4 Less. Call me when you change your mind."

"Don't—don't bother waiting by the phone." Her false bravado faded.

"I won't. I'll meet you at your place this evening. Perhaps we can renew our friendship."

"I won't be there."

"You will if you want to see this." Stan straightened and tugged a folded piece of paper from a back pocket. Slowly, he unfolded it and smoothed it with his hand. Holding the page in both hands so Birdie could see the torn upper edge, he grinned. "And I think you want to see this."

At first Birdie refused to look at the page. But Stan held it steady, unmoving, until her gaze focused on the sheet. "No." She grasped toward the page, but Stan danced away, laughing.

"Ah, so I was right. Think this will give you some missing information, Birdie?"

Birdie closed her eyes against the sight of Stan brandishing what looked like the missing page of nurses' notes from her medical file. Even with the brief glimpse he allowed her, she was sure the torn edge would match the bit of paper in the envelope at Garr's house. "How did you get that?" She held her hand out, palm up. Perhaps he could be fooled into giving it to her.

"Uh-uh, Birdie. Tonight." Stan refolded the page, stuck it into his pocket, and gave it a secure pat. "Let's just say, the receptionist is a good friend of mine."

A bitter laugh passed Birdie's lips. "I don't doubt that. You've always had plenty of that kind of friends. Stan, please give it to me. I... I need to know the truth."

"And what truth are you looking for, Birdie? Think that kid up in the big house is yours?"

Birdie shrank in upon herself. Stan had been following her. How else could he know so much? Was Rachelle in danger? Or Garr? "Stan..."

"Meet me at your place. I'll even bring a pizza. Still like pepperoni and mushrooms?" Stan chuckled and moved toward the office door. "Oh, and Birdie." He paused and glanced back at her. "Enjoy your talk with old nurse Ansley."

He disappeared before she could form an intelligent response. Dot rushed into the office as soon as the front door closed.

"Are you okay, Birdie?"

Unable to speak, she shook her head. She was confused, frightened, angry, and terrified she'd done something to put Garr and Rachelle in danger.

She had no doubt Stan was a dangerous man. Somehow, she had to find a way to appease him. Dot knelt beside her and touched her shoulder.

"Anything I can do?"

Uncontrolled tears pooled in Birdie's eyes. She hid her face in her hands and sobbed. Dot wrapped her arms around Birdie's shoulders and held her until she could cry no more.

Nodding his head in time to the music blasting from the car beside him, Garr tapped his fingers along the top of his steering wheel. Glad the driver had a reasonable taste in music, he glanced at the vehicle. Darkly tinted windows hid any hint to the driver's identity. Garr lifted his shoulders to ease a knot at the base of his neck and turned his attention to the railroad crossing. He found the underlying beat of the train inching through the crossing strangely soothing. What could have made Birdie take off so quickly? He shrugged. It was difficult to be in business on a good day, and he admired her dedication. Dealing with live creatures, especially if they were like the now calm monster bird in his sunroom, would be stressful in itself.

If her business interrupted their lives occasionally, he could understand. Hell, he got called away from time to time himself.

The sign of a local drugstore blinked through the gaps between train cars. He'd stop there before heading to the office to finish the model for his current project. A special evening was just what Birdie needed. And he needed Birdie.

Deep sorrow over the death of her child still resided within her. He ached to heal her, draw the pain of loss from her. Much as she had unknowingly taken the remaining pain of Melissa's death from him. Not sure how the possibility of another pregnancy might affect her fragile trust, Garr was determined to be responsible. Hopefully, they'd been lucky, but luck only went so far. The train passed and Garr eased his car over the rough crossing and into the drugstore parking lot.

It took a few moments to find the right aisle, then he stood staring at the multitude of small, square boxes. Had it really been that long? There were so many. Head cocked to one side, he read the box fronts without touching them.

"Boo." A feminine hand poked his side. Heat rising to his face, Garr stepped back and cleared his throat. The petite brunette chuckled. "Gotcha, coz."

"What are you doing here?"

"Shopping. Hey, I hear Aunt Esther's out of town."

"Yeah, and left her bird with me again." Garr wasn't sure he liked the sudden calculating look in his cousin's eyes.

"Getting along with the bird lady?"

"Does everyone know my business, Sara?"

"Naw. Rache told me about her a couple days ago. She loves her email, you know."

"She's not bothering you, is she?" Maybe the question would refocus Sara's attention. Uncomfortable, he glanced down and shuffled his feet.

"No, as usual, she's a joy." Sara glanced at the store display and pointed to a gold box. "Charlie and I like these. Comfort, sensitivity, and safety all in one little foil packet. Oh, that reminds me." Sara snagged a couple of boxes and dropped them into the red plastic basket over her arm. "And, if you really want to thrill her..." She pointed to a vivid blue box. "These have nifty little ridges."

A powerful surge of heat blasted across Garr's face. His sweet cousin was talking to him about— this? "I... umm."

Sara slapped his arm. "Come on, Garr. This is an important part of a relationship. It's nothing to be embarrassed about."

"I know." He reached toward the display, but his hand dropped back to his side, empty.

"Oh, here, you big baby." Sara plunked an assortment of condoms into her basket. "I'll pay for them. You try 'em out, then you'll know which ones you, and your lady, like the best. After this, it's all up to you." Giggling, she turned toward the checkout.

Garr followed and watched the wall while a young man checked them out. But he didn't miss the frank speculation in the man's eyes when Sara slapped the plastic sack into his arms and led the way from the store. His ears burned and all she did was laugh at him.

"Do you want me to call Rog?" Dot handed Birdie another tissue.

Birdie sniffed and dabbed at her eyes. "There's no proof he's up to anything, just my suspicions."

"I don't have to talk to him officially. Maybe he could give us some suggestions."

"I don't want you involved, Dot. I couldn't deal with the pain if anything happened to you."

Dot sighed. "You're not going to tell Garr either, are you?"

Fresh tears trailed down Birdie's cheeks. "N—no. And you won't either. I... I've got to leave his house. Stan knows I've been staying there."

"You'd be safer there than in your cruddy little apartment."

"I've got a deadbolt." Birdie tried to put on a brave face. But, at the skeptical look Dot gave her, she closed her eyes with a sigh. "I know." Her earnest gaze returned to her assistant. "He wants something from me, so he won't do anything until he gets what he wants. Once I find out what that is, I'll call Rog."

"I don't know—are you sure?"

"I'll be careful. Garr will probably try and call here. Can you put him off?"

Dot took her by the shoulders and bent until her face was inches from Birdie's. "Tell him. Everything. All your suspicions, what's happened, about Stan. Everything. Don't let the past make you hide your feelings, and not accept the help of the man you love."

"I don't lo—"

"You can try and convince yourself of that, Birdie. But you'll never convince me."

Birdie shook her head. If she admitted the truth, it would only be another tool for Stan to use against her. She took a deep breath and tossed her soggy tissue into the wastebasket. Dot's hands fell away from her shoulders.

"I was going to visit that nurse today, so I'd best get going. I'll stop by Garr's afterwards and tell him I won't be staying there. The birds are doing great. With Rachelle to take care of them, I'll only need to check in once or twice a day. Don't worry. Everything will be fine."

Dot gave a shaky laugh. "I thought that was supposed to be my line."

The parking lot was shrouded in shadow as thick, gray clouds moved with aching slowness across the sky. The fresh smell of coming rain blew through Birdie's open window. She stared at the nursing home's front entrance. Her fingers locked around the steering wheel, the knuckles white. Laying her forehead against the ridge of knuckles, Birdie struggled with her wayward emotions.

Everything had been fine. She could even deal with the suspicions she harbored about the death of her child. Until Stan appeared, and threw her already tenuous world into a maelstrom of confusion.

What did he know? What did he want from her? Would he threaten Garr or Rachelle? She pounded the steering wheel. What was she to do?

With a heavy heart, she cast a weary glance toward the nursing home. This was not going to be the day she would talk with Miss Ansley. It would be useless to try and prod the memory of an elderly, possibly confused woman about events of nine years ago. Certainly too many babies had passed through the maternity ward since then, and sadly, some of them had died.

Unable to control the shaking of her hands, Birdie fiddled with the ignition key before she could find the coordination to start her SUV. Backing from the parking space, she narrowly missed a sleek, yellow convertible. Stan smiled, waved, and motioned for her to precede him from the lot. The shaking moved up her arms and her heart beat in a syncopated, painful rhythm.

She pulled back into the parking space, rolled up the window, and locked the doors. Cautious, she turned her head to look back over her shoulder. A patch of sunlight broke through the gathering clouds and highlighted Stan's bright, white teeth and golden hair as he laughed. With another wave, he squealed the sporty car's tires and zipped from the lot.

In her mind, she heard the laughter, and choked back tears. He'd followed her, watched her. Frightened of the evil deeds her imagination attributed to the suave, manipulative man, she had to leave Garr's home. Garr's bed. And he must never know the reason why.

The warmth of fleeting thoughts, of the joy he'd brought her, chased the fear, but couldn't release her from the chill fingers of dread. If she stayed, something would happen, and her fear focused on the young girl she loved deeply. Stan really wouldn't hurt a child, would he? Birdic dashed tears from her eyes. She couldn't take the chance.

Continually scanning side streets and watching her rear view mirrors, Birdie searched for the shiny yellow car, unreasonably sure Stan knew her every move. Determination focused her drive across the city and up the long drive to Garr's magnificent Victorian. His car was gone and she heaved a sigh of relief. She could grab her things and leave without having to face him. One sight of Garr would test her fragile decision.

Molly and Brutus chattered happily at her when she peeked into the sunroom. Reaching back into the kitchen, she dug through the bowl of treats and clasped a handful to her belly. She would miss the crazy antics of the bonding pair, but there was no way she would take the chance and separate them now. Rachelle would take excellent care of them until the mess with Stan was settled.

Brutus took a treat carefully from her fingers, flapped his wide wings, then sidled toward Molly. She accepted the food offering as her due. But before Brutus made further advances, she reached out one claw and poked at him, forcing him back to the other side of the cage. Despite the sorrow hovering so close to the surface of her control, Birdie laughed.

"Here," she said, and dumped the rest of the treats into a heavy bowl on the floor of the cage. "Enjoy yourselves. I won't be seeing you for a few days. You be good for Rachelle and her dad. Okay?"

Two sets of intelligent avian eyes stared regally at her. "Forgive me, okay?" A tear trailed from the corner of her eye. She didn't know if she asked forgiveness from the birds, or from Garr.

Her gaze darted to a small wall clock. There wasn't much time before Garr and Rachelle returned home. And she had to be gone before then. She'd never be able to explain this to them—not when she couldn't even explain it to herself.

Returning to the kitchen, she found a sheet of paper and pen in the junk drawer. The pen hovered, poised above the clean white page for long moments. Somehow she had to find words could she write that wouldn't make him hate her.

Garr,
I'm so sorry. Something has come up and I must leave. I'll talk to you later.

The words meant nothing. Even as she paused before writing *love*, Birdie she knew it wasn't enough. How did she find words to tell him what he was to her, how he had brought her to the edge of complete joy, and gently nudged her beyond completeness? How could she tell him... she loved him more than life? And that was why she had to leave.

Crumpling the page into a tight wad, she lifted her hand toward the wastebasket. No, it would have to do. She smoothed the page on the counter and tried to soothe her jangled nerves as well. Creasing one single fold in the page, she lifted the pen and scrawled Garr's name. The crinkled, white page was an island on the dark countertop, a silent witness to her confused agony.

Minutes later she had her few belongings stuffed into her duffle bag. Memorizing the feel, the atmosphere of the home she was leaving, she hovered in the front entry. The house held the subtle essence of the man she loved. Inhaling the wood and spice scent, her memories added the wild musk of his lovemaking to the tantalizing mix. She had to leave. Now.

CHAPTER TEN

The threatening rain exploded in crashes of thunder and shocking streaks of lightning. Birdie parked in front of her apartment. The building looked strange to her, as dumpy and run down as Dot told her it was. The light by the door of her second floor dwelling was out, her doorway shadowed by the storm. The shaking returned to her hands and she tried to laugh away the terror.

She didn't mind getting wet when she ran through the huge, cold raindrops, it suited her mood. A hot shower waited, a haven of forgetfulness for a few moments. But the moments were far too short, and soon she faced the silence of the empty rooms. The odd, eclectic collection of furniture and decorations had once pleased her. Now, she wondered how she ever thought the tiny, mismatched apartment a home.

Dressed in a shapeless sweatshirt and sweatpants, her feet cuddled into fluffy socks, Birdie stood in the center of her living room. The late afternoon storm had darkened to an evening's continued rain. She hoped Stan wouldn't show up, but knew her luck couldn't be so good. He'd be there. In fact, he was probably delaying purposely to set her off kilter. It was working.

She flopped onto her lumpy couch and leaned over the coffee table and her scattered mail. Even the ragged bird magazines that had been crammed into her small mailbox didn't hold her interest. She stared at the door. A multitude of possible reactions when Garr found the note rotated like a carousel through her mind. Unfortunately, no brass ring waited at the end of this ride.

Garr stormed through the rain, splashing heedlessly through muddy puddles and reached *Birdies* door just as Dot turned the sign to closed. Wide-eyed, she stepped back and let him enter the building. Dripping onto the clean tile floor, he folded his arms across his chest.

"Where is she?"

Dot took another step back and bumped into a teetering stack of boxes. "Uh, who?" She reached behind her to steady the cartons and stepped forward again.

"Why did she leave?"

"Uh, Mr. Logan, what are you talking about?"

"Birdie." He shut his eyes and fought to control the anger and the despair. A deep breath did little to calm him.

"How would I know?"

Patience. He needed patience, right now. He took another deep breath and let his arms drop to his sides with a damp slap. "You called this morning and she came rushing over here. At some time during the day, she returned home." He paused and swallowed past the dryness of his throat. "She packed up her things and left. I want to know where she is and what's going on."

"Oh, no. I was afraid she..." Bright red infused the young woman's face. He'd come to the right place. "I thought she was gonna talk to you."

"About?"

"I promised, Mr. Logan. I can't break that trust and say anything more."

Garr muttered a fluent curse under his breath. "What was she going to talk with me about?"

"Please, I really can't." Dot shuffled her feet and looked at the floor. "But I think she probably went to her apartment." When her face lifted, a slight smile made her eyes sparkle. "Yep, I bet that's where you'll find her."

The pull of a responsive smile surprised Garr. "You're a sneaky woman, Dot."

"No, I just love my friend. I can tell you she's confused right now. She doesn't know what to think, what to do. You happened pretty fast."

"I happened..."

"Not only you, but you, as in the two of you. I'll always want the best for Birdie, and she's only been treated to the worst. You... you, Garr Logan, are best."

"I'm not so sure."

"Neither is she." Dot chuckled. "But I am. Trust me." Something in the young woman's manner relaxed the tension across Garr's shoulders and this time the deep breath gave him a positive feeling. She said a great deal for someone who'd promised silence. Maybe they would find a way to work through this mess. If he just could talk to Birdie.

"Now, don't go barging over there, slamming through the door like you did here."

Heat tickled the tips of his ears. "I... uh..."

Dot waved one hand at him. "Oh, don't worry about it. Actually, I hoped you would think to come here. Since Birdie has an unlisted number, you'd never be able to get her address that way. Come on back to the office for just a sec. and I'll give you directions. She doesn't live in one of the nicer parts of town."

"Thank you, Dot. You'll never know how much I appreciate this."

"No prob, Mr. Logan."

A chuckle startled the small birds in the nearest cage. "Please, call me Garr. I have the feeling we'll be seeing a lot of each other."

"Hope so, for Birdie's sake." Dot bent over the desk and reached for a pencil. It was refreshing to talk with a young woman and not have her fawning all over him just because he was unattached. He rolled his eyes toward the ceiling. According to her, he wasn't. It felt—good.

She turned back with a business card extended toward him. "Here's her address. And I put down a phone number where you can reach me—for any reason. Birdie doesn't know it yet, but I'm moving in with my boyfriend. Garr, call if you need us. Rog is a cop."

The unease returned and settled at the base of his throat. Why would the police need to be involved? He glanced at the card before tucking it in his shirt pocket. "Thanks, Dot. Everyone should have a friend like you."

She flushed prettily and made motions to shoo him from the building. "Get going. Be careful with Birdie. She's more fragile than she'll ever let on."

Garr nodded and spun on his heels. Once back in his car, he reached for the phone he'd left lying on the seat and punched the buttons for an automatic dial. He grinned when Rachelle answered.

"Hi, Daddy."

"Aunt Sara there yet?"

"Yup. She got here only a couple of minutes after you left. She's making tacos for supper."

"Sounds good, squirt. I'm not sure when I'll be home." Rachelle gave a soft sigh. "I know, Daddy. Just bring Birdie home."

His heart felt heavy as lead in his chest. "I will if I can, Rache."

"I know you will, Daddy. You have to." His daughter's voice dropped to a whisper. "I love her."

"I know, sweetheart. Me, too."

A soft knock at the door jerked Birdie to her feet. She stumbled around the coffee table, but her advance stalled in the center of the room. Turning first one way, then another, didn't help her decide what to do.

The second knock was louder, insistent. Still, she stood undecided.

Pounding on the door and Stan's, "Damn it, Birdie. I know you're there. Let me in. Now," spurred her to action. Two steps took her to the door. While Stan continued thumping heavily on the hollow metal door, Birdie fumbled with the deadbolt and the sticky doorknob.

Finally, she took a step to the side and gave the knob a final twist. The door slammed open under the assault of Stan's fist.

The grimace of anger on Stan's handsome face settled into a pleasant smile and he stepped into her apartment and looked around. Tossing a flat, greasy box onto the coffee table, he shrugged out of a light jacket and hung it neatly on the oak coat tree next to the door. "Damn me, but it's wet out there. Brought the pizza, babe. We can have a bite, and a good talk. Just like old friends, huh?"

"You were never my friend. And you're not welcome here."

After brushing at the couch seat, Stan sat and leaned against the back. He patted the upholstery next to him. "The place is still the same. Just like I remember it." A startled expression twisted his lips and he adjusted his position. "Right down to the broken spring."

"I want you to leave." Birdie remained standing in the center of the small room. The walls were rapidly closing in on her. She should never have agreed to see him. No, she reminded herself. She'd never invited him. He told her he would be there. So, why was she?

"I thought you wanted to find out about that little experience you had about nine years ago."

Little experience? Birdie frowned. He'd answered her silent question, to discover what he knew. And the price expected her to pay for that information. She'd do anything to keep him away from Garr and Rachelle.

"Show me the paper."

"Now, Birdie. Is that any way to treat me? Come on, babe. Sit next to me, share a bite to eat, then we'll talk."

There was no way she would let him control her. Not now. Not ever again. "No. Tell me and get the hell out."

The pleasant smile left his lips and he leaned forward. His bright blue eyes turned stone cold and calculating. "I'll give you those precious nurses' notes, after..."

His eyebrows rose as the words trailed away. Birdie took a step back. "Af... after what?"

"I want something. You can get it for me. You *will* get it. Then, we'll make a trade. That item for the notes."

"But, what do I have that you could possibly want?" She wracked her brain, trying to think of anything she owned of value enough to be of interest to Stan Davis. The only thing—*Birdies.* "No, you can't take my birds."

Stan relaxed against the back of the couch and laughed. "What the hell would I want with those stupid, shitting creatures? No, Birdie. You don't have what I want, yet. But you'll get it for me, have no doubt about it."

With slight, subtle movements, the only denial she had the strength to give, she shook her head back and forth. "No," she whispered, "No, I won't do anything for you. Get out."

"Fool. You should remember how I always get what I want." Stan stood, took a huge step over the coffee table, and clasped her shoulders in vise-like grips. His manicured nails pressed deeply into the muscles and increased in pressure forcing her to look up into his face.

A sarcastic smile touched his lips, but his eyes remained icy. "You will return to that large house, rejoin that happy family. I will contact you there."

"Th... this is my home."

"You can't fool me, Birdie. You've become very comfortable at Logan's Hollow. And you will be again, until I'm ready for you." The pressure of his fingers changed abruptly to tiny, caressing circles. "God, I've missed you, babe."

Feeling dirty and used, Birdie jerked away from his hands. He hadn't changed. He'd never miss anyone, unless somehow he lost himself. "Get out of my apartment."

Stan chuckled, held both hands up in surrender, and pursed his lips to kiss the air. "Oh, babe, you don't know what you're missing. Don't you remember?"

Unfortunately, she did remember. Any good times she may have had with the city councilman disappeared the moment he forced himself on her. The memories she'd thought long buried blasted to the surface. Taking a step back, she covered her mouth to hold back the scream vibrating silently in her throat. Her vision blurred and panic clawed away her rational thoughts. It was going to happen again.

"I see you do remember, babe. Don't worry. I don't have time to renew that part of our relationship. Maybe when all this is over, I'll come to you again." Stan rubbed one hand over the bulge in his slacks.

Birdie couldn't help but watch the slow, sensuous curl of his fingers over the rise beneath the expensive fabric. Tearing her gaze from the morbid fascination, she glanced around the room. He was between her and the phone. Even her purse and cell phone were miles away across the room. Her lower lip hurt and she released the tender flesh from the tight bite of her teeth. She could do this. "Get... out."

The sound of Stan's laughter sent tremors of fear through her. He would be capable of hurting her since she continued to defy him. She took a long, slow breath and let the air escape as silently as she could. If being hurt saved Rachelle and Garr, then it didn't matter. Anything she could do to protect them would be done gladly, willingly. But she'd never do anything willingly for Stan.

The laughter died away and Stan reached for his jacket. "You'd better lock the door after me, babe. You never know..." He left the threat hanging and looked at her expectantly. "Come on, babe, walk me to the door."

"Don't call me babe. Don't ever call me that again." Birdie took a reluctant step toward him. If closing the distance would get him to leave faster, she'd take the chance. A broom leaned against the kitchen counter and she grabbed it as she passed the narrow door. Holding the slender wood before her like a fighting staff, she hesitated before moving closer to the entrance.

"Oh, babe, you have become a wild woman. I could enjoy this. But not now. Go back to Logan's Hollow and wait for my call." His fingers closed around the doorknob.

"I'm not gonna wait for anything from you. Get out." Birdie shook the broom handle toward him.

"I'm going. How about a kiss for old time's sake?"

Birdie's fear surged into anger. "Get the hell out of my house. Now. And don't ever bother me again. I'll... I'll..."

"You'll do nothing, babe. Not if you want to see those nurses' notes." The door shuddered with the force of being thrown open. Stan hovered in the shadows of the open doorway.

Taking a tentative step closer, the desire to shove him over the flimsy metal railing flared hot and urgent through her. Too bad she only lived on the second floor. A slimy character like Stan Davis would probably bounce. Still, the idea drew her another step closer.

Stan grabbed her arm and pulled her full against his slender body. He jabbed his hand into her hair and tipped her head back. The broom clattered to the concrete walkway outside her door. Shadows hid his face. "Oh, babe, what a tempting sight." His head lowered toward her.

By twisting violently, she startled her captor and he loosened his grip. Birdie shoved in the center of his chest, backed away and slammed the door in his face. The click of the deadbolt gave her only a tiny sense of safety, but the fading sounds of Stan's laughter stole any security the heavy bit of metal could provide.

Dry, wracking sobs tore through her chest, and she collapsed by the door with her face hidden in shaking hands. Unable to control the trembling, she curled into a ball on the worn carpet, chewed on her fist to stifle the terrified cries, and wished for someone to save her from the pain. She cried for Garr, all the while knowing she could never see him again.

Partially hidden by an overgrown bush, Garr sat in his car and watched Birdie's door. Just as he'd driven into the cracked, pothole riddled parking lot, a man had entered her apartment. Jealousy burned through him, cramping his tense muscles to inactivity. So, she'd left his home, his bed, and run to another. If she was already involved with someone, why hadn't she said anything? As much as he desired her touch, the feel of her body pressed against his, he would never knowingly intrude on another's relationship with her.

Although tempted to simply drive away and forget her, Garr knew he never would. And, how could he explain to his daughter what he didn't understand himself? So he waited and watched. He would wait all night if need be.

The confused and pained swirl of his thoughts pounded through his brain until a dull ache pressed behind his eyes. He rubbed at his temples. What in the hell was he doing? If Birdie wanted to talk to him, she would. He was acting like a teenager— spying on his first crush, sitting in a car and staring at a closed door through a film of drizzle. But he couldn't make his fingers loosen their grip on the steering wheel and reach for the ignition.

So, what was he going to do? Nothing that made any sense without talking to Birdie. She'd be back sometime, if for nothing more than to get her bird.

He replayed every moment with Birdie, from his first sight of her on Rachelle's birthday, until they drove separate directions that morning. But he couldn't catch hold of anything that might have driven her away.

Leaning his head against the headrest, Garr stared into the faintly fuzzy material of the car's upholstery. Maybe she found intensity of his feelings for her frightening. He certainly frightened himself. If Birdie's past had been as... painful as her assistant hinted at...

A rectangle of light illuminated the damp pavement and drew his attention. Her door was opened, silhouetting the man in the brightness. Garr squinted through the drops scattered over his windshield. He couldn't see enough of the man's features to identify him.

The man reached back into the apartment and drew Birdie against him. Garr wanted to look away, but couldn't force his gaze from the woman he loved. The man leaned to kiss her and Garr licked his lips, tasting the memory of Birdie's mouth against his. He had to look away.

Birdie twisted from the man's embrace, shoved him away, and slammed the door. She hadn't welcomed the advances. A wash of relief made Garr feel lighter, happier, even more confused. If she rebuked the other man, she might easily rebuke him as well. Garr watched through narrowed eyes as the man walked away, his steps light and stealthy.

A second man stepped from the deep shadows at the edge of the parking lot. A hat, pulled low, hid his features. He confronted the first man, who spread his hands in a conciliatory manner.

Garr leaned over the steering wheel as far forward as he could. The hat man seemed to be threatening the other. A terse smile of righteous satisfaction froze on Garr's lips. Served the man right. Too bad he wasn't the one with a fist raised to the blonde's face.

When both men gestured toward Birdie's door, Garr glanced quickly at the apartment. The door remained firmly closed. Wishing he could hear what the men were saying, he returned his attention to the men. Hat Man had the blond by the front of his jacket, his face so close the brim of his hat touched the other man's forehead.

Who were these men? Garr concentrated on the first, willing him to turn enough so he'd be able to see his face. There was something about how the man moved, how he threw his shoulders back as if in defiance, that was familiar. He rolled his shoulders and tried to concentrate on the sense of that familiar.

Hat Man shoved the blond and turned away, one hand moving in a sharp, cutting motion. He disappeared back into the shadows. The blond stood defiantly in the rain for a few moments before his shoulders slumped and he moved toward a car.

Fear for Birdie coalesced and poked sharp shards of concern through Garr. He jerked the keys from the ignition and waited, his hand clenching around the door latch.

As he waited until the dark blue sedan squealed from the parking lot, Garr replayed a multitude of scenarios in his mind. Once the vehicle was out of sight, he took a shallow breath and slid from his car. The rain had finally stopped, and the air remained cool and damp. A chill of dread he couldn't attribute to a drip from the overhanging tree branches traveled down his spine. Had Hat Man gone as well or was Birdie in danger from either of the men?

He stood before Birdie's door for long moments before he felt brave enough to lift his hand and knock softly on the worn metal door.

Birdie gasped, gulped, and stared at the door. He was back. She scooted across the carpet, cowered behind the thick arm of the couch, and pulled her knees up to her chest. "Go away," she whispered, the words strained and cracking as they passed her lips.

There was another soft knock and she reached for her bag to dig for the cell phone. Her hand froze at the hesitant voice from outside her door.

"Birdie? It's Garr. Please, let me talk to you."

"Garr?" Birdie crawled from behind the furniture. "Garr?" Her voice was stronger and she stretched one hand toward the door blocking her savior. "Garr?" Using the coffee table to support her wobbly legs as she stood, Birdie lurched toward the deadbolt and cried out at the sticky movement.

"Garr?" The door swung inward and he was there, hand lifted to knock again, his hair disheveled with droplets of water sparkling at the tips. She flew into his arms, and knocked him back a step. The fierce pressure and strength of his arms made everything momentarily all right. "Garr." The speaking of his name opened a tightly closed floodgate and tears flowed.

He eased her back into the apartment and released her only to close the door behind them. Then, she accepted the comfort of his arms, the tender pressure of his lips against her hair, the meaningless words that thrilled through her numbed senses. But the tears weren't enough to cleanse her soul.

Birdie tried to ignore the thoughts cascading through her mind. She had no idea how much danger Garr and Rachelle might be in from Stan, and she didn't want to know. Knowing how Stan loved to manipulate, the contents of the nurses' notes might not show any new or worthwhile information. She couldn't she be sure—of anything.

No, she was sure. Sure of her love for Garr and his beautiful daughter. Through the pain, a light of hope shimmered for a brief moment. She'd talk to Miss Ansley, and see if the old nurse remembered anything. Then, hard as it might be, she'd forget her suspicions and... and try to get her life back to normal. Birdie shuddered and Garr's arms tightened around her. She couldn't even get her own thoughts straight.

Resting her head against the beating of Garr's heart, she glanced around her apartment. She couldn't stay here. Stan would be back. Now, she had no home. Why? Why did everything have to revolve around a single sheet of paper? Ruthlessly, Birdie sniffed back her tears. She'd get through this, somehow, and keep Rachelle safe.

When her eyes dried and the soft, hiccupping gasps of her sobbing faded, Garr stepped back slightly. His hands were gentle on her shoulders. "What do you want to do about this, Birdie?"

Silent, she turned to gather her purse and the duffle bag she'd dropped onto a chair, and moved to the door. "I won't stay here."

Garr took her free hand. "Baby, are you sure?"

After her nod, he kissed her cheek. "Birdie, honey, let's go home."

Due both to the rain-slicked streets and the shaking of his hands, Garr drove carefully. He had questions, hard questions, and he needed to know the answers. From the corner of his eye, he glanced at Birdie. Huddled in her seat, she clutched the shoulder strap of her seatbelt as if it was a lifeline and she was a drowning woman. A passing car's headlights illuminated her pale face and the wide, vacant stare of her blue-gray eyes. It would be some time before he got those answers.

Why had Birdie left in the first place? Who was the man who frightened her so badly? And now, why was she coming back, terrified and lost?

Waiting at a stoplight, Garr expelled a long breath and scrubbed his hand over his face. He couldn't find a way to protect her, to help her, when she wouldn't tell him what was wrong.

A large, baby blue and white Fairlane eased to a stop next to them. Garr admired the old car a few seconds before turning back to Birdie. "Baby?"

Slowly, her head turned and her gaze lifted, but she stared past his shoulder. He didn't think it possible, but her eyes grew even wider, her face white. She covered her mouth with a tightly closed fist.

"Birdie, what's wrong?" He winced at his sharp demand. But perhaps that would get through to her.

Her head shook slowly from side to side and her lips moved behind the fist, but no sound passed her fingers. A glistening of tears pooled along her lower lashes; a single droplet trailed down her cheek. She shrank in upon herself, and cowered against the door.

Garr angled in his seat and reached for her. The sound of the classic automobile racing through the intersection barely registered, but the impatient blare of a horn behind them shocked him back to the city streets. He drove through the intersection and stopped next to the curb.

"Garr?" Still muffled behind her hand, Birdie's voice was tiny. "It was him."

"Who, baby?"

"In that car next to us. It was St... it was the man from my apartment."

Garr shook his head and stared straight ahead. "No it wasn't. That man drove a late model sedan. Who is he, Birdie? What does he want from you?"

A solid link to the reality threatening to slip away into confusion, the steering wheel was cool and firm against his forehead. "How can I help you if I don't know anything?" He tried to keep his voice calm and steady, but a tremor vibrated through the words. "Let me help, Birdie. Please."

As much as she wanted to confide in him, tell him of the terror churning in her chest—she couldn't. There was no doubt in her mind Stan would make good on his promise to harm him—or Rachelle—if things didn't go his way. She couldn't take that chance, at least not until she found out what Stan really wanted.

The hand she rested on Garr's shoulder trembled. She offered a compromise. "I will—when I can." *When it's safe.* After she silently watched the rise and fall of his breathing for immeasurable moments, he lifted his head from the steering wheel and slowly turned toward her.

"I'm here when you need me, Birdie. Please trust in that. And in me."

"I know. I do." Stan's threats returned to taunt her and her hand slipped from the warm comfort of the simple contact. "I really should go back to my apartment."

"No. You belong with me, with Rachelle. With us."

"You don't understand—I can't go to Logan's Hollow."

Anger rose from him in waves, and she winced at the restrained frustration simmering in his dark eyes. "Why not? Tell me, Birdie. Make me understand. Convince me you're better off somewhere else." His jaw tightened and the pulse of his heartbeat throbbed at his temple. He stared at her for a long moment. "Fine. Don't tell me anything. But you're going home—to Logan's Hollow."

Slamming the car into gear, Garr pulled back into traffic. Every plane, every line in his rugged face, remained solid and immobile as stone.

Birdie cringed in her seat and stared out the side window. A long, single streak of lightning blazed from sky to ground. A rolling crash of thunder faded into the distance. The few large drops of rain turned into a deluge, sheeting against the window and filling the gutters on the buildings they passed to overflowing. It took forever to reach Logan's Hollow, yet they were there much too soon.

She didn't know what to say to the young girl she already loved dearly, knowing her presence in the house created danger. Her lip was raw from the imprints of her teeth, but she continued to gnaw on the tender surface, hoping the pain would show her an answer.

At the top of the drive, she leaned desperately into Garr's side and pointed to an ancient, bright yellow Volkswagen. "Wh... who?"

Unable to get into the garage because of the little car, Garr pulled as close as he could to the front of the house. "My cousin, Sara. She came over to take care of Rache." He peered toward the front entry. "We're still going to get pretty wet. I'll take your bag and we'll run for it."

Reaching over the seat to grab her duffle, he gave her a quick kiss on the cheek. "Let's go." He opened his door and sprinted for the porch.

Birdie grasped the door handle and methodically opened the latch. When she stood outside the vehicle, she froze and let the cold rain wash over her. Maybe it would wash away—what? She closed her eyes and lifted her face to the storm. Thunder boomed, and lightning burned colors behind her tightly closed eyelids. The storm suited her, matched the raging of her confused emotions. Arms spread, she welcomed the rain, and hoped against hope it would cleanse her.

Garr stopped before his front door, fumbled for the key, and with a roll of his eyes realized he'd left them in the car. He wasn't going back out into the downpour, so he rang the bell and turned to Birdie.

The space beside him was empty. Panic touched his
soul and he whirled to see her standing in the rain.
Just standing. Head tilted back, arms spread wide,
standing. Afraid for her, he leapt back onto the path
and rushed to her side.

"Birdie, what the hell are you doing? You're
soaked. Come inside. You can't get sick now.
Birdie? Birdie, look at me."

Slowly her face lowered and she opened her
eyes. "What?" Garr took her arm and gently tugged
until she followed him to the house. Sara and
Rachelle stood at the open door by the time he'd
gotten Birdie to the porch. Sara whispered to
Rachelle and took Birdie's other hand to pull her
into the foyer. Rachelle returned at a run, a pile of
fluffy towels clutched in her arms. Sara handed one
to Birdie, but all she did was stare at the thick
terrycloth.

Concern filled Sara's eyes. "What happened,
Garr?"

Taking a proffered towel, Garr wiped the worst
of the drips from his face and hair. "I don't know,
Sara. There was a man at her apartment.
Something's frightened her terribly. I'm not sure
what to do."

"Hey, Rache," Sara turned to the young girl,
"Would you take Birdie to the bathroom and help
her get dried off?"

"Sure." Rachelle took Birdie's hand in her
small one and led her toward the stairs. It barely
registered his daughter was taking Birdie upstairs,
to his room. Garr watched the slow, heavy steps
taking Birdie away from him.

Sara touched his arm. "What did the man do to
her?"

"I don't know. She won't talk about it. She was afraid to come home."

"This is home?" A smile pulled one corner of Sara's lips.

A deep breath filled his chest with longing. "I was beginning to think so. Now, I'm not so sure."

"Be sure, Garr. Listen. I think you two need some time alone. You know, Charlie and I haven't given Rachelle a birthday present yet. How about if we take her to Kansas City for the weekend? Go to the zoo, the amusement park, shopping, the whole spiel." Garr's eyes remained focused on the empty staircase. "I guess that would be okay."

"And, I'm sure we'll want to leave bright and early in the morning."

"Fine."

"I'll take Rache home with me tonight, then."

"Okay."

"And I'll bring her back with green and purple striped hair."

"Whatever."

Sara planted her hands between his shoulder blades and gave a firm shove. "Get up there and take care of your woman. She needs you right now, more than either of you know."

"Sara, I..."

"No need to thank me, coz. Just find out what's wrong with Birdie, and together I know you'll be able to make it right. Now, you get on up there." Sara pushed him again. "Rache and I will be fine. We'll see you early Sunday evening."

Garr started slowly up the stairs, taking one step and pausing before lifting his foot to the next. He glanced back at his cousin. With a wave of her hand and a soft smile, she shooed him away.

Taking the remainder of the stairs two at a time, Garr rushed headlong toward his room. Stopped by the closed door, he took a few deep breaths and let conscious thought seep into his brain. He couldn't go slamming into the room; he'd scare her even further into her frightened withdrawal.

Undecided on his next action and throbbing with an adrenaline-enhanced need to do something... anything... Garr gripped the doorknob tightly, but didn't turn the ornate orb. Just how was he going to get Birdie to confide in him? He sucked on one side of his cheek. She wouldn't say anything until she was ready. Pressing her for answers and information could cause her to withdraw more into her shell, and he'd never be able to reach her. And that, he decided with a snorting release of breath, was not an option.

The knob turned under his fingers and the door opened. His beautiful daughter stood there, eyes wide and sadder than a nine-year-old's had a right to be. Tears glittered on her pale golden lashes.

"Daddy?"

Garr crouched and gathered her into his arms. She clung tightly to him for a moment, sniffed back her tears and pulled away. With one small palm against his cheek, she looked back into the room. A sodden mess, Birdie stood in the center of the bedroom, absently patting a towel along her arm.

"I don't know what to do."

Garr jerked at Rachelle's forlorn statement. "I'm not so sure either, squirt. Sara'd like to take you to Kansas City for the weekend."

"I know. We talked about it. I'm all packed. But, Daddy, what about Birdie? Will she be okay?"

He couldn't convince his intelligent daughter everything would be all right, when he wasn't sure himself. Pasting a half-smile on his face, he tried anyway. "I think, maybe, with some quiet time, some rest, she'll be back to normal. So, you go and have a great time. Ride a roller coaster for me, 'kay?"

"Sure, Daddy. But I'll worry about Birdie—and you."

"I know, sweetie. Just like I worry about you when you're away from me, and I hope everything is okay. Do you have the phone card I gave you?"

Rachelle nodded.

"And you remember how to use it?"

A tiny grin sparkled her somber expression. "Of course, Daddy. I'm not a little kid, you know."

Garr engulfed her in a fierce, protective hug. "I know, Rache. I love you, more than anything."

"I love you, too. So does Birdie."

They both glanced at the woman hovering at the center of the room, arms wrapped tightly around herself.

"Do you think so?"

"I know it, Daddy. Just like you love her."

"Out of the mouths of babes, huh, coz?" Sara stood in the doorway. "I've got your things Rache, and there's a break in the weather. Should we get going?"

Holding his daughter in another powerful hug, Garr stroked her long silky hair and forced back a shudder. He couldn't imagine what life would be like without his daughter. "You can call me tomorrow night if you want."

Rachelle giggled and Birdie's head snapped toward the sound. Her eyes met Garr's and he was unable to control his shudder at the dull lifelessness of the gray depths.

Rachelle squirmed from Garr's embrace and ran to wrap her arms around Birdie's hips. She looked up, bright blue eyes meeting dusky gray.

"I'm going to Kansas City, but I'll be back on Sunday." Rachelle bit her lip. "Will you still be here?"

A gentle smile that didn't quite reach Birdie's eyes shone down on the young girl. "I don't know for sure, honey. But, I'll try."

"I... I love you." Rachelle turned and ran from the room. Birdie stared after the girl then lifted her gaze to Garr. He hovered near the door, a young woman at his side. Shaking away the heavy lethargy consuming her muscles, Birdie shuffled toward them and glanced at the woman before looking expectantly at Garr. Her lips twitched when he took the hint.

"Uh, Birdie, this is Sara."

Birdie extended her hand, dropped the towel to the floor and shrugged. "Aunt Sara?"

Sara chuckled. "Actually, I'm Garr's cousin. Rache doesn't have any aunts, so I got the job. And now, my job description states I've got to get her to my house before it starts to rain— again. It's nice to meet you, Birdie. Hope to see you again soon." She turned to Garr and touched his arm. "We'll be back Sunday evening, and I'll give you a call before I bring the kid home. If you need anything…"

Rachelle returned, a stuffed, lumpy backpack cradled in her arms. A few moments were spent with her before Sara tugged on her long hair and herded her from the house. Birdie shivered in the sudden quiet of Garr's intense, questioning gaze. She rubbed her arms.

"I'm so cold."

In a flash, she was in Garr's arms, her soggy clothing pressed tight against his. Warm breath brushed her cheek as he whispered her name.

"I'm okay. Really."

He pulled back. "Are you telling me the truth?"

Unable to hold his gaze, Birdie glanced toward the bathroom. "Do you think it would be okay if I took a bath?"

"Of course." A hint of disappointment colored the tone of his response. "Would you like me to run the water?"

"Please." She couldn't tell him the truth and she didn't know if she'd ever be okay again. The despair ran so deep, the bottom hovered high above her head. When she tried to smile, her cheeks felt rigid and tight, and she knew she'd failed.

Garr turned with a sigh. Watching his movements as he entered the bathroom and turned on the water both solidified her determination to protect him, and created an ache that begged her to tell him everything. It was too much like a cartoon angel and devil, each sitting on her shoulder arguing incessantly over her fate.

Wiping his hands on the thick towel he picked up from the floor, Garr stepped close to her. "It's all ready, baby."

"I... thank you."

Garr paused as if trying to make a decision before turning toward the hall door. "Call me if you need anything." His flat, emotionless voice returned the sting of tears to her eyes.

"Garr?" He stopped but did not turn back to her. "I don't want to be alone. Will you stay with me?"

"If that's what you want." His shoulders drooped.

"Please. I... we need to talk."

"Yes, we do." He swiveled back, his face relaxed in a gentle encouraging smile. "Don't let your water get cold. I'll change into some dry clothes and come sit with you."

She welcomed the caress of his hand along her arm when she passed him. Moments later, she eased into the warm water. Garr had set the whirlpool controls for a gentle bubbling swirl that soon began to relax her muscles. Leaning back, she let her eyes drift closed. It would be easy to let the churning water chase her doubts and concerns so far away. A happy family picture colored her imagination. Another muscle relaxed.

"Birdie. Oh my God, baby. What happened? What did he do to you?"

She jerked upright and water sloshed over the edge of the tub. "What?"

Dressed in sweats and a ratty T-shirt, Garr fell to his knees by the tub, soaking the legs of his sweats. Birdie frowned and watched his trembling hand reach toward her. Carefully, his fingers touched her shoulders and ran lightly along her collarbone. He leaned to one side to look at her back.

"Garr, what is it?"

His eyes were dangerous swirls of anger and pain. His jaw clenched. "What did that bastard do to you?"

Confusion kept her silent until Garr reached toward the counter and slid a small mirror into his hand. Holding it out toward her, he stroked one finger over her shoulder to direct her gaze.

A sharp gasp passed her lips before she could bite it back. Still, she tugged her lower lip between her teeth and bit hard enough to keep from crying out again when Garr gently probed the worst of the bruises and rested his fingers over the discolorations.

"These are like fingerprints, baby."

"He... he held me. Shook me."

"What else?" He pushed her hand and the mirror to one side, took her chin in his hand and made her look at him.

"N... nothing. Really, Garr. He just shook me."

"That's enough. When I find out who he is..."

The rush of panic made her grab for Garr's shoulder. "No. You can't do anything. Please, promise me, Garr. Stay away from him. Stay out of it."

"I can't." Garr cradled her face in his hands. Tentative, he leaned closer and brushed his lips across hers. "By God, I love you, Birdie

 The sharp ring of the phone in the bedroom startled Garr and he jerked, landing with both arms up to his shoulders in the deep tub. It would have been funny, if the bottom hadn't dropped from Birdie's churning stomach. She had to get to the phone, but Garr was in the way, his arms trapping her in the tub.

"Garr? The phone."

Pushing himself backwards out of the tub, he grabbed for a towel and stood. "I've got it." The growl of anger still vibrated in his voice and he stomped from the bathroom.

Birdie chewed a knuckle raw. What if it was Stan? She scrambled out of the tub, pushed impatiently at the whirlpool control, and wrapped herself in a bath sheet. The knuckle found its way back between her teeth and she hovered, undecided, in the doorway. Garr's back was to her when he reached for the receiver, the T-shirt stretched taut across his shoulders.

He grunted hello and listened for a moment. "Fine." After slamming the handset into the cradle and rocking the nightstand, he turned and spread his hands in apology. "Sorry. It must have been a wrong number. There was no one there."

But Birdie knew he was wrong. There had been someone on the other end of the line. Stan. And he would call again, and again, until she answered and he could continue to make demands. She'd never be able to talk to him without Garr overhearing. Trying to appear calm, she shrugged. "It happens." Tossing the towel back toward the bathroom, she slipped into the thick terry robe lying across the end of the bed.

Ready to move into the comfort of Garr's still open arms, she froze at the distant sound of thunder. A single squawk rose from the home's lower level. Her hand flew to her mouth to cover her distress. "Oh, no. I forgot all about the birds. Molly must be terrified by the storm. I've got to go check on them." She whirled, but stopped at the gentle touch of Garr's hand on her arm.

"Would you like me to come with you?"

'No, that's okay." She stroked his damp arm and tried to smile. "You probably should change clothes...again. I'll be okay. But, you know, I am kinda hungry. Would it be okay if I brought something back from the kitchen?"

A true smile graced Garr's face and smoothed the double line of tension engraved between his brows. "This is your home, baby. Feel free, but bring back enough for me, too?" He rubbed his stomach. "It's been a long day."

Silent, she left the room, rushed down the stairs and into the sunroom. The huge cage was covered and only soft rustlings welcomed her. Lifting one corner of the quilted cover, she bent to peek at the two birds. Huddled together on the high perch, the two heads turned toward her. Molly made a contented chirp and lifted one foot to scratch her belly. The birds were fine. Brutus obviously kept Molly from being frightened of the storm.

Birdie stretched her fingers and the cover fell softly back into place. She left the sunroom and turned out the light behind her. She shivered at the black night making deep, bottomless pits at the windows. Somewhere... Stan watched her even now?

Opening the refrigerator door exposed a pleasant surprise. A plate, covered with plastic wrap, held bits of fruit and chunks of cheese. Two large bottles of designer water tied together with a bright blue ribbon stood behind the plate. A box of assorted crackers waited on the counter. Sara had been busy. Birdie tucked the crackers under her arm, wove her fingers around the bottlenecks, and reached for the plate of cheese.

The phone rang. The box of crackers crashed to the floor. Tossing the water back into the fridge, she stumbled over the crackers and snatched the phone from the wall. Juggling the receiver, she shouted, "I've got it."

A deep breath steadied her nerves. "Hello?"

"Birdie?" The woman's voice was soft and cautious. "Are you okay?"

An uncontrollable giggle bubbled from her lips. "Is this Sara?" Relief washed over her at the affirmative response. "Is anything wrong with Rachelle?"

"Oh, no. I just wanted to check up on you and my coz. Things were a little tense when I left. But you sound better now."

If she only knew. Thank goodness they weren't on some sort of video chat. Birdie could control the tremor in her voice, but not the shaking of her hands and arms. "I—we've talked a bit..."

"I won't keep you. I'm sure you'll probably talk long into the night. I left you a surprise."

"I just found it. Looks great, Sara. Thank you, so much. Give Rachelle my love, will you please?"

"You got it. Don't worry about us. We'll have a great time." Birdie stared at the receiver clutched tightly in her trembling hand for a long moment before she tried to replace it on the wall. Missing the hook twice, she sighed in frustration and leaned on the counter. Her nerves couldn't stand too many more phone calls. Resting her forehead on one palm, she bit back the fresh sting of tears. Somehow there had to be a way to handle this situation and get rid of Stan over the weekend while Rachelle was away from home and safe.

Muffled footsteps traveled down the stairs. Straightening, Birdie rubbed at her eyes and tried to paste a smile on her face.

"Who was on the phone? Is everything okay? Talk to me, baby." Garr's concern sounded from across the kitchen.

"Sure, everything's fine." She turned, kicked the cracker box and bent to pick it up. "That was Sara. She wanted to let us know she left something for us in the fridge."

The slight tremor of her hands and the waver in the soft-spoken words gave her away. Birdie was nervous and still frightened. There was too much she wasn't telling him. Garr managed an easy smile. "Sara's always been thoughtful. Did you want to take her surprise back upstairs?"

A nod shook her still damp hair. "Sure. The birds are fine. Maybe having Brutus nearby makes Molly feel safe. The protective male kinda thing, I guess."

If only she'd listen to her own words. Garr turned to the fridge. Retrieving the expensive water and snack plate from the shelf, he took a deep breath. He could keep her safe, from whatever—whoever—was frightening her. A strange rush of adrenaline mixed with jealousy made him choke on a tight exhalation of held breath. He was jealous of the way a damn bird protected his mate?

Watching the slow twirl of the cracker box in her restless fingers, Birdie stared at her hands. Balancing the plate on his fingertips over the bottles dangling from his bent fingers, Garr reached out to still her hands.

"Baby, I know you don't want to talk about what happened tonight. That's okay. I will be patient. As much as I can— patience is not one of my virtues."

Finally, a timid smile brought faint sparkles to her dull, gray eyes. "You've been very patient with me. I'm sorry for being such a bother."

"Bother? Oh, Birdie, not a bother." Unable to resist the soft invitation of her lips, Garr leaned to close the small distance between them and kissed her gently. Meaning only to offer a brief moment of comfort, the touch of warm, moist skin shot jolts of mind melting electricity through him. He angled closer, the plate held far out to one side. The cracker box crackled when Birdie molded herself to him, squeezing the cardboard between their bellies.

Who needed food when he had the sweet taste of her mouth, the silken flavor of her tongue against his? No other sustenance for him now. He increased the pressure of his kiss, slanting his lips first one way, then another, encouraging her nearly silent sighs of surrender. She was his, and he would protect her.

Their bodies swayed together, only the heat of the kiss holding them together. And what heat. He burned with it. Like a fever raging out of control, her responses fueled the power pooling in his groin. The press of her hip against him produced nothing but pure, intense feeling.

The plate tilted dangerously, the slide of cool china against his fingertips registered just before their snack slipped to the floor. His startled jerk broke the contact between them. Even dazed, her eyes a whirl of stunned desire, Birdie reached and steadied the plate.

"The crackers already met the floor." Her laugh was husky with repressed passion and emotion. "We should save the cheese."

The touch of her dry palm against his cheek drove any thoughts of cheese from his head. Dumping the plate on the counter with a loud clatter, he practically ripped the cracker box from her hands. He pressed her one step back and captured her against the island with his hands braced on either side of her hips.

"To hell with the cheese." He took her mouth, teasing the soft inner lips with light scrapes of his teeth. It was agony to keep his body from hers, letting only their lips touch, but he would not frighten her. If he chased her away now...

Birdie twisted her head only enough to barely separate their mouths. Gasping, she whispered against his cheek. "Let's go upstairs."

"For cheese and crackers?" His whispered response stirred the hair near her ear and he resisted the intolerable urge to trace his tongue along the fine, pink shell.

Pulling back enough to look into her eyes Garr watched surprise fade back to the heat of desire. Birdie chewed on the swollen pout of her lower lip. "Well..." She stroked one finger along the side of his jaw. "Maybe later. Will you make love to me?"

"I will never make love *to* you, baby. As I've told you before, I will only make love *with* you."

"Make love with me then? Now? Tonight?"

In answer, he took her hand, stopped only long enough to shove the cheese back into the refrigerator, and tugged her along behind him. Up the stairs. Into the room he no longer considered his. It was, and would always be, theirs.

The mattress was soft against her back when Garr eased her down. With one gentle finger, he loosened the terrycloth tie of the robe and eased the lapels apart. He traced the bruises along her collarbone. "Are you sure?"

Slipping her hands under his T-shirt, Birdie circled her palms slowly over his chest and abdomen. The cushion of crinkly hair tickled her palms. "I'm sure. What happened today had nothing to do with you." Afraid Garr could see the lies in her eyes, she turned her face to the side. "Or with us."

The touch of his finger turned her face back to him. "Someday, you'll tell me the truth, baby."

"The truth?" He read her so easily. That she even considered lying to him amazed her.

"The truth. With a capital 'T'." Garr molded his firm body to her side, angled one knee between her legs, dipped his head, and continued the assault on her lips and her senses. The path of his tongue over the bruises left jolts of electric tingles that expanded, traveling across her skin to quiver at her aching nipples. And when his mouth closed over one of the turgid peaks, she arched off the bed with a cry of delight. One of Garr's arms slipped beneath her shoulders and pressed her upward against the fierce suckling of his wonderful mouth.

"Oh, babe." Muffled by her breast, it took a moment for her to decipher his mumbled words.

Not baby—*babe*. Perhaps he did call her baby, but she didn't understand. It didn't matter. Stan found the way to intrude on their time. Struggling against the fierce need to run, Birdie froze.

Garr knew the instant her responsiveness vanished and he held a being of stone, this woman who was now so afraid. Easing his mouth from the lingering heat of her skin and putting an inch of cold air between their bodies, he propped his head on one hand and gazed at her, waiting for her to speak.

The tight lines of her face eased momentarily before twisting into confusion when she opened her eyes to him. The deep gray had returned, smothering the desire present only a few seconds before. Garr took a deep breath and inched his hips, and the evidence of his raging need, further from her.

"Don't you want me anymore?" Birdie reached up to touch his face then pulled back her hand.

Snatching at her retreating hand, Garr held her fingers and pressed his lips to the palm. Her hand quivered. "Want you? Birdie, I want you more than life itself."

"Then, why stop?"

"Ah, baby. Because you're afraid." He kissed her palm again and closed his eyes against the rush of sensation of her soft, trembling skin.

"That doesn't matter, Garr. I'm here if you need me."

Rough, harsh laughter barked from his lips and, startled, she jerked her hand from his. It was just as well, he didn't know how long he could tolerate even that innocent contact and not bury himself deep within her. And he would not do that while she was afraid, while he was not the only presence in her mind.

"You offer to satisfy my needs, with no thought of your own?"

"Of course."

"Haven't I shown you, I won't take from you?"

Hesitant, she stroked a lock of hair back from his forehead. "Yes."

He took a deep breath and silently asked for strength. If he ever found the man who'd hurt her so...

"Garr?"

"Turn over, Birdie. Lay on your stomach."

Fear sparked in the depths of her eyes, and her muscles tensed visibly. What *had* that bastard done to her?

"Will you let me rub your back? Help you relax?"

Doubt replaced the fear, but Birdie nodded slowly and turned over even more slowly. She hid her face in the depths of a fluffy pillow.

"Tell me if anything I do makes you uncomfortable, Birdie."

Garr brushed her hair to one side and gently pressed his thumbs into the base of her neck, rotating small circles in the tight muscles. "I need to slip the robe off your shoulders to do a good job, baby. Is that okay?"

"Mummphf."

Taking the unintelligible sound as an affirmative answer, Garr eased the terrycloth from her shoulders but tucked the material tightly around her, just below her shoulder blades. Patiently, he spoke soft syllables to her as he stroked her smooth skin, carefully avoided the bruises, and worked the tight muscles. A subtle change in her breathing and the relaxing of the fingers clutching the pillow let him know she finally slept under his tender ministrations.

Not wanting to disturb the easy slumber, he lay flat on his back next to her and tugged the comforter over them. Trying to ignore the throbbing, hard muscle at his groin, Garr bit back a cry of surprise when she turned toward him and wrapped one arm over his chest. The rise of his desire twitched like a compass seeking north and his hips angled minutely toward her.

Willing his body to obey the restrictions his mind decreed, Garr chewed on his lower lip. His stomach growled. Closing his eyes, he pictured the plate of cheese downstairs. On top of everything, he was hungry. But, he couldn't leave Birdie's side, not now. He'd survive without food.

His stomach answered with another growl, the tremors of the rumbling chasing each other through his body to vibrate along the length of his erection. Swallowing heavily, he rubbed a hand over his face. At least things couldn't get any worse.

"Garr..." One quick glance at Birdie confirmed she still slept. The rapid movement of her eyes and her softly fluttering lids told of her dreams. A silly grin stretched his lips. She dreamed of him. Her lips pouted as if in a kiss and her sigh pressed the softness of her breast to his side. The rebellious, insistent part of his body grew harder.

He ached, ached with a need so great he had to gulp back his wild cry of frustration. He had to get away from Birdie, but needed to stay at her side. Maybe things wouldn't get worse.

They did. Still sleeping, Birdie traced her hand across his chest and tugged on his shoulder until he

angled to face her. One long leg slipped over his
hip, captured his length between them and pressed
him against her moist heat. He groaned, and Birdie
snuggled closer. It was going to be a long, long
night.

The long hours awake attuned Garr to each
nuance of Birdie's sleep, so he knew the instant she
woke. And, when she woke, so did his barely
dormant need. He tried to stifle a groan, but the
vibration of sound escaped his tightly clenched lips.

Birdie angled one arm under her and lifted her
shoulders to look down on him. "You look terrible."

"Thanks." His dry, scratchy eyes closed briefly
then opened to Birdie's shy smile.

"I can help." Without another word, she leaned
forward, tugged up his shirt, and pressed cool lips to
the center of his chest. He tore the shirt over his
head and tossed it to the floor. Placing small kisses
in a path toward his throat warmed his skin. Birdie's
lips grew softer, each kiss held a moment longer.
Until, pliant, those lips touched his mouth, coaxed
his lips to part, and she chased his groan with her
tongue.

Silent, she touched him, caressed his body, and
ran her fingers lightly over his trembling skin. His
body screamed for him to take control, to bring a
rapid release to the long night of denied passion.
Knowing the fierceness of his ardor would frighten
her, he held back, letting her explore and find her
way with his body.

Birdie made slow, passionate love to him. She
pushed his sweats down his legs, straddled his hips
and rode him with gentle motion. After Birdie's
loud moan preceded the tightening of the hot, wet

sheath encasing him, he arched deeply into her with a sharp cry and clutched blindly at her waist. His very essence drained from him into her.

She stroked his cheek until the violent shuddering passed, then lay forward and rested her weight on his chest. A tiny smile graced her reddened lips. "It's still early. Go to sleep, Garr." She rolled from him and his skin cooled. Stroking her fingers over his face, she encouraged him to close his eyes. "I'm gonna take a shower and make us some breakfast."

The bed dipped in a familiar way when she moved to the edge, stood, and leaned back to draw the comforter over him. Her form was blurred slightly as he watched from under barely opened eyelids. She moved toward the bathroom, but stopped just before passing through the doorway.

Quiet, her voice still carried across the room. "Garr? Thank you for watching over me, for protecting me." The door closed behind her with a soft click.

Rolling to his side to watch the door, Garr lost the battle to keep his eyes open. As he drifted toward sleep, a single word flashed neon behind his heavy eyelids. Protection. Only then did he remember the small boxes tucked in the drawer of the nightstand.

 Following the smell of fresh brewed coffee down the stairs, Garr wondered how Birdie felt in the light of a new day. Her refusal to tell him what happened, to even just name the man, held him in check. Without a hint of information, he couldn't figure out some way to help.

Frustrated with forced inaction, he paused near the kitchen island. Birdie stood at the sink, staring out the window, unmoving except for the slight, jerking rise and fall of her shoulders. She was crying. His frustration melted to helplessness. Now, what to do? Did he try and comfort her again or leave her alone to her thoughts a while longer?

"It's okay, Garr."

Her voice sounded stuffy and rough, she'd been crying a long time. Protective anger rose to fill his chest and moved up to tighten his shoulders. The rapid shift in emotions kept him in place. He couldn't fight the memories.

Birdie turned toward him and leaned back against the sink. "Yes, I've been crying. But I'll be okay. I've gotta be. I need to try and talk to the old nurse today." She gestured toward the empty countertop. "I couldn't find anything to fix for breakfast. It's been a while since we went to the grocery store, I guess."

Garr crossed to the counter and as he reached for a coffee mug, knocked the box of crackers to the floor. Bending to pick them up, he turned a smile to Birdie. "I think cheese and crackers would make a fine breakfast. Besides, if we don't eat these crackers soon, they'll be nothing but crumbs."

Her chuckle brought a wider smile to his face and he relaxed and turned toward the refrigerator. Maybe, maybe they could work through this. "How about we take this out to the sunroom so you can spend some time with the birds, too?"

Grabbing both coffee mugs, Birdie nodded. "I'd like that. But, I warn you, Molly loves crackers. We may not get any."

Garr enjoyed the time spent with the two large birds perched on the backs of chairs next to the table. He hated to admit it, but Brutus was growing on him. He actually liked the monster bird. Having a female around certainly had made a difference.

Watching Birdie over the rim of his mug, he agreed with himself. Having a woman around did make a difference. Although there were secrets and pasts that needed working through—he admitted part of him still clung to his memories of Melissa and a guilt she'd shake her finger at—he knew Birdie belonged in his life. Forever.

Uncomfortable with the way Garr watched her, Birdie fumbled with the cracker she offered Molly. Eyes lowered, she wondered what he was thinking about. Her behavior lately would be enough to send most men running for cover, but he was still here. Of course he was still here, this was his house. Still, he remained patient, kind, understanding. She'd never felt lucky in love, and now this wonderful man fit into her life. Maybe this wasn't his true self and once he knew her better...

She shook her head and received a questioning lift of his eyebrows from Garr. No, this was the real Garr Logan. One only had to watch him with

Rachelle for a few minutes to know. A heavy, wavering breath lifted her chest. Rachelle. It was time to find out the truth.

"I should get going. The sooner I talk to Miss Ansley, the better."

Garr gathered the last of the cheese and the empty cracker box and stood. "I'll take you."

"Oh, no. You don't need to do that."

He grinned down at her. "I think I do. Your car isn't here."

"Oh. You could just drop me off at--"

"No. You don't need to do this alone. If you want to talk to the nurse alone, that's fine. But I want to be close by in case you need anything. Let me do this for you, please?"

The soft pleading in his voice loosened the bands around her heart. It would be nice to have company. And, maybe his presence would keep Stan away. She chewed on her lip and made a decision.

"I'll get Molly and Brutus settled and we can go. Okay?"

With a sharp nod, Garr entered the kitchen and disappeared toward the front of the house. Moving slowly, Birdie returned the birds to the huge cage and made sure their water and food dishes were full. Not that they needed anything to eat after all the crackers and cheese Garr fed them.

By the time she reached the kitchen, Garr waited with a light jacket in one hand, and her bag sat on the island. He'd propped the manila envelope against the small leather purse. "It's cool out since all the rain last night." His gaze followed hers to the envelope. One of his shoulders lifted with a shrug. "I thought you might need that, too."

"Thank you. The nurses at the home where Miss Ansley lives told me she's confused most of the time. I thought, maybe, if she saw some of the old nurses' notes, she'd remember what was on the missing page. I hope."

Holding the jacket by the shoulders, Garr helped her slip into the light garment. When his hands lingered on her shoulders, Birdie leaned back against him. "I know it's probably a pipe dream to think she'd remember something from nine years ago. But I have to try."

Garr's hands slid down her arms and around her waist. "I know, baby."

The warmth of his breath tickled her ear and she giggled. "Thank you."

A quick line of tender kisses followed the path of his breath. "You're welcome. Shall we go?" Garr released her and jingled the keys in his pocket. "I'll drive, you give the directions."

When he offered, Birdie took his hand. A sudden welling of peace and joy filled her. Everything would be okay.

When Garr pulled into the parking area of the large retirement community, Birdie finally relaxed the hard grip she had on the armrest. She'd spent most of the trip across town peering into neighboring cars and glancing in the side mirror at the cars following them. No taunting smiles, no shining blond hair, no Stan. She breathed a sigh of relief.

Garr unfastened his seat belt and angled in the seat to face her. "Are you sure you want to do this alone?"

Nodding, she clutched the envelope to her chest. "Will you walk to the building with me? I'm sure they'll have some sort of a lobby or something where you can wait. If you don't mind." She glanced at him from under her lashes.

"No problem, baby. You'll know where to find me if you need anything."

During the silent walk to the building Birdie took comfort in the warmth of Garr's hand surrounding hers. He gave her strength. If only she could give him the answers he deserved. If Miss Ansley confirmed her suspicions, her next dilemma would be how to tell him. About her. And about Rachelle.

Thank goodness Rachelle was out of town. At least Birdie didn't have to worry about her safety as well. She didn't trust Stan not to hurt the child, or at least frighten her in order to get Birdie to do what he wanted. What did he want? What did he want with Garr?

"We're here." Startled by Garr's soft voice, she stared up at him in alarm. "Are you sure?"

When she nodded, he opened the door and ushered her into the cool foyer. As she suspected, there were comfortable chairs arranged around an ornate fireplace. Garr gestured toward the seating area and she nodded again. He squeezed her fingers gently and brushed a soft kiss on her cheek. "Take care, baby."

Birdie watched until he settled on a loveseat and reached for one of the magazines spread over the mission style coffee table. Hoping the magazines were fairly recent, she turned toward the information desk.

"May I help you?" An elderly woman with bright white hair leaned on the counter.

"Uh, yes. I called a couple of days ago asking to see Miss Ansley. Could you direct her to her room?"

A sad smile stretched the wrinkles of the woman's face. "Ah yes, Cynthia. Such a sad situation. She used to have an apartment on the third floor, but since she's become so confused, they had to move her into the care wing. If you go straight down that hall and take a left at the end, you'll be there." She pointed down a clean, brightly-lit hallway. "When you get there, just ask one of the aides which room Cynthia is in. Have a good visit, dear."

Birdie nodded her thanks. Facing the hall, she needed to inhale a deep, calm breath before she could take a step forward. The hallway lengthened, each light fixture spotlighting a circle on the utilitarian carpeting. The doors lining the hall tilted; stretching, wavering, telling her to turn away.

No. She couldn't let panic take over, wouldn't allow her fears to keep her from the possibility of the truth. Briefly closing her eyes, Birdie focused on a mantra of truth and found her mind's eye picturing Garr's concerned smile. Her eyes opened and she strode purposefully down the hall.

Garr kept his head lowered over the magazine, but watched Birdie's internal struggle take an external form. He had to hold himself still to let her do what she needed to do, without him. Hopefully, this would be the last time she felt the need to face an uncomfortable situation alone.

He tossed the slick magazine back to the table, stretched his arms along the back of the loveseat and leaned back against the firm cushion. No matter how long Birdie's meeting actually lasted, it would seem to take forever. He snorted softly to himself. After last night, he should be an expert at long, uncomfortable waiting.

An aide, dressed in a teddy bear adorned smock, paused outside Cynthia Ansley's room and turned her face toward Birdie. "I don't know if Cindy will even realize she has a visitor, so don't be disappointed."

"I understand. But I've got to try."

"Okay, then." The aide led the way through the wide door and crouched in front of the room's only occupant. "Cindy, you have a visitor." She rose and indicated a second chair before patting the old woman's arm.

"Thank you," Birdie whispered as the aide passed.

"Good luck." The door closed silently behind the aide.

After moving the hard-backed chair next to the old woman's recliner, Birdie studied Nurse Ansley. Soft silver hair had been swept into a neat bun. She wore a delicately flowered housedress and fuzzy blue slippers. She cradled a doll in her arms, stroked its messy hair, and crooned softly. Birdie sighed, the old nurse was the picture of a gentle confusion. Maybe the nurse was reliving her past in the maternity ward. Sighing, Birdie crossed her legs. She wouldn't learn anything today.

"Miss Ansley?"

Clear brown eyes glanced up at her and the old woman laid the doll on the bed at her side. "Call me Cynthia."

Startled by the clarity in the woman's expression, Birdie was unable to form a response.

Cynthia chuckled, a raspy, unused sound. "I heard the aides talking, so I know why you're here, dear. I do remember that day. So much tragedy in a place meant for happiness." She shook her head sadly.

"But..." Birdie waved vaguely at the doll.

"Oh, my confusion?" Cynthia narrowed her eyes to peer at Birdie. "You look like an honest young woman. Let me tell you a story before we get to the heart of your visit."

"Okay..." Birdie drawled the word out slowly. So many people had warned her about the woman's confusion, yet Cynthia seemed totally coherent. Birdie didn't know what to do and wished Garr was at her side. His calm presence would help her think. Maybe she was the confused one, not Miss Ansley.

Cynthia leaned forward in a conspiratorial manner. Keeping her voice low, she began. "About, oh, I'd say six months ago, my niece started seeing a new young man. He seemed nice enough at first, with his striking good looks and pleasant manner."

Birdie tried to hide a grimace. The description reminded her too much of Stan.

"Now, my niece looks after my affairs and such. I've made some fairly lucrative investments over the years. No doubt she told her suitor about them. And he... and he..." Cynthia growled in the back of her throat. "Oh, just thinking about it makes me so angry."

She reached over to pat Birdie's hand. "Anyhoo, somehow he gained control over my niece, and got her to do things she normally wouldn't. And, he got some doctor to prescribe a new blood pressure medication for me. Fool that I am, I took it without looking into the side effects myself. That's when the confusion started.

"I may have been a foolish old woman, but I'm not stupid. Before the drug could really take hold, I stopped taking it. Flush 'em down the toilet each time they try to give me one." Crinkling more wrinkles around her eyes, she winked. "After being a nurse for so long, I know all the tricks to keep from taking a pill."

A noise from the hallway interrupted Cynthia's chuckle. She reached for the doll and pressed her finger against her lips. "Shh."

A crisply white uniformed nurse entered the room and knocked softly on the open door. "Time for medications, Cindy."

Cynthia rocked the doll slowly back and forth, but lifted her head and opened her mouth. The nurse placed a small paper cup against the old lips and tilted it. Removing the empty cup, she handed her patient a plastic cup of water. "Drink it all now."

She watched until the water was gone and glanced at Birdie. "How's it going?"

"It's—umm—interesting."

"Yes, Cindy's a sweet old thing. Let me know if there's anything else I can do for you."

Birdie said, "Sure," to a retreating, white back. The door closed.

She turned her attention back to Cynthia when the old woman sighed. Then, she stuck out her tongue and displayed a small, greenish-blue pill. Spitting the offending medication into a tissue, she sighed again. "Sweet my old ass. God, I hate being called Cindy, makes me feel like a teenager. And I don't want to do that again." She rolled her gaze to the ceiling.

Birdie chuckled.

"Ah, that's better, dear. Now, they shouldn't need to bother us for a while, so on with my story."

Cynthia shook the wadded tissue at Birdie. "The effects of this pill are subtle and cumulative. I'd taken it for nearly a month before I started noticing changes in my behavior. I forgot things, found myself in different parts of the building, not remembering how I got there. It was frightening. Now I have a true understanding of how having Alzheimer's must feel."

"Do you think you would have noticed if you weren't a nurse?"

"Probably not. And even if I had, I doubt I would have associated what I was going through with a pill. Medications are supposed to help. Drugs harm." Cynthia tucked the tissue into her pocket. "And this, at least for me, is a drug."

Confused, Birdie leaned forward. This was a fantastic, unbelievable tale. But why shouldn't she believe it? She was trying to find out if her daughter had been switched at birth.

Cynthia continued. "The symptoms lessened almost immediately when I stopped taking the pill. However, I wanted to know what my niece's boyfriend was up to. So, I came up with a plan. I've been pretending the confusion since then."

"The lady at the desk told me you used to have an apartment in the complex."

"Still do." Cynthia nodded. "When I came into this community I bought my condo. One of the perks of living here is the varied levels of care. When I came up with this plan, I contacted my attorney to make sure no one sold off my condo. And, my niece has tried. I know it was at the instigation of that man. I'm going to foil his plans, though. I expect to make a miraculous recovery soon and go home."

"Have you found out what you needed to know?" Birdie's curiosity overcame her own search for information.

"I'm close. That man even showed up here a couple days ago." Cynthia chuckled happily. "Did I give him a show. Total confusion, didn't even recognize the dear man." Then, she became serious. "He really gave me the willies though. There was so much greed and lust for power in his face when he looked at me. I can't let him continue to control my niece." She closed her eyes and sighed.

Birdie didn't know how to comfort the old woman, but reached out, took her hand, and caressed the dry, thin skin.

Cynthia's eyes flew open. "Now, you know my story. You have questions about your stay in maternity nine years ago?"

"Yes, I..."

A warm palm covered her hand and Cynthia gave her fingers a slight squeeze. "Shall I tell you what I remember about that day? Then, you can ask me specific questions."

Maybe that was a safer way to discover what she needed to know. Birdie was afraid she wouldn't be able to form the questions or make her need for information coherent. She nodded and closed her eyes to listen to the slightly wavering voice.

Cynthia's recollections were vivid enough to send Birdie back in time to the day her daughter was born—and died. The old nurse remembered how the infant had rallied after some initial difficulties with breathing. But complications arose with a post-partum mother and the tiny girl was not monitored as closely. So, when her gentle breathing stopped, no one noticed.

Through the blur of tears Birdie watched Cynthia dab at her eyes as well. "I recently looked at my chart and read the nurses' notes. Only," Birdie paused and took a deep breath, "I think there was a page missing. A page that might tell me what happened to my child. It would be a page covering the time between when she was fine and when she... wasn't."

"Oh, dear. I can't tell you anything about that. Something probably happened when the files were transferred from the hospital to the archive building."

"Probably." Birdie had one more question, one she didn't know how to ask. So, she blurted it out is a breathless rush. "Do you remember any cases of babies being switched at the hospital?"

"Here in town?" Startled by the question, Cynthia slowly shook her head. "No, I can't say that I do." Her eyes twinkled merrily. "Wait. There was one time babies were placed in the wrong cribs. But we figured it out when it was time to change their diapers."

Birdie joined the woman's soft laughter. "Thank you," she gasped. "Thank you. I think you've helped me put my own thoughts into perspective. I was giving my baby up for adoption. I was afraid the child of the woman who died didn't live either. And my healthy child was given to the father to ease his loss."

"Oh no, dear. That would not happen. There have been, unfortunately, many men through the years who lost both their wife and their child.

There's no way one of my nurses would switch a healthy child for an unhealthy one."

"But you couldn't watch every nurse all the time."

"One learns to judge people well. And to trust. You don't believe in your ability to know a person's true worth, do you, Birdie?"

Unable to deny the woman's astute observation, Birdie shook her head. "I once knew a man who turned out to be like the man your niece is involved with."

"No need to say more." Cynthia reached for her doll. "Unfortunately, the nurses will start wondering how you could spend so much time with a crazy old lady. I'm sorry I couldn't help out more."

Light hearted, Birdie rose and hugged Cynthia. "You've helped more than you know. Would it be okay if I come back to visit you again?"

Cynthia kissed her cheek. "Of course. I'd like that. Now, scoot. I'll follow you out. This is about the time I usually wander out to the nurses' desk. Shift change, you know. Get lots of gossip that way."

Taking Cynthia's hand, Birdie led the way from the room, but paused slightly when the woman's steps became shuffling and hesitant. At the nurses' desk, Cynthia patted her hand and turned toward an aide, holding out the doll for a kiss. The aide air kissed the doll and lifted her gaze to Birdie. "Have a nice visit?"

"It was very nice." Birdie angled away, but turned her face back to the aide. "And, she doesn't like Cindy. She prefers to be called Cynthia."

Cynthia covered her bark of laughter by coughing.

The aide grimaced at Birdie and focused her attention on her patient. "Are you okay, Cindy? Uh, Cynthia?".

A sad smile graced Birdie's lips when she approached Garr, her footsteps heavy and slow. Had she discovered the information she needed, or would the search continue? More than willing to assist in whatever way he could, he stood and stepped around the coffee table to meet her.

"Everything okay?"

Birdie nodded. "Yeah. I think so."

"And..."

"I need a little time to assimilate what I found out today." She touched his arm and looked up at him with moist, blue- gray eyes. Love overwhelmed him and his knees threatened to buckle. "I'll tell you soon. I promise."

Unable to resist the closeness of her body and the warmth of her touch, Garr engulfed her in his arms. "I'll hold you to that promise, baby." He slanted his lips across hers, pressing gently.

The tightening of her hand on his arm was her only response, so Garr reluctantly released her.

She took his hand and played with his fingers. "I don't really want to go home yet. Especially since Rachelle isn't there."

Leading her toward the door, Garr nodded. "Yep, we've got a free day. Do you trust me?"

"Trust?" Her eyes sparkled when she grinned. "With a capital 'T'."

 Traffic on the interstate moved at a steady pace, but passing semi-trailers shook Garr's lighter car. He'd been closed mouthed about where they were going, only grinning at her questions and shaking his head. So, Birdie stared out the window and watched fields and small towns rush by until Garr turned off the highway and traveled into one of those small towns.

After parking on a narrow side street, he angled in his seat and swung his arm to indicate the three block long main street. Tiny shops lined the walkways, their signs proclaiming a wide selection of antiques and crafts. Birdie smiled. She loved wandering places like this, able to lose herself for hours in browsing.

"How did you know? I love antiques."

He shrugged. "I didn't. But I've always found this a great place to think. And to study the century old architecture. Come on. Let's get started."

A few hours later Birdie settled on a park bench and kicked off her sandals. Wiggling her toes felt so good. She shaded her eyes with one hand and scanned the crowds milling about the sidewalks. Garr had wandered off, giving her strict instructions to stay put. Earlier, she'd found a few small items that caught her fancy, so while she waited, she unwrapped her treasures.

A few tiny figurines of cartoon characters would make Rachelle laugh. Oh, how she wished the young girl was her daughter. It hadn't taken long to fall in love with the vivacious nine-year-old.

Or with her father. Stan's threats surfaced in her mind, snatching away her breath and tightening bands of fear around her heart. In fact, she wasn't convinced Stan would ever leave them alone.

As much as she'd tried not to that afternoon, she'd peered warily at each passing car and jumped each time the bright sunlight highlighted a slender man's blond hair.

Birdie had given up trying to imagine what Stan might want from Garr and couldn't even think how Stan would know Garr. Unless there was some contact in the past while Stan was still a city councilman. She shook her head, that assumption just didn't feel right.

A cool shadow fell over her, and a crackling paper sack dropped into her lap. Garr stood silhouetted against the afternoon sun, but she could feel his pleased smile. Setting aside her packages, she lifted the heavy sack. "What's this?"

Garr sat, his thigh comfortably pressed against hers. "A present."

"What kind of a woman do you think I am? I don't accept presents from strange men." Birdie couldn't hold her serious expression.

Garr leaned back with one palm pressed to the center of his chest. "Strange? Strange? Me, strange?" He shrugged. "Okay, you got me. But you've also got a gift to open."

The excitement in his eyes was contagious. Carefully untwisting the top of the bag and peering inside, Birdie found a thick wad of tissue paper. She lifted it from the bag and held it up to Garr.

"Open it, baby."

Curious, and slightly uncomfortable under his intense gaze, Birdie slowly unwrapped the tissue paper. Finally, a cobalt blue macaw rested in the nest of white tissue. She couldn't speak.

"Well?"

"Oh Garr. It's beautiful." She held the figurine high in the sunlight. The magnificent detail in the glasswork sparkled in the sun. "I can't believe it. I've never seen anything like it." Angling to face Garr, she caught her breath at his expression. She didn't know what his smile or the glint in his eyes meant, only that it thrilled her from the roots of her hair to the tips of her curling toes.

"I'm surprised you didn't see it earlier, but I'm glad you didn't." Garr stroked the side of the figurine and Birdie shivered in anticipation. His finger moved to trace the line of her jaw to curl around the shell of her ear. "I think it will look great on the mantle, don't you?"

"I... oh, yes." Birdie leaned into his caress and closed her eyes. Blocking the brightness of the sun, Garr leaned closer and brushed his lips over hers. Heedless of the people passing the bench, Birdie threaded the fingers of one hand through Garr's hair and held him in place against her lips. "Oh, yes," she whispered when the kiss ended.

"Uh, baby. Maybe we should go."

Her eyelids were heavy, her body heated and tingly. "Okay." She had to blink twice before she could draw her gaze from his and rewrap the macaw. Taking his offered hand, they rose together and ambled toward the car.

"How about we head to the boats for supper? They've got a fantastic buffet, and I'm starved." Garr opened the car door and waited until she was seated before he moved to the driver's seat.

"The boats?" Under the influence of Garr's kiss, Garr's presence, she didn't understand what he meant.

"Yeah, the boats. The casinos on the river."

"Oh. I've never eaten there."

"Like I said, the buffet is fantastic. And since it's Saturday, they should have prime rib and peel and eat shrimp." He smacked his lips and pulled into traffic.

"You know all the places to eat, don't you?"

"I told you, I'm a lousy cook."

It was full dark by the time they returned home. Birdie sprawled in her seat, only the seatbelt keeping her upright. She rubbed her belly. "I can't remember ever eating that much. I'm still stuffed."

The deep warmth of Garr's chuckle lulled her to a comfortable, relaxed state. He reached to the side and unbuckled her seatbelt. "Think you can waddle into the house?" Shoving playfully at his shoulder nearly toppled the plastic cup propped on the seat between them. Birdie grabbed the casino's cheap promotional item and jiggled the quarters. "I can't believe I won so much with just a dollar." She stirred the coins with a finger. "Thanks for giving me my stake."

"Yeah, I'm a big spender. If you would have lost that dollar, we would have had to wash dishes to pay for dinner."

"Ooh, dinner. How dare they have such wonderful desserts. I should have run home."

"Come on. Let's get you into the house." Garr exited the car and met Birdie by her door. Wrapping an arm around her shoulders, he pulled her tight against his side. Before he unlocked the front door, he gave her a scorching kiss.

Lips burning with pleasure, she followed Garr into the dark house. She leaned back to close the heavy door and found herself trapped by Garr's arms. The wood pressed hard against her back and he was firm, hot, and welcoming before her. The touch of his mouth against the base of her throat brought a vibrating moan from the churning depths of her body.

His palms skimmed her sides, moving subtly inward until they covered her breasts. She arched her back and her head fell to the side. Garr's kisses traveled slowly along the rounded neckline of her shirt. "Garr." She gasped. "I can't."

He jerked back and lifted one hand to cradle her cheek. "Baby?"

Seeking to relieve his concern, she smiled and when she realized he probably couldn't see her well in the darkness, she matched his cheek cradling gesture. "I'm too full. What I'd like to do with you, what I need, would be truly uncomfortable until I digest more."

Garr laughed. He caressed her breast, kissed her forehead, and laughed. He turned away and laughed.

Birdie swiped at the wall and activated the foyer light. Planting her fists against her hips, she stomped one foot. "It's not funny. I really did eat too much."

Hands spread in apology, and snorting once with the effort, Garr bit back his laughter. "I'm sorry. It isn't funny."

Unable to control the rise of joy, Birdie burst into laughter. Bending forward, she clutched her stomach. "Oh, my. Oh, don't make me laugh. Stop."

But the laughter continued and they leaned against each other. When the laughter faded to nothing, the silence cocooned Birdie. No matter what, no matter how Stan tried, he couldn't take these feelings from her. And, she wouldn't let him destroy the moment. She snuggled into Garr's embrace. "We can continue this later, yes?"

"Yes!" Garr's enthusiastic response curled like a caress low in her body. It made her knees watery. He turned them toward the great room. "How about a cup of peppermint tea? It always seems to calm Rachelle's stomach aches."

"Umm, sounds wonderful."

After settling her on the couch, Garr moved into the kitchen to prepare the tea. While waiting for the water to heat, he peeked into the sunroom. Both birds huddled in a corner of the cage peering the patio door. The huge birds looked frightened. He would ask Birdie about it when he took her the tea.

The phone rang. Birdie shrieked. His forehead tightened in confusion as he reached for the phone.

"Hello?"

Birdie entered the kitchen and he turned to her with a smile. He mouthed 'one of my partners,' and was vaguely surprised when she visibly relaxed. His attention returned to the phone.

"What are you doing working on a Saturday night? That's too bad." He winked at Birdie. "Sure, I've got it here in my office. Hang on. Let me get you that information." With a shrug, Garr nodded toward the boiling water and strode quickly across the great room, the handset pressed to his ear.

He'd stepped behind his large, mahogany desk before noticing the safe standing wide open. "David, I've got to go. I'll call you back."

Crouching next to the thick metal box, he peered inside. An envelope lay on its side, a fan of bills peeking from one end. The folder containing important documents appeared untouched. Careful not to disturb the safe or the surrounding furniture, he leaned closer. There didn't seem to be anything... no, the wooden box containing the antique left to Rachelle by her grandmother was gone.

"Birdie?"

A moment later she appeared in the doorway and reached to rest one hand on the frame.

"No. Don't touch anything. There's been a break-in. I'm calling the police."

 While Birdie waited for the police to arrive, she wandered into the sunroom to check on the birds. Molly gave her a tentative squawk of welcome, but remained cowering in the corner of the cage. Brutus stood beside her with wings slightly spread, angrily clicking his beak and stamping one foot. Birdie moved forward slowly, and keeping her voice soft and calm, spoke to her feathered friends.

The calming attention began to sooth the birds, but Birdie restrained the urge to take them from the cage for cuddles. Afraid to touch anything, just in case, she kept her hands clasped tightly. What else would happen? After his demands, it made sense Stan might have had something to do with the break-in.

A cool breeze carried a breath of fresh air through the sunroom, raising a shiver across Birdie's shoulders. She turned toward the French doors. Jagged glass shards edged the near the latch. That must be how the thief entered the house. The chime of the doorbell startled her and she moved cautiously toward the kitchen.

A uniformed officer and a suit clad detective followed Garr into the great room. She stared at the men for a few moments before rushing forward. "Rog. What are you doing here?"

The suited man turned to her with a smile. "That's Detective Roger Corley to you, ma'am."

"Detective? When did that happen?"

"A couple days ago. The same day I asked Dot to marry me." His proud expression gave way to concern when Birdie only opened and closed her mouth soundlessly. "Oops. Looks like you didn't know. Dot will be upset I spilled the beans before she got a chance."

Recovering her wits, Birdie grinned. "I'll be surprised when she tells me. And, congratulations— on both accounts." She turned to Garr and pointed back toward the sunroom. "I think I know how someone got into the house. There's glass broken out of the French door. That's probably why the birds were so frightened."

Rog nodded toward his fellow officer. "Check it out, while I take statements here."

Silently, they watched the officer leave before Rog spoke. "I'm sorry my first case has to involve you, Birdie. Now, Mr. Logan, the questions."

Birdie touched Garr on the arm. "I'll go back with the birds. Another stranger in their room might frighten them more. I'll be there if you need anything from me."

Garr gave her a brief smile and sighed as he watched her walk from the room. The sway of her hips was delightful and heaviness filled his groin. Jerking his attention back to the detective, he closed his eyes briefly. Their relationship needed a break— some simplicity to erase all the complications.

He led the detective into his office and pointed to the open safe. "As far as I can tell, there's only one thing missing. Although an envelope containing cash was disturbed, it doesn't look like any was taken. But I can't tell for sure without counting it."

"Of course, Mr. Logan. What was taken?" Rog had his pad held in one hand, a thick pen poised over the page.

"A wooden box about ten inches long and four inches square. It's rosewood with a cross carved on the top. The cross is of an ancient design, supposedly from around the time of the second crusade. The box holds a small scepter. The staff is wood with a gold overlay. The head is gold, encrusted with jewels."

Garr chuckled at the detective's expression. "If you ask me, it's really ugly. But it's part of my daughter's inheritance from her late mother. This artifact is purported to have been given to one of her ancestors for service during the crusade. It's been passed from mother to daughter since then."

"So, it is quite valuable?"

"Yes. The insurance documents are in the safe as well."

"Do you have any thoughts on who would know of the item's existence and want to steal it?"

Garr took a deep breath and wished he could sink into his chair. He pressed his lips into a thin line and nodded. "Unfortunately, I do. My wife's brother caused many problems right after her death, including insisting the scepter belonged to him. But, as far as we could trace it, the item was never given to a son—only to the eldest daughter of a family. Rightfully, the scepter belongs to my daughter now."

Taking a few short steps around the desk, Garr continued. "My brother-in-law disappeared after that. I was hoping he'd never return. But I suspect he has. Although he hasn't tried to contact me yet. Maybe he planned on using a more direct route and just take what he wanted."

"A name, sir?"

"Davis. Stan Davis."

Comforted by Birdie's presence, the macaws had quieted. With the confusion, fear, and uncertainty roiling within her, she was surprised to discover the calmness of the sensitive avians. And they sent that calmness back to her. She accepted it gladly and was smiling softly when Rog stepped into the sunroom and cleared his throat.

"Come on in, Rog, uh, Detective."

"I need to ask you a few questions, too. Birdie, I'm sorry."

"Don't be. I've been expecting them. All a part of your duty, isn't it?"

Rog nodded and sat close to Birdie. "I wanted to talk to you alone, without Mr. Logan. I've sent him off to check the rest of the house to see if anything else is missing. Though I doubt there will be. The perp seemed to know exactly what he wanted." He cleared his throat again and tapped the end of his pen on the notepad.

"What is it, Rog?"

"I hate to ask this... could this break in have anything to do with the man who's bothering you?" He held up one hand, palm forward. "Don't be mad at Dot. She was so distracted, I convinced her to tell me why."

Birdie slumped in her chair, relieved she didn't have to go into the whole story. "I'm not angry. And yes, I think it may have everything to do with him. He wanted something from me, something from Garr's house. He never told me what."

Rog leaned closer, elbows on his knees. "Who is this man and do you know where he's staying?"

"I don't know where he's at." She paused and crinkled her forehead in thought. "Wait. He did mention a motel. It was... yes, the Inn 4 Less. And he must have some connection to lots of cars since each time I've seen him, he's been in a different vehicle." She shuddered and stared at her tightly clasped hands.

Maybe now this nightmare would end so she could go on with a reasonably normal life.

A thick-fingered hand covered hers and Rog gave a slight squeeze. "I know this is difficult, Birdie. We'll watch Mr. Logan's house until we catch the thief." His voice lowered. "Give me the name, Birdie."

She took a deep breath and lifted her gaze to Rog. His expression was expectant. "He used to be a city councilman. Stan Davis."

Rog's eyebrows shot high on his forehead and he quickly bent his head to write on his notepad. Before Birdie could ask about his reaction, the uniformed officer hurried into the room.

"Detective, come take a look at this."

Birdie followed the men out the broken doors to the edge of the dark patio. The uniformed officer crouched on the bricks and directed his flashlight beam toward the soft, wet earth of a flowerbed. "There, Detective."

Crouching beside his fellow officer, Rog moved the man's hand slightly to change the angle of the light. "I'll be." He glanced up toward the sky. City lights reflected on the low- hanging clouds. "Better get a cast made of that right away. Looks like it could rain again any minute." The officer handed Rog the flashlight and rushed toward the squad car.

A presence warmed the air behind Birdie before Garr's hand rested on her shoulder. She angled her head to rub her cheek against his fingers.

Rog rose and faced them. "Have you been wandering around your garden barefoot, Mr. Logan?"

"Huh?" Garr moved around Birdie to peer at the small circle of highlighted ground. "A footprint?"

Rog shone the flashlight over Garr's loafers and answered his own questions. "No, I doubt it. Your feet are too big."

Staring down, Garr lifted one foot, shrugged, and motioned for Rog to shine the light back on the footprint in question. The outline of the foot had been preserved perfectly in the firm, damp earth. The indentation of five toes could be clearly seen. "This is a good clue?"

"With the information you two have given me, I'd say it'll seal the deal—or the perp's fate at least. I... uh..." Rog cleared his throat. "I hate to ask this. Is there somewhere else you could stay? At least until we finish up our investigation tonight?"

Moving beside Garr, Birdie entwined her fingers in his. "We can stay at my place." She grinned at Rog. That way, you'll know where to find us."

Relief washed across Rog's features. "That'd be great. It doesn't appear anything's been disturbed other than the safe in the office. Is that right, Mr. Logan?"

Garr nodded and pressed Birdie's hand to the side of his thigh. The smooth weave of his jeans did little to tame the heat of his body against her skin. Her hand trembled and his fingers tightened around hers in immediate response. Thankful for his presence, she leaned closer to his side.

"Just try not to disturb anything as you leave. And, thanks for your cooperation."

Garr shouldered two bags and followed Birdie to her apartment door. She had become increasingly quiet the closer they got to her place, and his worry grew with leaps and bounds. She'd almost completely closed down her last time here. When that bastard attacked her. He winced with his own memories of the bruises on her body, the evidence of rough handling she barely admitted had happened. This time, though, he'd be with her. And nothing would happen to her. He'd give his life to insure it.

Birdie's hand was slow and shaking when she lifted it to fit the key into the deadbolt. Before she opened the door, Birdie turned her face toward him. "It's not much of a place, I guess. Nothing like your home."

Bracing one hand against the doorframe, Garr leaned closer. "It doesn't matter, Birdie. If I wanted glitz, I'd stay at one of those fancy hotels downtown." Tiny splatters of the renewed rain ran under his collar. "As long as it's warm and dry."

Her eyes lowered. "I'm sorry. Come on in."

Garr stepped into the small living room and glanced around while he dropped the bags to the floor and shut the door. The room was utilitarian and crowded with an assortment of mismatched furniture. Under a greasy pizza box, a pile of bird related magazines and catalogs covered an end table. This was where she spent her energies. Her

dedication to her business and her love of birds
filled him with pride.

Still standing in the center of the room, Birdie
stared at him. Her blank expression contradicted the
fear and agonies flashing through her eyes. "Garr...
I..."

"What can I do, baby?"

She sniffed and chewed on her lower lip. "Hold
me? Just hold me."

Across the short distance in a fraction of a
second, Garr engulfed her gently in his arms. The
tight muscles of her back shuddered with each
breath, but she didn't cry. Rocking her from side to
side, he stroked her back, giving silent comfort.

When her shuddering eased, he angled back
minutely and caressed her cheek with his palm.
"Can we sit down?"

"Oh, I'm sor—"

Garr stopped her speech by pressing his index
finger against her lips. "No apologies necessary."
Together they moved toward the couch. Garr waited
for her to settle near the middle of the long piece of
furniture and eased down next to her.

"Yeow." Garr jerked to one side and passed his
hand over the surface of the seat. The sharp point of
a broken spring jabbed his palm.

"I forgot." Birdie giggled, her laughter tinged
with hysteria. "That spring's been broken forever."
She slid to the far end of the couch and Garr moved
into the space she vacated. "Are you okay?"

"I'm fine. It surprised me more than anything.
Come here. I'm not done holding you yet." Garr
cuddled Birdie to his side and pressed her head
against his shoulder. She fit perfectly and, despite
his concern and worry, he leaned his head against

hers and smiled into her silky hair. This was all he needed.

Silence surrounded them for long moments. Garr stroked her back using long, lingering movements of his hand to ease the tension from her muscles. Reluctant to do more, he placed soft kisses on her head.

A quiet snore passed Birdie's lips. Garr's smile grew to a wide grin as he eased her to a more comfortable position. All those tears, cried and unshed, had stuffed up her nose. For some inexplicable reason, it endeared her to him even more. He tugged an afghan from the back of the couch, draped it over them, and closed his eyes.

But his mind would not rest, or even be quiet. His thoughts centered on the woman at his side and how she had suddenly appeared in his life. His lonely life. Rachelle resided in a huge part of his heart and soul. But he had ignored the emptiness caused by Melissa's death for far too long. He could no longer.

He couldn't lose Birdie. He opened his eyes and studied the tiny living room by the dim light filtering through the drawn blinds. Would she miss this place? Be willing to give it up? Garr vowed to do anything within his power to convince her she belonged with him—and with Rachelle.

Birdie's hand snaked over his stomach and curled around his side. Her fingers clutched at his shirt and she mumbled softly and sighed before settling into deeper sleep.

Garr's chest lifted with a responding breath. Would his love be enough to conquer the pain and terror the recent events caused her? Love. Yes. He loved her and it was past time he showed her how much. Tomorrow he would...

His planning lasted late into the night. Garr held Birdie and comforted her when dreams disrupted the peace of the darkness. It was all he wanted. It was enough.

 A cramp knotting the muscle in her calf woke Birdie and she jerked upright. Confused, she stared around her, hardly recognizing her own apartment. She leaned back, rested her head against the high back of the couch, and massaged the tight muscle.

The memories of the previous day returned as the calf muscle relaxed. She took a deep breath and snorted to herself. Garr brought her here—and they didn't even make it to the bedroom.

A line of bright light edged the dusty blinds in her front window. She closed her eyes. They'd slept on this uncomfortable, broken-spring couch all night. Garr was nowhere to be seen. Perhaps he'd found the comfort of the bed?

Rising carefully to prevent a repeat of the cramp, Birdie tested the muscle before taking a lurching step forward. She was stiff from the awkward night and stretched her joints slowly to loosen them.

"Garr?" She received no answer, but an appreciative inhalation brought her the aroma of fresh coffee. She grinned and stumbled wearily toward the elusive scent.

The galley kitchen was empty, but half a pot of dark brew waited on the counter. A folded sheet of notebook paper leaned against a large mug. She snatched at the paper and crinkled the edge tight in her fist while she poured some morning stimulation.

The hand holding the paper shook. Despite the waiting coffee, she feared he'd left her. But then, if

he'd left her, making coffee was silly. She was
being silly. There was only one way to find out why
he'd gone. She flattened the paper on the counter,
opened it and smoothed the crease without looking
down. A large mouthful of coffee burned her tongue
and she tried to cool her mouth before she took a
deep breath and glanced at the page.

It was upside down. She rolled her eyes toward
the ceiling and set the mug on the counter with a
loud thump. Coffee sloshed to the rim, but stayed in
the cup. It was a simple movement to turn the page
so she could read. Still, it took all her willpower to
make that move.

A tiny smile pulled at her lips as she read.

Baby,
I had some urgent errands and didn't want to
wake you. I should be back before 11:00. I'll take
you to the OK for dinner—great Sunday specials!
Then we can see if the detective's found out
anything and be home—hopefully—before Rache
gets there.
See you soon. Love, Garr

Love. Did he really love her? She hoped so, for
she loved him more than she ever imagined
possible. How had this wonderful man come into
her life? She wasn't sure if she believed fate might
be finally giving her a chance.

Wishing for a donut or even a piece of toast to
go with the coffee, Birdie opened the tiny pantry,
but her cupboards had done the Mother Hubbard
trick and were bare. She decided a shower was in
order, along with a change of clothes. And she
knew just what she wanted to wear. In the depths of

her closet was an outfit she'd bought on a whim and never worn. It probably still had the tags on it.

Her shower was quick in the claustrophobic tiny cubical so unlike the wide openness of the shower in Garr's master bath. Wrapped in her one large towel, she leaned over the sink and tugged a comb through her hair. The roots were beginning to show, the mousy brown making a thin, dark line against the fading golden-red. She pulled the length back and stared at her face in the mirror.

What could anyone see in her plain features? Granted, brightening her hair color helped accent her eyes, but still. Shaking her head, she grinned as the damp ends of her hair tickled across her shoulders and sent sensuous shivers tickling down her spine. With a final shake of her head, she dropped the towel and reached for her clothing.

The light gauze pants and tunic flowed over her skin much like her hair had done. Garr would like this outfit. Birdie opened the small wooden box where she kept her few pieces of jewelry. She'd never felt she needed much; besides, the shiny metal was a huge temptation for the birds. And not good on their insides if they happened to swallow an earring or bead. Now, she wished she had more pieces to choose from in the carved box. She wanted to look special for Garr.

Finally choosing a silver chain that hugged her neck and nestled nicely into the vee of the tunic, she was as ready as she'd ever be. A glance at the clock propped at the edge of the counter made her blow out a frustrated breath. It was only ten.

She returned to the living room and tried to interest herself in one of her favorite bird magazines. But the moment seemed too much like when she waited for Stan. The magazine went sailing across the room. Unsure what to do to keep her mind occupied, Birdie stood and sidled around the low table. Maybe more coffee?

The phone rang. She jumped back against her armchair, fell into the seat and reached for the phone. It had to be Garr. "Hello?"

"Birdie, this is Rog."

"Hi. What's up?"

"Birdie, this is official business. We've got a suspect under custody and he wants to talk to you."

Birdie's heart fell to the pit of her stomach. "Me?" Her voice squeaked.

"Mr. Davis refuses to cooperate until he sees you."

"I... I understand. As soon as Garr gets back, we'll come down."

"Uh..." Rog's discomfort was evident over the phone line.

"What is it, Rog?"

"He told me to have you come alone."

A nervous gasp escaped before Birdie could contain it. She tried to cover her discomfort with humor. "That sounds like a ransom drop or something."

"Can you come?"

There was no avoiding seeing Stan. Birdie closed her eyes. At least Stan couldn't be in control at the police station. "I'll come right away." With one finger she disconnected the line and dialed Garr's cell phone number. Her couch rang. Holding back a sigh, Birdie hung up her phone and searched through the cushions until she found Garr's tiny phone. She held it up in front of her face and spoke to the black plastic. "Guess I'll have to leave an old fashioned note."

With the note telling Garr she'd gone to the police station taped to the outside of her door, Birdie climbed into her SUV and drove slowly across town. She had no idea why Stan would demand to talk to her. There was nothing she could—or would—do to help him out of this situation. If he had broken into Garr's house and stolen something, he deserved what he got. And secretly, she hoped he got a lot.

She was ushered into a small waiting area and offered a foam cup filled with thick coffee. Staring into the dark liquid, she decided the television shows and movies were right about the quality of coffee cops drank. It even smelled old and over-brewed. But the cup warmed her hands, and she gained a modicum of comfort from the solid presence keeping her nervous hands occupied.

The ten-minute wait while they brought Stan from lock down seemed hours long. Finally, just as she contemplated tossing her cup into the trash and escaping the station, Rog appeared in the doorway and beckoned to her. She rose, smoothed the front of her slacks, and followed the detective down a long, wide hallway. Rog held a door open and, feeling as though she was about to step into an arena to face a pride of hungry lions, she moved through the gaping entry.

Instead, one man sat at a table. He lifted his head and smiled. Still the same Stan, always the charmer. This time, it wouldn't work. Birdie eased into a hard, metal chair across the table from Stan and clutched her hands tightly in her lap. She relaxed a bit when Rog pulled a chair to the third side of the square table and sat with his arms crossed over his chest.

Birdie took a deep breath while trying to decipher the strange glints flitting through Stan's eyes. Even under arrest, he was planning something. She cleared her throat. "What do you want?"

"Ah, babe. I just wanted to talk to you before they send me up the river." Stan chuckled.

"Don't call me that. Ever. I'll ask you again, and if I don't get a truthful answer, I'm leaving." Birdie placed her palms flat on the tabletop in preparation to stand.

"Thought you might like to know what was on those nurses' notes. Seems I can't give 'em to you—evidence you know."

Stan glanced at Rog from the corner of his eye. The detective remained solid and impassive. "I *can* tell you, however, that all that's on the page is a few notations about the sudden decline of our daughter. There was nothing they could do." He shrugged and sadness, an emotion Birdie had never seen from Stan Davis, filled his eyes. "She must not have been meant to live. I... I really am sorry, ba—Birdie."

The sadness and regret left his eyes and the calculating glint returned. "To bad she wasn't switched. Maybe you could have a kid after all." Stan chuckled and leaned back in his chair.

"Why do you enjoy taunting me—hurting me?"

"Aw, I don't mean to hurt you. I do have fond memories of our time together." Inviting her to place her hand in his palm, Stan reached across the table.

"Don't even go there. Did you break into Garr's house?"

"Why would I do such a thing?" Wounded innocence filled his expression.

Rog gave a quiet snort. Birdie pointed at Stan and jabbed her finger in the air to make her point.

"You were blackmailing me to get me to find something for you. Don't even bother to deny it, Stan."

"All right, I won't. There was an ancient artifact in the safe. I need that piece to repay a debt."

Rog leaned forward one fist resting on the table. "Who do you owe?"

Stan glanced at the detective and remained silent for a moment. When he came to a decision, the grin faded and he grew serious. "I need to cut a deal."

Rog relaxed back in his chair with one arched eyebrow and a satisfied grin. "And why is that, Mr. Davis?"

Squirming, Stan hemmed and hawed a few moments before turning in his chair to face Rog. "The man I owe is the head of a large... umm, shall we say… conglomerate. And although I owe him a great deal, he's trusted me with the operations in this part of the country."

"Drugs?"

"I can't say."

Rog slammed his fist on the table. "Can't—or won't?"

Stan hung his head. "I don't honestly know. I'm not that far up on the totem pole, so to speak. Although I suspect illegal substances are involved somewhere along the line. However, I just do little jobs, mostly acquiring rare art and collectable items for his private hideaway."

Birdie rose and paced the length of the room before swinging around to face him. "You're a burglar?"

Stan placed one hand over his heart and bowed. "At your service, ma'am."

Birdie shook her head. Obviously not a very good burglar. She couldn't believe this. A question popped from her lips. "How did you get so many different cars?"

"I'm honored you noticed. I have a friend who runs a used car lot for classic cars. He lets me borrow whatever I need. I need that artifact. It's been in my family for generations, since the second crusade. It's a scepter that was given to a wife to honor the service her husband was doing at the front, so they say. I made the mistake of describing it to... the boss, and he wants it. Wants it badly. If I don't get it for him, I'm a dead man."

Birdie leaned against the wall, crossed her arms and lifted her eyebrows at his unbelievable story. "So?"

The rustle of papers as Rog flipped through his small notebook drew her attention from Stan. Rog nodded and said, "That corresponds to the info we've gotten from federal law enforcement. I'll let them know about your desire to make a deal." Rog slipped a photograph from a folder and shoved it across the table toward Stan. "Know this man?"

Color drained from Stan's already pale face. "Can't... can't say that I do." He pushed the photograph back at the detective.

"Uh-huh." Rog lifted the photo to show Birdie. After she stared at it a few moments and shook her head, Rog explained. "The feds have reported this man to be in our area. He's a cartel hit man. Sure you haven't seen him, Davis?"

A sharp knock delayed Stan's answer. The door opened to reveal a thin, lanky man dressed in jeans and a wrinkled button-down shirt. He carried a long narrow box cradled in his white gloved hands. Rushing into the room, he set the box on the table and collapsed into the chair Birdie had vacated.

"This is amazing," he said between gasping breaths. "This isn't just an honorarium, it holds another secret. Watch." Grinning, the man fumbled with the box lid and removed a thick wand from a cushion of fabric. Curious, Birdie stepped closer while Stan slumped in his chair with a groan.

"The head of the wand is removable, although because of the difficulty I had, I don't think anyone's opened it for a very long time."

Birdie gestured to catch Rog's attention. "Who is this guy?"

"Historian. From the college. Helps us out occasionally. Doctor Nels Smythson."

The professor waved one hand at Birdie. "Nice to meet you. Now look." He twisted the scepter's jeweled head and it released into the palm of his hand. With careful, exacting movements, he set the top aside and stuck one thin finger into the barrel of the wand. When he removed his finger, he brought with it a rolled piece of paper.

Even with her untrained eyes, Birdie could tell the page was old. Possibly very old. Dr. Smythson set the wand back into its box and took a deep breath. Holding an end of the parchment down with one of his fingers, he unrolled the document. Birdie looked over his shoulder, but couldn't read the faint scratchings. However, the illuminated designs around the edge of the page were startling and bright. Amazement kept her speechless.

But not Stan. "So, that's what he really wants. Maybe that's what he meant when he spoke of treasure associated with such pieces. He was always studying old, smelly books." Stan sighed. "Not the scepter at all, but what was hidden inside."

Dr. Smythson bounced in his chair. "This is Italian, a very old dialect." He traced the words with his finger and a faint red infused the tips of his ears. "Uh, this is... uh... a love poem. Written by a woman to her husband. It's... uh... rather graphic. I must study this further." Without another word, he carefully returned the parchment to the wand, and left the room with the box held reverently before him.

Rog chuckled into the silence left by the man's abrupt departure. "A strange one, but he knows his stuff. We've just never been able to get him to follow police procedures. So, Mr. Davis, does this shed any more light on our situation?"

Stan stared at the scarred tabletop. "If you can get me some kind of protection, I'll tell you—the feds—what I know. Like I said, it's not much." His expression took on a self-deprecating smirk. "I'm smalltime in the operations. I can't go to prison for this. You know he'll find me there."

Nodding, Rog rose. "A common scenario for lowlifes like you. I'll see what I can do. There is one thing I'm really curious about."

Stan nodded for Rog to ask his question.

"Why were you barefoot? Didn't you know footprints are just as individual as fingerprints?"

One of Stan's eyebrows lifted. "Really? Ah well. I was barefoot because I used my socks to cover my hands. So I wouldn't leave any fingerprints. I never..."

The door burst open and Garr filled the doorway. He took two long strides across the floor, reached over the table, wrapped his fist in Stan's shirt, and jerked him to his feet. "I told you never to bother my family again."

"Hold it, Mr. Logan." Rog angled one arm between the two men and eased around the table to stand next to his prisoner. "Mr. Logan?"

Garr growled low in his throat, but loosened his hold. Stan slumped back into his chair, trying to smooth the front of his jail issue T-shirt. "What did you think you were doing?" Garr turned to where Birdie hovered uncertainly behind him. "And how do you know this... this piece of shit?"

"Oh, she's known me for a long time, haven't you, babe?"

Birdie stared at Stan. His old bravado had returned and his smile mocked her. Slowly, she turned her face to Garr. "Yes. I knew Stan many years ago."

"Years ago. Yep. About ten, wasn't it, babe?"

Silent, Birdie watched Garr. Stone-faced, no emotion but anger flickered in his eyes.

Stan continued as if no one else were in the room. "Yep. Had quite a wild time of it, too. You see, my dear brother-in- law, I'm the father of Birdie's child."

"Is this true?" Face turned only slightly toward her, the question was forced through the tight, straight line of Garr's lips.

Birdie hung her head. "Yes. I told you the truth about how it happened." She turned a glare on Stan. "It was date rape. I didn't consent." She spread her hands and pleaded with Garr. "I didn't."

"And that's not all, Garr. She actually thought your daughter..."

Garr whirled on Stan. "Leave Rachelle out of this."

"Aw, come on, Garr. She's my niece. I'd never do anything to hurt her. But Birdie..."

Stan glanced meaningfully at her and Birdie's heart sank lower than her churning stomach. An evil, vindictive intent lingering in his eyes.

"Birdie thought her child, and yours, had been switched at birth. So, it was your child who died, and hers lived on with you. She's been trying to find her child, even talked to that crazy old nurse. She was searching for answers, and she found Rachelle."

Birdie's world collapsed in the long moments it took Garr to turn back to her. He took a threatening step forward, his hands clenched into tight fists at his side. "Were you planning to steal my child? Were you planning on insinuating yourself into our house before we met? Is that why your card was in the phone book that day? How did you do that?"

"No, Garr. I never... it's just she looks so much like Stan. Can't you understand how the circumstances..."

"I trusted you in my home!"

And in your bed. Wrapping her arms about her waist, Birdie cringed in on herself. Stan smiled pleasantly at them. Rog was open-mouthed and speechless. No one could help her now. She had to make Garr see reason, to see she would never do anything to cause him hurt. She'd never hurt Rachelle in any way.

Taking a huge, shaking breath, Garr turned and pointed at Stan. "I don't ever want to see you near my home or my daughter again." He angled his upraised finger toward Birdie. "You..." His hand slapped to his side and he strode from the room. The door slammed behind him.

Deep chuckles roused Birdie from shocked inactivity. She pressed her hands to her temples to contain the fierce pounding. But Stan's laughter continued. Without thinking of the consequences, she marched to the table and drew back her hand. The sound of the slap echoed in the sudden silence. Stan covered his cheek with his palm and stared wide-eyed at her.

Birdie turned to Rog. "Do you need to file assault charges against me, Detective?"

Rog shook his head. Giving Stan one final, scathing look, Birdie backed toward the door and fumbled for the knob. She had to get away before she lost control. She bit her tongue to keep from sobbing out her pain. Stan would never see how he'd finally hurt her, how once again he'd ruined her life and any chance of happiness.

Turning away, she stalked from the conference room. The sound of Stan's whine followed her down the hall. "You can't let her do that to me."

CHAPTER SIXTEEN

Birdie could barely force her brain to function, let alone her aching body. Dry-eyed now, her tears spent, she could find no energy within herself to perform even the most mundane chores.

She couldn't blame Garr. Realizing how her actions and her secrecy must look to him curled her into a tight ball of misery. With her head resting against the hard arm of her couch and her arms wrapped tightly around her, she tried to focus on the opposite wall.

Staring at the blank space on her living room wall didn't help. The crack in the plaster moved until it formed Garr's profile. The spider-web lines shouted out her foolishness. And her guilt.

Why couldn't she have left well enough alone? Until the day she met Garr, she'd never considered her daughter may not have died, never thought about a switch of babies at the hospital. Why, when she met Garr, did she suddenly think about such things?

Now she couldn't even think at all. She tried to make her mind as blank as the wall, but thoughts of Garr, and what might have been, kept slipping through the ever-widening cracks. Cracks forever marring her—heart and soul.

She could offer no excuses for her actions— couldn't explain the near obsession she'd discovered in herself when trying to find the truth about the death of her child.

The truth. With a capital 'T'. Truth was, she hurt Garr by not trusting him and by not sharing her suspicions from the very beginning. Hurt him deeply. Her gaze dropped to the coffee table. The greasy, now smelly pizza box hovered at the top of a pile of bird magazines like a vicious accusation. This was all Stan's fault. If he'd never shown up, bringing with him the intensity of emotions she'd worked long and hard to conquer, most of this new pain, as well as the pain she'd caused Garr, would never have happened. She would have told Garr her suspicions sooner. And later, later maybe they would have laughed over the absurdity of her fanciful ideas.

Stan would get what he deserved. For once, he had to face his comeuppance. With a growl low in her throat, she lurched to her feet, snatched the pizza box from the table, and ran from her apartment.

Tears poured down her cheeks as she stood at the complex's shared garbage Dumpster, ripping the soggy box and hard pizza to shreds. She imagined tearing Stan apart, and shouted her anger as she tossed each piece to the bottom of the Dumpster. When the box was gone, her tears dried. She ran her greasy hands through her hair and glanced around. Luckily, her screams had caused no disruption to the quiet Sunday afternoon. No curious faces peered from windows or peeked from open doors.

Relieved, and ashamed of her childish tantrum, Birdie slunk back to her apartment. Staring at her filthy hands only brought fresh tears. So many tears. At that moment she doubted they'd ever stop. Birdie wandered into the bathroom, stripped and stepped into the shower. At least with the water pouring over her, she wouldn't be able to tell how much of the wetness on her face was tears.

The door slammed behind Garr and rattled the glass sidelight. Leaves of the plants the receptionist lovingly kept alive fluttered in the wake of his fierce passage. He jabbed the key into the lock of his private office, wrenched the door open, and tossed a small package to the messy desk.

He stomped around the huge, oak desk to a display table arranged in one corner of the office. His latest project, a new addition to his house, was spotlighted by a shaft of sunlight filtering through a crack in the blinds. The anger flushed from him like a clogged drain, suddenly opened. He backed away from the table and sagged against the edge of his desk before slumping into the leather chair.

What in the hell had he done? A renewed rise of anger brought heat to his face. She'd played him for a fool, used him to fulfill her need to find a child long dead. He shook his head and captured his temples between his palms. No, that wasn't right. With a groan of frustration, he slapped his hands on the desk.

The small package bounced on a thick file. Garr stared at the tiny box, a treasure he'd removed from his mother's bedroom safe that morning. He'd planned to hand the velvet box to Birdie, had even pictured the room filled with candles and romance. But now, he'd ruined his chances.

He opened the box and stared at the ring once belonging to his great-grandmother. A diamond, surrounded by strange, bluish-purple stones graced the simple gold band. As a boy he'd loved the way the stones seemed to change color in different lights. Now all he saw was the shifting colors of Birdie's expressive eyes. No other ring would do for her. He sighed and took the ring from the box. Holding it to the light, he watched tiny spots of prism colors float around his office.

The sparkles of color bounced off the white foam board he'd used for the model of his addition. A slow, hesitant smile spread across his face. That might do the trick. He couldn't talk to Birdie, not yet. He had to be able to prove his feelings and show her his hastily spoken words were built from surprise and anger at his brother-in-law. Would it work? The rainbow lights bobbed up and down. Garr took it as a sign and reached into his jacket pocket for his phone.

His fingers closed around a tiny bit of lint. His brows drew together in confusion. Where? He sighed. At Birdie's. The phone must have slipped from his pocket. He'd lost more phones that way.

A tense shrug lifted his shoulders. He couldn't make the calls he needed today, anyway. Shoving a stack of papers to one side, he glanced at the clock angled on a corner of the desk. Rachelle would be home soon, and he needed to be there. He closed his eyes against the knowledge he'd be forced to admit his foolishness to his daughter. He could only hope she was old enough to understand.

"Please, Dot?" Pleading with her assistant, Birdie clasped her hands before her and shook them.

"You should do this, Birdie. You know that."

"Yes, I know." Birdie sank into a chair. It had been over three weeks since Garr accused her of trying to steal his daughter. She knew—hoped—the moment had been only his anger talking. But she'd not heard from him since then. Rachelle called her once, but the whispered conversation was rushed and she hadn't had the chance to ask Rachelle about her father. Now, using the fact she still carried his cell phone next to hers in her purse, she was trying to persuade Dot to make the dreaded first contact.

Dot sighed and picked up the phone. "What do you want me to say?"

"Umm, that I have his phone. Umm, that I'm sorry... that... oh, I don't know."

Dot's eyebrows lifted dramatically. "Did you know someone else tried to break into Garr's house a few days after you left?"

"Oh, no! Is everyone okay? Dot? Why didn't anybody tell me?" Birdie sank onto her chair and covered her mouth with one of her hands. Was this connected? Stan was still in jail— wasn't he?

With her hands lifted in a conciliatory manner, Dot sat on the edge of the desk. "Rog couldn't tell anyone—until yesterday. Seems it had something to do with the FBI. And no, no one was home. And yes, they caught the would-be robber immediately. Don't you want to talk to Garr about it?"

"I... I can't. If he wanted me to know, he would have—"

"Called you?" Dot chuckled. "You're both simply stubborn idiots. She slowly punched in the number to Garr's home. Birdie gave no thought as to how Dot knew the number and held her breath. When the barely audible rumble of a deep voice answered, she let the breath escape. She wanted to hear his voice and experience the wonderful tremors caused by the low tones. One of her hands lifted as if with a mind of its own and reached toward the receiver. She jerked her hand back, turned away, and stared into the bird room while still straining to hear anything of his side of the conversation.

"Hi, this is Dot. No. No. Did you know Birdie has your cell phone? You did? But..." There was a long pause. Curious, Birdie turned her face toward Dot. Her assistant quickly squelched her grin and nodded soberly to Birdie. "Yes, I understand. Oh, I think that's best. Sure, whatever I can."

What were they talking about? Birdie turned to fully face the desk and lifted her eyebrows in question. Dot waved away her concerns. "How's Molly? That's great. Uh-huh, no problem. Thanks. Bye."

"Well?"

"He'll call in a week or two to arrange a time to get his phone. Molly's doing fine, she and Brutus seem to be getting closer. Rachelle is enjoying taking care of the birds and Garr says she's doing a wonderful job. Not to worry."

"I miss my baby, though." *Baby.* How she longed to hear the simple endearment. But, only from Garr.

"You could go get her any time. I'm sure it could be arranged."

"No, not now. She and Brutus were bonding. I'm amazed it happened so quickly, but I wouldn't want to take the chance on separating them now. No, I'll wait."

Dot's forehead scrunched with the effort of trying to keep a grin from her face. Birdie jammed her hands against her hips and leaned toward the younger woman. "What's going on? You're getting pretty good at keeping secrets from me."

Dot shrugged, but the grin remained.

Tired of thinking about her hopeless situation with Garr, Birdie crossed the office and sat on the corner of the desk. "So how's Rog? His first case has turned out to be bigger than anyone thought, huh? Even more important, girlfriend, how're the wedding plans coming along?"

"Let me show you the dress I'm thinking about." Dot reached for her bag and tugged a thick folder from the depths. Soon the women were lost in wedding plans. Birdie's hopes and dreams were relegated to a far, safe corner of her mind while she celebrated her friend's love and happiness.

"No, I need it done yesterday. Last week would have been even better." Garr shook his head and spoke more terse words into the phone. "Yeah, yeah. Of course I understand. Sure, as soon as possible." Frustrated, he tossed the cordless phone to the far end of the couch.

His project was taking longer than it should. As an architect, he had a fair idea how long it took to obtain building permits and arrange sub-contractors, but he'd never been faced with the number of delays continually slowing the addition. Now, when the area was nearly complete, the plumber bailed on him until the following week. He closed his eyes and shook his head. He could only call in so many favors.

The sound of his daughter settling on the leather cushion next to him made him open his eyes and smile. The smile faded at her serious, older than nine expression.

"Daddy, can I talk to you?"

"Of course, squirt. About anything. You know that."

"I miss Birdie."

Inviting her into his embrace, Garr sighed and held out his arms. Rachelle crawled over his legs and curled onto his lap. He sighed again. It had been a long time since his little girl cuddled with him. Part of him wished she would never grow up. "I know, honey. So do I."

"Are you ever gonna talk to her again?"

"Soon. When the addition is done." Garr stroked Rachelle's slim back and felt the shudders accompanying her tears. "Honey, don't cry."

"I can't help it, Daddy. I love her so much. I want her to be my mom. I need her." Rachelle leaned back and touched his face with her fingertips. "You need her too, don't you, Daddy?"

"I do." Garr ran his hand down the length of her silky hair. A flash of inspiration made him smile. "Let's see if we can hurry this along, shall we? There's just a little plumbing to be done. I'd say this is an emergency, wouldn't you?"

Rachelle nodded, slipped from Garr's lap, and stretched to reach the phone. As she did, Garr angled to pick the phone book up off the floor. He flipped rapidly through the pages, pointed to a number and let Rachelle dial.

"Hello, yes, I have a plumbing emergency. Yes, I understand that. No problem, I'll pay whatever it takes to get someone out here right away."

After giving directions to the plumber, Garr disconnected and smiled at Rachelle. She squealed and threw herself back into his arms. "Thank you, Daddy. Thank you."

Garr kissed her fresh smelling hair. Sometimes adults really needed to listen to their children.

Twice that week Birdie found herself on the road to Garr's house. And it was only Tuesday. She pulled her SUV into a Gas'n Snack and turned around. Forcing back the deep, agonized breath hovering in her chest, Birdie stared into the distance. Then, she shook her head and gave a wry chuckle. There was no way she could see Garr's house from here.

She ached to know how he was doing after the second robbery attempt. Ached as well, with the longing to feel his arms around her and his lips against hers. Just the thought made her breasts tingle and heat pooled low in her belly. It wasn't just the physical part of their relationship she missed. She longed for their stimulating conversations, the way he laughed, and the fact he couldn't cook.

And she missed Rachelle. The emptiness she'd carried with her for nine years had been filled with a sunny disposition and long golden hair. If she could wish for any child, she'd hope for Rachelle. It didn't matter that she'd not borne Rache. It only mattered Garr thought she wanted to steal his child. That had to be the reason he never contacted her.

A month was a long time to miss someone, miss a family so desperately. She'd told herself over and over, then over again to get on with her life.

Birdie parked in front of her small business and leaned her forehead against the steering wheel. It seemed all she'd done since she met Stan ten years ago was have to get over something and move on emotionally. She was tired of moving on. It was time for her emotions, for some part of her life to be settled.

When she finally released the sigh, it returned with a dry, hopeless sob. Only one thing would do now. She had to talk to Garr and bring Molly home. Then there would be closure for another painful— no, a wonderful—part of her life.

Her courage and determination failed her in the short walk to the building. Lightening her mood, Dot's smile greeted her.

"You had a phone call while you were gone." Birdie's heart leapt painfully in her chest. *Garr.*

Dot continued. "That old nurse you visited a while back called. She wants you to come visit when you have the time."

A fresh wave of guilt flowed over Birdie. She'd promised to visit Cynthia, but had focused on her own sadness and problems, and left the old woman alone. Tucking the guilt into a mental strong box, she smiled at Dot. "That sounds like a great way to spend the afternoon. Unless I'm needed here?"

Dot stretched and shook her head. "The only thing scheduled is a delivery of seed. I think I can handle that."

Birdie chuckled and felt her eyes widen at the nearly forgotten sound. Had it really been so long since she'd laughed? The cheerful sounds were unusual to her ear. "I'm sure you can. If you want, I can take an extra shift..."

"Don't worry about it." Dot waved her away. "You'll get more than your share of work when I'm on my honeymoon. So get going. Have a nice visit. And, Birdie..."

In the act of turning away, Birdie looked back over her shoulder.

"Relax. Have a good time. Be happy."

"Thanks for caring, Dot. I'll be fine soon."

"I'm sure you will." Dot's grin held more secrets Birdie didn't have the energy to weasel out of her. So, she waved over her shoulder and left the office.

Birdie took a quick tour of the bird rooms before she left, making sure each cage was clean and its inhabitants well fed and watered. Most of the time she spent with the birds lately had been barely dealing with their basic needs. Although the college students had been doing an excellent job, she really needed to give the birds more personal attention.

So she spoke softly to each feathered creature and gave caresses to those who would accept them. When her route led her back to the door, she stepped into the sunshine of a bright day. A faint flutter of hope and peace surrounded her. Maybe things were turning for the better.

Garr disconnected the speaker phone, leaned forward with his elbows resting on the desk and steepled his fingers. Tapping his fingertips together, he grinned. The plan was in motion.

Sara would pick Rachelle up after school. Rache would wait at Sara's until he went to get her. He knew where Birdie was. Now, all he had to do was get there and convince her to return to Logan's Hollow with him. And then...

Needing to wait half an hour before he left his office, Garr tried to keep busy. But his gaze strayed continually to the model of his home's addition. And his thoughts strayed to Birdie. Would she be willing to listen to him? It had been exactly one month since that fateful day at the police station. He took a deep breath and closed his eyes. His memories filled with Birdie, her smile, her joy, her comfortable presence and the way she fit perfectly into his arms.

He glanced at the clock for the fiftieth time, grabbed his jacket from the back of a chair, and rushed from the office, pausing only a few moments to give instructions to the receptionist.

The need to see Birdie pressed his foot against the accelerator, driving him faster than the speed limit. The retirement home wasn't far from his office, but even with a new friend on the police force, Garr didn't think he needed to tempt fate. He relaxed the pressure on the gas pedal. Meeting Birdie this way was a chance no matter how he looked at it, and he needed all the help from fate he could get.

An empty space waited next to Birdie's vehicle and he slid his sedan easily into the parking place. He thought about waiting in the car, but decided to sit in the lobby instead. If he angled the chair just right, he could watch both the lobby and the SUV. Just in case Birdie used another exit.

He waved to the elderly man at the reception desk and settled into a reasonably comfortable wing back chair. Laying a magazine across his lap, he opened the slick pages to somewhere near the center of the publication. Then, staring casually around the lobby, he waited.

 "I can't believe you're back in your own home." Birdie perched on the edge of an overstuffed couch after a quick tour of Cynthia's large condo.

Cynthia chuckled and winked. "I made a sudden, miraculous recovery. The doctors and nurses are still trying to figure it out. I'll let 'em stew a while, then I'll spill the beans. If nothing else, maybe it will help the professionals realize the need to explore all the avenues when a person's health or behavior suddenly changes."

"So, something must have happened between your niece and the man."

"Appears he got caught after robbing a house. A pretty quick way to end a relationship, don't you think?"

"Well..." A niggle of apprehension churned behind Birdie's heart.

"My niece is an intelligent woman. She told me she suspected something was up, but had no idea what that man was doing. She was going to drop him anyway."

"So, he's a thief?"

"A dumb one, too. Seems he took off his shoes so he could put his socks over his hand. To prevent fingerprints, you know."

Birdie gasped, then began to laugh. "And he... he left a footprint... in the mud."

"How did you know?" Cynthia leaned forward and reached for Birdie's hand.

"It was... he robbed a friend's house. Oh, Cynthia. I'm so glad you're back home. It must feel great."

"It does. Now, how about a cup of coffee? You don't impress me as a tea drinker."

The women laughed together and moved into the dining area. Cynthia stepped through a set of swinging café doors and started the coffee. They sat at a contemporary dining set and talked until the pot was empty.

Promising it wouldn't be a month before the next time she came for a visit, Birdie hugged Cynthia. Her steps down the long, carpeted hallway were light. Even her heart felt lighter. She'd hidden in her lonely misery much too long. It really was time to move on. But, even as her mind logically planned her future, her heart cried out for Garr.

As if in answer to the summoning of her heart, Garr sat in the lobby. Birdie froze, blinked, and blinked again to make sure he wasn't a figment of her imagination. Even the tight, tense lines of his jaw and the undecipherable glint in his eyes looked wonderful to her. How she missed him.

She stepped into the lobby and Garr rose. The magazine slipped to the floor with a sharp rustle of pages. He held out one hand.

With her breath hovering in her throat, Birdie closed the distance between them, but only looked at his hand. She couldn't meet his eyes. "I'm so sorry, Garr. I never meant to cause you problems. I would never, ever consider trying to take Rachelle from you."

His hand lifted to touch her chin and raise her face. "I know that, baby. I was so angry with Davis I couldn't think straight."

"He said those things on purpose. He wanted to hurt me because I refused to help him."

"I should have expected it. His behavior never changes." Garr tilted her head back infinitesimally. His eyes pleaded; hers must have given an answer. He closed the distance between their lips with a soft kiss.

A soft moan of assent accompanied Birdie snaking her arms about his neck and pressing against him. The kiss deepened and sent her spinning until she clutched his shoulders to stay upright. Garr's hands tightened on her waist, arching her hips to his. His lips moved slowly, teasing, until she allowed him entrance to her mouth. Time stood still.

The harsh sound of the clearing of a throat popped Birdie's eyes open and she pushed at Garr's shoulders. What was she doing? When Garr released her, she turned toward the reception desk. The gray-haired gentleman grinned at them, nodded once, and winked.

Garr bent to whisper in her ear. "Come home with me?" He didn't wait for an answer, but returned the man's nod, took Birdie's hand and led her from the building. They stopped in front of the cars.

Birdie glanced at him. "I'll drive my SUV."

"Are you sure?"

She nodded. Afraid something would go wrong, she didn't want to be without transportation of her own. Garr squeezed her finger and cupped her chin with his other hand.

"Don't worry, Birdie."

"But... but do you forgive me for lying to you?"

His eyebrows rose to hide under the shock of hair that had fallen over his forehead. "Lying?"

"Well, maybe not really lying, but I kept things from you. If I would have told you my suspicions, maybe we could have worked through them earlier."

"Hmm. Perhaps. I understand, however, why you kept silent. Now, when we know the truth…Rog showed me the nurses' notes Davis had in his possession. Seems your friends were distressed by our separation."

Not as much as me. Before she could speak, Garr pressed another kiss to her lips.

"Come home with me. There's something I need to show you. And we can work through any issues you find important now." He grinned. The expression lit his face and stole her breath.

She could manage only one word. "Yes."

"Follow me, baby." After a lingering kiss, Garr turned toward his vehicle, unlocked the door and slid behind the steering wheel.

Birdie remained standing where she was, stunned by the past few minutes. It really couldn't be so easy, could it? The sharp sound of Garr's horn startled her from her reverie. She waved and climbed in her vehicle.

Following Garr's sedan would have been difficult in the late afternoon traffic if she hadn't known the way to the development. She grinned and waved at the Gas 'n Snack when she drove past—no turning around this time. And by the time they reached the top of Garr's drive, she'd decided to pursue whatever relationship Garr was willing to share with her. She didn't want the bare survival of another month like the past weeks.

Garr opened her door and took her hand as she slid from the seat. "Welcome home, Birdie. I daresay the birds will be happy to see you."

"Ah, I've missed them and their crazy antics."

Stopping her at the front door, Garr turned a serious expression to her. "Did you miss anything else, baby?"

She swallowed heavily. Following the movement, Garr's eyes were intent on her throat. His eyes darkened and heat spiraled through her. "Oh, yes."

Inside, she waited for him to take her in his arms. The desire rising between them electrified the air and lifted the fine hairs on the back of Birdie's neck. She took a step toward the stairs.

"No, baby, come this way." Garr's smile smoldered with sensuous promise, but his eyes glinted playfully. "I want to show you my latest project."

Wrapping one arm around her shoulders, Garr led her through the great room and out to the sun porch. The birdcages—were missing. Birdie jerked to a stop. "Garr?"

"The birds are fine. Come on."

He took her through the long, narrow room to a new doorway partially hidden by tall, potted plants. Thin blinds covered the double doors. Birdie glanced at Garr in question.

"I was designing this addition before you... before all the trouble with my brother-in-law." He cleared his throat. "I wanted to surprise you. Close your eyes."

"Oh, just like one of those surprise decorating shows, huh?"

"Close your eyes, Birdie."

When she covered her eyes with her hand, Garr opened the door and guided her through the opening. The squawk of greeting told her the birds were here and safe. Contented chattering surrounded her and made her smile.

"Okay, now you can open your eyes." Garr stood back and held his breath. She *had* to like this room, so much depended on her reactions.

"Oh, my…Garr? You built this for the birds?"

Releasing his breath, Garr nodded and tried to see the room through her eyes. Behind wrought iron bars dividing the room in half, the two macaws perched high in a bird's paradise. Multi-levels of perches, a variety of toys and a thick, rope swing provided plenty to keep the curious birds occupied.

Birdie pointed to a far corner. "A nest box? You built them a nest box?"

Heat burned the tips of his ears. "They, umm, acted like they needed one. I did a lot of research. I hope everything is okay."

Birdie flew into his arms and he stumbled back three steps. "Okay? It's the most beautiful habitat I've ever seen. If I were a macaw I'd never want to leave."

"What kind of habitat would keep you here, baby? I've got to know."

"All I need is you—and Rachelle of course." Bright pink filled her cheeks. "Anywhere you are, that's my habitat." Pressing him back against the counter he'd installed to hold supplies, Birdie kissed him boldly. Her tongue traced patterns over his lips until he groaned and she danced her tongue along his. Heat followed the path of her hands when she stroked his arms, his back, his sides, until she slid her fingers under his shirt.

Surprised and delighted by her ardor, Garr returned her caresses. The sound of their harsh breathing became a counterpoint to the joyous chattering of the birds. Garr wrenched his lips from hers, but hugged her more tightly. "Not here, baby."

Her eyes had turned deep blue. Now, confusion warred with desire. Garr chuckled. "I don't think the stone floor would be too comfortable."

Birdie's eyebrows rose. "Hmm." She turned from him, but kept hold of his hand, tugged to get him to move and led the way back to the sunroom. Halfway through the room she glanced at the floor. A thick, braided rug covered the wood planks. "This will do."

Birdie returned to her sensual assault. Her hands on his shoulders, and her kisses, forced him to his knees on the colorful rug. She eased him to his back and stroked his hair from his forehead. "Thank you, Garr. For so much."

Growling, he turned them so she lay beneath him and hovered over her. "Not the time for talk, baby." He trailed a path of kisses over her face and down her neck. He suckled her nipples through the thin material of her T-shirt. Birdie arched to his mouth and frantically twined her fingers through his hair.

She jerked his head back and he gave a low grunt of pain. "Garr, what about Rachelle?"

Dazed by the feel of her against him and the tingling of his lips, he stared down at her. His hips slid against her, seeking the heat at the juncture of her thighs. She gasped and slapped at his shoulder.

"When does she get home from school?"

Pinning her beneath his full weight, Garr nibbled at her ear lobe. "She's at Sara's. We'll pick her up. Later. Much later."

They rolled around the rug and undressed each other. Garr wondered at how the moment could be both frantic and leisurely, sweet and torrid, and so totally Birdie. The abandonment with which she cried out when he entered her stilled his body. Her legs wrapped around his hips to hold him tight.

Then, she moved, and his cry echoed with the joy of the long awaited moment. It would be like this every time. Arching into her, Garr accepted the gift of her body, giving back with each stroke, each adjustment of his hips.

Birdie met his thrusts, moaning out her sudden release. Garr's hips moved in tempo to the pounding of his heart. Spilling into her with a choked cry, he held her tight against him.

"Oh, God, baby."

CHAPTER EIGHTEEN

"We should go get Rache, soon. I'm getting hungry."

Birdie stroked her fingertips over Garr's bare chest and chuckled. Then, her stomach rumbled. "Oops, guess I am, too."

Garr crawled over her and out of bed. "Our clothes are still downstairs. I'll go get them and call Sara while you get dressed. How about going to the OK?"

A faint twinge of apprehension made Birdie blink. They had planned on going to the OK Café before she'd been called to the police station. She took a deep breath. She couldn't avoid a good eating place because of a memory. "Okay on the OK."

Fifteen minutes later they were on the way. When they pulled up in front of Sara's federalist style home, Rachelle ran to the car. She clamored into the back seat and fastened the seatbelt. "Everything okay, Daddy?"

Garr glanced in the rear view mirror. "Almost, squirt."

"Good."

"Say, we thought about the OK for supper? Thought maybe you'd like to visit the pigeons before we eat."

"Oh, yeah, right, Daddy. That'd be great. I'll even let you order for me so I can spend extra time outside."

Birdie frowned. Something about their brief exchange seemed forced. She worried at the notion for a few moments until she realized strange noises were coming from Garr. "What are you doing?"

"Singing." He glanced sideways at her and began again, a bit louder. "Birds do it, bees do it, even educated..."

"Daddy, please." Rachelle covered her ears. "Don't sing. You'll scare Birdie away. Along with all the dogs in the neighborhood."

"I think Rachelle is trying to tell you I'm totally tone-deaf."

Birdie grinned. "She didn't have to tell me. I figured it out for myself. Gee, can't cook, can't sing. What are you good for?"

A smile tugged one side of his mouth and the corresponding eyebrow lifted. He glanced over at her. "I'm sure there must be something."

The burn of renewed desire blazed through her. Birdie was saved from responding when they pulled into the café's parking lot. Rachelle rushed off to the fenced in windmill and the collection of pigeons. The café was sparsely populated and Garr chose a booth in the far corner. After ordering, Garr took Birdie's hand and caressed her fingers.

"Birdie. I want more than just a physical relationship with you."

She chewed on her lip. What was he getting at? "We do have more. We have a growing friendship."

"That's true, and very important. Birdie, baby, I need you in my life." A strange desperateness colored his tone, but she couldn't read his eyes in the restaurant's florescent lights.

"I'm not going anywhere."

Holding her hand with one of his, the other hand disappeared under the table and returned with a small, velvet box. Birdie gasped. There were only a few things that could be in the tiny jeweler's box.

Flipping the top back, Garr exposed a ring. The clear center stone sparkled, but the purple-blue stones surrounding it danced in the light. He turned her hand over and set the box in the center of her palm.

"This ring belonged to my great-grandmother. She was happy for many years while wearing it. I hope, I pray, you'll spend happy years with it upon your finger. Birdie, I'll get on my knees if you want me to."

Numb, Birdie shook her head.

"Baby, will you marry me?" He closed her fingers around the ring box. "I love you, desperately. I love you with a heart and a half."

"That sounds like a movie line."

Garr ducked his head. "It is. But it's how I feel. Birdie, *Vous et nul autre*."

Startled, Birdie lifted her gaze from her hand to Garr's face. "French?"

"I suppose I pronounce French as well as I sing. I saw the phrase in a catalog."

Birdie grinned at him. "Do you know what it means?"

"You and no other. If you deny me now, there will be no other."

"How could I sentence you to such loneliness? My whole being is filled with love for you, Garr. I love you so much, I could just burst. Of course I'll marry you."

Birdie opened her hand and Garr took the box. He removed the ring from its velvet bed and slipped it on the appropriate finger. It slid sideways. Birdie took his hand and kissed his fingers. "Looks like we'll need to have it sized." She placed it back in the box and handed it to him. "Keep it safe for me until then."

Out of breath, Rachelle rushed to the table. She glanced expectantly at her father, then at Birdie. Garr patted the seat next to him. "The ring's a little big, but as soon as it's sized..."

"Yay! Really, Birdie? You'll be my mom?"

"If you want me."

Rachelle slipped from her seat and crawled on the bench next to Birdie. She wrapped her arms around Birdie's neck and hugged her tightly. Birdie returned the embrace and smiled at Garr over Rachelle's head. Rachelle pressed a kiss to Birdie's cheek and swung around to sit close to her.

"Oh, Daddy, guess who I saw outside?"

Before he could say anything, an older woman slid next to him. "I knew I'd find you here. Just wanted to let you know I'm home."

Birdie stared at the white-haired woman. A frequent visitor to *Birdies*, she had often invited Birdie to speak at the bird lovers club.

Garr cleared his throat. "Birdie, I'd like you to meet the owner of the monster bird. My mother, Esther Glenn."

"You're Garr's mother?" Disbelief made Birdie's voice squeak.

Esther reached over to pat Birdie's hand. "Of course, dear. Oh, you didn't know. Glenn is my third husband."

"You're the one who left my business card in Garr's phone book?"

"I suppose I did. I'm often leaving them places. Hoping to improve your business." Esther glanced at her son. "She's quite remarkable with birds, you know."

Garr chuckled. "I know, Mom. I know."

Esther rested her palms flat on the tabletop. "So, anything interesting happen while I was away?"

DEAR READER

Thank you for reading this tale. Bringing stories to life is one of my greatest delights and I hope you enjoyed your time in one of my worlds as much as I enjoy creating them. Readers like you spark the energy needed to tell these tales. Again, thank you.

With today's world of vast reading choices, word of mouth is the best advertising. So please let others know about this book. Tell your friends, relatives, acquaintances, the dog next door (hey, you never know...).

And if you're so inclined, please leave a review so others can discover the worlds of *lizzie starr.

To keep up with new releases, sign up for *News From The Starr*. Yes, it's a newsletter, but will appear in your email only occasionally. Your email is safe with me, will never be shared, and you can, of course, unsubscribe at any time.

Sign up for the news or just stop by and visit me online at *www.lizziestarr.com*. There you can read first chapters, discover more about the Keltic Multiverse and other worlds in my tales.

I love connecting with readers!

Happy reading,

 *lizzie always made up games and stories to keep her company. So, a cunning witch lived in Grampa's weather research station and was only held at bay by waving a certain weed. An ancient road grader morphed into a boat carrying wild adventurers to islands filled with fierce lions and dangerous cannibals, which really looked a lot like sheep. Now, filled with fantasy, love, and romance with a sparkling twist, the stories of her imagination swirl their way into the mundane world. When *lizzie must return to a more routine life, she's *the Lunch Lady* at a private school.

Author and lunch lady~~what a combination!

THE STARR LIBRARY

FANTASY ROMANCE

The Double Keltic Triad
By Keltic Design
Fires of a Keltic Moon
Keltic Flight
Wild Keltic Carouselle
Keltic Dreams
A Faire Keltic Renaissance

Children of the Keltic Triad
Blue Keltic Moon

The Keltic Multiverse
Prince of Dark Ness
(Double Keltic Triad 5.5)

CONTEMPORARY ROMANCE

Birds Do It!

SHORT STORIES
Available as ebooks

At Death's Gates
Dead Lily Blooms
Death and the Dryad

From the Keltic Multiverse
Candy Guy and the Chocolate Brownie

Futuristic Romance
Written in Stone

JOURNALS AND COLORING BOOKS

The Cosmos Journals
Moonstruck
Star Gazing
Fires in the Sky

Coloring Books Coloring Book

Journals for Writers and Makers
Creating Super Characters
Name Collection Journal for Writers